THE DESERT'S SHARE

SHANNON BAKER

SEVERN RIVER

PUBLISHING

Severn River Publishing
www.SevernRiverBooks.com

ISBN: 978-1-64875-507-1 (Paperback)

ALSO BY SHANNON BAKER

Michaela Sanchez Southwest Crime Thrillers

Echoes in the Sand

The Desert's Share

The Kate Fox Mysteries

Stripped Bare

Dark Signal

Bitter Rain

Easy Mark

Broken Ties

Exit Wounds

Double Back

Bull's Eye

The Nora Abbott Mystery Series

Height of Deception

Skies of Fire

Canyon of Lies

Standalone Thrillers

The Desert Behind Me

To find out more about Shannon Baker and her books, visit

severnriverbooks.com/authors/shannon-baker

To the brave men and women of the Border Patrol

1

The first shot sent a jolt through me, amplifying all my senses at once. The pungent scent of creosote and mesquite filled the air. Even the scuff of boots in the sand seemed as loud as a siren. As I climbed the side of a narrow ridge, surrounded by thick brush, only my training and discipline kept me in line behind Steve Brody as he cautiously waved us forward. Like a racehorse in the gate, I wanted to burst ahead.

The moon provided just enough light for me to pick my footing. Since we didn't want to signal our location to the smugglers, the flashlight dangled on a strap at my side. When we'd tacked up earlier, I'd pulled out a heavy strap, clipped it to my flashlight, and flung it over my chest. Brody had pointed to my strap and snickered, his craggy prune of a face irresistibly smackable. "Look at that. Grandma has to have help carrying her flashlight. Maybe you ought to hit the gym and build up enough muscles to hold your gear. Or better yet, stay home and bake cookies."

Brody didn't warrant my irritation. That's what I tried to tell myself. The honest truth was that I'd like to take this flashlight, nearly as long as a toilet plunger and heavy enough to break concrete, and tap it not so gently on Brody's head. Maybe it could bang some sense into him.

The second shot was followed by a sharp yelp of pain and return fire. Brody hesitated, and I'm sure both of us following him wanted to shove him aside to get to the action. If I'd been with the team longer, I'd have probably been able to identify the voice of the man who'd been shot. All I could do now was assume it came from an agent and not someone from the cartels.

I didn't see the point to our slow progress. We had to be visible to scouts with their high-power night-vision binoculars situated on the tall peaks hemming us in. Which peaks and how many scouts we could only guess. We did know that the cartels had the same equipment as Border Patrol. Our MSC—mobile surveillance capable unit—located a few miles away, used infrared camera to track this group of seven men, each with a seventy-pound pack of drugs strapped to his back. They'd been feeding the information into our ear pieces.

But at some signal from their own scouts, the group had scattered like cockroaches when you slap on the kitchen light. Our surveillance team was scrambling to find them in the thick mesquite and brush.

I held my M4 ready. At any moment we could come upon the group or be ambushed. That last scenario was unlikely. Packers wanted to avoid us, and most of the time, didn't even carry weapons. All I knew is that one of our own had been injured and I needed to join the fight.

Brody, in his late forties and with a soft belly too big to perform all a Border Patrol agent might have to, pulled his uniform cap low and kept inching toward the shots.

Something shifted in the brush to my left. I only saw a hint of movement, a suggestion of something different from the shadowed lumps of desert cactus and creosote. I couldn't see anything out of the ordinary and stopped to let my eyes take in a wider view. The other rookie behind me, Luke Manifold, smacked into me and stopped, clearly confused.

Like trying to zero in on a particular star in the night sky you can only see by looking to the side, I let my eyes soften. My skin pricked when my gaze narrowed to a shadow on the base of a creosote bush. I studied it for a split second before tightening my grip on my flashlight and pushing it on.

Two forms sprang away from me, lunging up the side of the mountain and heading to the top of the ridge. They wore camo and neither seemed bigger than my fourteen-year-old daughter. Without thought I took off after them.

Manifold didn't follow and Brody probably didn't know I'd broken rank. We'd been instructed to stay close. If I'd been following orders, I'd have alerted Brody and let him make the decision. But these guys were slippery and protocol took too much time.

The voice in my ear from the MSC unit came to life. "Runners on the east slope. Three heading down to the valley floor."

Those weren't the guys I was after.

"Sanchez!" I had no trouble recognizing Brody's booming voice behind me. He should know not to shout, marking our location for anyone out here. It didn't make me stop pursuit, but it made me worry I'd be the next one to feel the burn of a bullet.

The two smugglers scrambled up the scree, sending an avalanche of pebbles and a few rolling rocks down on me. Luke caught up to me as I fought my way to the top, still gaining on the runner.

The MSC agent spoke rapidly in my ear. "Lots of action on top of the ridge. Looks like two running and two pursuers. One of the runners on the east slope is down."

No sign of Brody. I whispered back at Luke as I kept running, "I'll go after these two. You get the guy that's down."

The voice from MSC shouted in my ear like an annoying gnat, telling me the obvious. "Runners heading north along the ridgetop." I kicked it into overdrive, digging my boots into the loose gravel and charging after them.

Suddenly, one peeled off from the flat of the ridge. He jumped off the side, maybe hoping to run into the darkness. But the side of the ridge was steep and covered with loose rocks and sand. He immediately lost his footing and fell. He rolled, probably collecting cactus spines, smashing his bones on sharp rocks and scraping exposed skin. He shouted into the night. I could probably go after him and at least grab one. But from the look of the fall, he might not be jumping up and scampering off. If Brody ever caught up maybe he'd have a shot at him.

Somewhere along the line I'd let go of my flashlight. It dangled from the strap, creating a strobe as I ran and sending light up and down in a crazy show.

"One dropped out of view on the west side of the ridge." The MSC communication buzzed in my ear but I barely paid attention. They were telling me what I'd already seen in the scant moonlight.

I kept after the other runner. My flashlight bounced beams as I hurtled and dodged cactus. He darted around a cholla and I followed, a few needles grabbing my shirt and sticking my arms, poking my skin but not registering pain.

"Agent chasing the northbound runner, stop." The words rumbled in my ear, not making sense. I was less than thirty feet from the runner and closing.

A stand of manzanita slowed our progress, but I zigged and zagged, picking up a few more feet as we raced along the narrowing ridge.

"Repeat, stop pursuing the northbound runner." The voice sounded louder but adrenaline kept me from comprehending the message.

The runner brushed his bare arm across a barrel cactus and yelped. I closed the gap another five feet. I'd be able to tackle him in a few more seconds.

"Agent. Stop chasing!" the MSC unit shouted in my mic.

The manzanita created a wall in front of the runner. I had him.

He did a home plate slide between the base of two plants, squeezing through an impossibly narrow gap.

"STOP!" The word exploded in my head but only as useless noise.

If he could make it through the gap in the manzanita, I could too. I ducked my head, closed my eyes, and bulled through the manzanita, smelling the spiced scent of crushed leaves. My boots dug in as I pushed myself forward.

I accelerated several inches before a band sliced into my neck. As my feet went out from under me and I pitched forward, my hands instinctively flew out to brace my fall.

They hit nothing. I tipped headfirst. The strap of my flashlight pulled across my windpipe, my knees buckled, and I pitched into the dark emptiness.

Absolutely nothing. Air below me. But I wasn't a bird soaring on a thermal. I was only plain old me, mother, wife, about to plunge to my death. I'd followed like a dog on a rabbit's tail without using the brain I'd been given, and now I was falling, about to smash into a thousand pieces on the desert floor.

Except I wasn't falling. I was dangling by the strap that had tangled in the manzanita. My toes tipped into the sand at the edge of the ridge but the rest of me swayed in the air. My hands couldn't grab anything and my arms waved helplessly. The ground below was shrouded in shadow.

The ridge had petered out just beyond the stand of manzanita, and only the sturdy strap of my flashlight, now caught by a feeble branch, kept me from sailing off into emptiness. The beam rocked across the darkness.

The thrill of the chase ratcheted up with a flash of panic at the realization I was swaying from the edge of the cliff. How hefty was the strap? How strong was the manzanita branch? If I pitched myself forward to create momentum to pull myself back to the ridge, would I strain the hold enough to snap it and send me flying to my death? My children motherless. Deon a widower and so angry I'd put myself in this position. All of these thoughts took less than a heartbeat to whoosh through my brain before I acted in the only way possible.

Wedging my feet and using momentum to swing myself backward, I grabbed a manzanita branch and pulled myself back to the ridge.

"Shit. Agent. Are you okay?" I understood these words shouted in my ear.

Okay? My hands shook. My blood beat with hot life. I keyed my mic. "Okay."

I untangled my flashlight from the bush and leaned over the edge. The man I'd chased lay in a heap on the desert floor fifty feet below me, moaning and writhing. Alive, but probably not in good shape. He'd had no backup yelling in his ear to stop. Not that it had done me any good. That's the funny thing about adrenaline. I'd heard the MSC but only now understood what he'd said.

Below me ATV headlights crossed the desert toward us. Those agents would get to the body before I could scramble down, so I crawled through the manzanita, snagging my clothing and feeling the burning sting from the cholla I'd collected earlier.

It didn't take much to find the disturbed ground where the other guy had bailed over the side. I climbed down after him. He lay on his back, leg twisted beneath him. He moaned when I approached but didn't make any moves to fight. Aside from the scrapes and cuts from his fall, there wasn't much blood. I keyed my mic and gave the location of the runner. "Looks like a broken leg. Gonna need a stretcher."

Within an hour the ridge was crawling with agents. I checked my watch, noting our shift had ended three hours ago.

Luke walked over, all arms and legs like a gangly colt. He looked nervous, though not at all winded. "Have you talked to Brody?"

What I had in law enforcement experience, Luke had in youth. We'd gone to the Border Patrol Academy together, and though it'd be a stretch to say I was old enough to be his mother, I could at least have been his much older sister.

Luke made a movement with his eyes to indicate Brody's approach. "Don't look now, Michaela, but I think we're about to get in trouble."

Brody stopped in front of me and put his hands on his hips. The way he pursed his lips and drew in his eyebrows made him look like a Shar-Pei, only not as cute. "You were to stay behind me."

"Yes, sir." Sir. Brody had been Border Patrol for six years. That made him my senior. I had been under his rotation for a month, my last before I qualified for solo duty. My admiration for Brody hadn't grown since the moment I'd walked into the sector office three months ago and he'd mumbled under his breath, just loud enough for me and a few of his cronies to hear, "Didn't know they recruited grandmas these days."

I tried to look contrite. It's not my best look, but I thought I might be able to pull it off in the darkness. "I saw movement and was the closest. I didn't want to alert everyone to our position, so I apprehended the suspect." If I used a little cop lingo maybe it would sound official enough.

Brody took in Luke with disdain. "You damned rookies were lucky. You don't go running off in the dark. You could have ended up shot, like Beeman."

Luke sounded clueless, though I suspected otherwise. "Hinkin said Beeman is fine. Just a flesh wound."

"Did I hear my name?" Liz Hinkin was probably a couple of years younger than me but had ten years of experience on the Border Patrol. At thirty-six, I was the oldest recruit in my class at the academy. My few years as a Tucson cop and then six years volunteering for the Arizona Rangers gave me some law enforcement experience, but Border Patrol was a whole new scene.

She turned to Brody. "Good job chasing those two but what took you so long? While we were waiting for you, scouts must have spotted us and alerted the packers because they squirted. Maybe we could have held on to them if you'd shown up on time."

Luke's eyes were wide, and bright patches of rosy skin slashed across his cheekbones. This was his first time with enemy fire. I couldn't tell if he was excited, terrified, or both. "We heard the shots and then Beeman yelled," he said.

Hinkin eyed me. Obviously, she knew more about Brody than I did. She had seniority on him, but that didn't carry much weight in an organization where agents mostly patrolled alone and had an amazing amount of autonomy.

I couldn't tell her Brody did everything to keep us from the scene but sit down and read a book. I looked her in the eye and said, "Brody must have known they'd scatter, and he positioned us well. They practically ran right to us."

"Of course they did. Two rookies and Brody weren't going to actually track them." She turned away.

Brody took a step closer to me and said in a harsh whisper, "Don't congratulate yourself on saving my ass. If you hadn't run off on your own, Hinkin wouldn't need any explanation." He stomped off.

Towering over me, Luke gave his head a sad shake. "I don't think he likes you."

I didn't care about being friends with Brody, but having an enemy at your back was never good.

2

The moon cast little light as I climbed into my Honda Pilot outside the station in south Tucson. At least at this hour I wouldn't have to contend with much traffic as I made my way up I-10 to Oro Valley and the Tucson suburbs we called home.

What I'd done today, apprehending bad people in the desert, was good work. I'd been where I was needed, doing work that made a difference. We'd stopped heroin from hitting the streets, maybe kept someone from killing themselves.

It was a drop in the bucket. I knew that. But it was a drop. And that mattered.

Lights from houses pockmarked the neighborhood. It was that time of night when many had already turned in, while night owls were gearing up. A light glowed in our master bedroom and the blue flicker of the TV told me Deon was still up. Or at least he was dozing in front of some war movie.

I parked the Pilot and lugged my lunch cooler into the house. Famished after the adventure on the ridge, on my way home I'd mowed through almost everything I'd packed, even the emergency food. Since my parents died when I was a kid, I'd been managing my diabetes, and it was generally as natural as breathing. Out on patrol, I'd have to pay close attention.

I caught the door from the garage into the kitchen before the spring slammed it shut. On a school night, the girls ought to be asleep by now. Deon had left the light above the stove on for me, and it gave the kitchen a cozy glow. Setting my lunch cooler on the island, I made my way to the back door to make sure it was locked.

The door's glass acted as a mirror for my movements. The family room took up the space opposite the kitchen, the floor littered with body pillows and who knows what else. It looked like maybe Deon and the kids had watched a movie before bed but I couldn't see much in the dim light. As I checked the lock, the glass reflected movement on the sofa.

"Sami?"

She sat up, her tousled hair outlining her thin face. "Hi, Mom."

I flipped the lock, noting that Deon had forgotten again, and made my way toward her. "What are you doing up?"

She leaned her elbows on the back of the couch and rested her head on her arms. "I was waiting for you."

"Does Dad know you're down here?" I walked over and placed my hand on her head, letting my fingertips massage lightly. Sami always loved to be touched. As a baby she'd snuggled into every hug, seemed never to tire of being rocked, and as a toddler, she'd often climbed into my lap. Nothing like her older sister, whose affection was more selective. Josie was definitely more cat to Sami's dog personality.

Sami shrugged. "Don't know."

I sat down and put my arm around her, letting her cuddle into me. At eleven, she didn't have that sweet baby smell I missed. Now she carried around a combination of citrus shampoo and playground dirt. Even this comforted me in a way. At least some little girl was left in there. "What's going on?"

"Nothing." Her words were muffled in my uniform shirt.

I rubbed her head for a few seconds, letting her figure out how to start.

"Nikki is having a slumber party on Friday and she invited everyone but me." The words squeaked out like tiny daggers into my heart.

Nikki. My least favorite of Sami's friends. She'd hurt Sami's feelings so many times over the years I'd have gladly used her as a practice dummy for my self-defense classes. "I'm sorry. But there's no way she could have invited everyone. Her house isn't that big."

Sami sighed. "Okay, she asked Sujata and Bella and Pauline. But not me. And she knows those are my homies. We're a group and she left me out on purpose."

Nikki's mother wasn't any great prize, either. Mean girls grow up to be mean moms and raise more mean girls. "That's not nice. We can't change other people. Sometimes what they do hurts and that's all there is to it. But you have a choice to move on and make yourself feel better. Or you can let it keep hurting you." I said all those nice words and hoped they'd help Sami. They didn't do much for my outrage.

She hiccuped and the tears started even as she burrowed closer into me. "But they're my friends and now they won't like me."

If those shallow idiots wanted to throw over my kind, smart, funny kid for the likes of Nikki, then they didn't deserve Sami. But me saying that wasn't going to help Sami right now. "I've got Saturday off. Why don't we plan something fun. Maybe we can hike to Seven Falls."

She sniffled. "I don't know."

I clenched my teeth before making the next offer. Hiking would be my first choice, but Sami had other priorities. "Well, then, how about we have a spa day. I'll make an appointment for you to get those purple streaks you want in your hair and we'll get pedicures. Then have lunch. Maybe go to a movie afterward."

She sat up, wiping her eyes. "Can Josie come with us?"

What kind of mother was I that I cringed at the idea of convincing Josie to spend the day being silly with me and Sami? Turning fourteen had taken all the fun out of Josie. Maybe she'd rally for Sami, though. "Absolutely. If she wants to join us, she's welcome."

Sami stood up, rubbing her eyes and sniffing a bit. "It still hurts my feelings I wasn't invited to Nikki's."

Life hurts. I'd rather take on any pain than have to witness one of my girls get hurt. But you can't protect your kids. Also, I still wanted to punch Nikki's lights out. "I know, Bug. But we're better than letting it keep us down."

She considered. "Yeah. We're better than that."

We climbed the stairs together and I walked into her room, waiting while she slipped into the bed still crammed with dozens of stuffed animals. She was growing up so fast and now balanced on the ridge before plunging into teenage years. I wanted to keep her on this side of the mountain for a little while longer. But she tugged away and I'd have to loosen my grip.

Tonight, though, she didn't mind letting me pull up her covers and lean down to kiss her forehead like I used to do every night.

I hesitated outside Josie's door. With careful movements, I slowly turned the knob and eased it open. Her covers rustled and she snarked at me. "Thanks for waking me up. It's not like I have to get up early for school or anything."

"Sorry. Just wanted to say good night."

"Whatever."

I stepped into her room. "Can you cut the crap? Maybe you're not a fan of me working but I'm—"

"Yeah," she mumbled, faking sleepiness. "You're following your heart. Got it."

Maybe I'd given that speech a few too many times. At any rate, I wasn't going to straighten out her attitude this late at night, and frankly, I was too tired to try. I backed out of her room without responding and thudded down the hall to the master suite.

Deon lay sprawled on our bed while the TV droned on low volume. He blinked when I opened the bedroom door and walked inside. With one look at my face, he opened his arms for me.

I didn't stop to take off my boots or shed my clothes but climbed next to him and let him pull me close. His subtle scent of shaving cream and deodorant mingled with the unique smell of his skin, made it all feel familiar and safe. Like Sami when she snuggled into me, my tears broke loose when I felt that security.

"Hey, hey. It's okay," he murmured into my hair. "Rough day on the border?"

I didn't sob so hard I couldn't get words out. "Yeah. No. I mean, that's not why I'm crying."

"Okay." The way he said it sounded like a question and now I needed to tell him.

I sat up and scooted to the edge of the bed to take off my boots. "Sami was waiting for me downstairs."

"She was? I thought she went to bed." He pointed the remote at the screen and punched it off.

My boots thumped on the floor one after the other and I stood to strip off the grungy uniform. "That little piece of garbage, Nikki, didn't invite Sami to her party even though she invited everyone else."

Deon raised an eyebrow. "Everyone?"

My shirt and bra hit the floor and Deon seemed to lose the thread of conversation. I pulled him back in. "All her friends anyway. I swear, Nikki better watch her back."

Deon brought his focus to my face as I unzipped my pants and pushed them off my hips. "I thought Sami seemed upset tonight but she didn't say anything."

I stood naked in front of the bed, tears clogging my throat again. "She's growing up and moving away and I'm not here when she needs me. What am I doing starting this new career that's taking so much time?"

He leaned back, and I suspected he battled with the idea of a naked woman standing in front of him and what he could do with that, and a distressed wife and what he should do with that. He chose correctly. "We all talked about this before you went to the academy. You've done all the training. We survived."

"But I feel like our family is coming apart. Josie will barely talk to me." I didn't even mention my split with my sister.

He sighed. "Josie is fourteen. Whether you started with the Border Patrol or waited at home for her every need, she's going to find some way to rebel. Sami is a preteen. God is to blame for that situation. He should never have designed adolescents like he did."

The tears fell warm down my face. "They used to need us."

Deon's eyes grew misty. "It's the way of the world. We always knew they'd grow up, right? It's not a surprise."

"But maybe I should be here for a while. Maybe I shouldn't have joined the Border Patrol right now."

Deon watched me. "I wouldn't argue if you wanted to quit. I can make enough money to support us. But is quitting what you want?"

Deon hadn't been overjoyed with me going back to law enforcement. He was the one who'd asked me to quit the Tucson Police Department when Sami was little. He worried about me getting injured. But being on the job seemed such a part of me that after the kids quit relying on me to tie their shoes and fix their peanut butter sandwiches, I'd grown so reckless I'd nearly cost us our marriage.

I wiped my eyes. "No. I don't want to quit." I hadn't even begun the work that had prompted me to sacrifice so much to become an agent. The country needed protection against criminals and terrorists. Though you could argue that everyone crossing the border illegally was a criminal, many weren't out to cause harm. There was a need for compassion to act against the desert's cruelty. Even more, I wanted to finish the work my brother, Chris, abandoned two years ago when he resigned from the Border Patrol.

"The girls are going to grow up and have their own lives. It won't matter if you're volunteering for the Arizona Rangers or stopping drug smugglers on the border."

He leaned over and reached for my hand. "Now come over here and I'll see what I can do to relax you."

I pulled back. "Give me two seconds to shower, but relaxing isn't what I have in mind."

3

I jerked awake in the dim morning light to the sound of Josie's demand. "Get out of the bathroom. I'm going to be late."

Sami's voice sounded muffled by a closed door. "I'm brushing my teeth."

Deon's footsteps pounded on the stairs. "Get in the car. It's time to go."

Josie groaned in frustration, then stomped down the stairs.

The bathroom door banged against the wall and Sami said, "I don't want to go early. Mom can take me."

The bedroom door swung open and Deon spoke over his shoulder. "Mom can't. She's barely got time to get herself to work."

Sami whined, "Then why didn't she get up earlier."

Deon strode across the bedroom and leaned over to kiss me. "Because she worked late so she got to sleep in a little."

Sami's groan matched Josie's and she did the same stomp down the stairs.

Not that we didn't have our share of frustrating mornings before I went back to work, but I still felt a stab of guilt for not directing the proceedings. "Sorry," I said to Deon.

He waved it away. "No big deal. Josie has some project and needs to be at school early and Sami can go to early club. We've got this." He gave me another kiss. "See you at Josie's game. Starts at six."

"Yep," I said, acting as if I'd already planned on it. Truth was, I'd forgotten.

My phone showed six forty-five. Damn it. That gave me fifteen minutes before I had to hit the door myself. I checked my blood sugar monitor and jumped out of bed. A quick shower, my food for the day tossed into my lunch cooler, and a cold boiled egg and apple snatched from the fridge on my way out the door. I pulled out of the driveway only five minutes late.

Tonight, we'd meet up at Josie's game, and afterward, all four of us would have dinner together. I'd make up for being late last night and not seeing them this morning. A deep breath in and out and I settled into the commute.

I hit typical morning traffic as I drove from my quiet suburb through downtown and to the station located just outside the gates of Davis-Mothan Air Force Base. I had one more day with Brody. One last shift and I'd be on my own. While the thought of getting away from Brody brightened my mood, the idea of being solo made me nervous. Out on the desert making my own decisions on where to go and what to do, and possibly running into situations I might not be prepared for, created anxiety and excitement. This was what I'd trained nearly two years for.

Toward the station the traffic slowed, and all three lanes seemed suddenly congested. An accident on Golf Links? No blue and red lights flashed and no siren blared. A quick glance at the clock told me I wouldn't be late. Probably not. Hopefully. God, it would be bad to be late to muster this early in my career.

I rolled down the window of my Mom-mobile Pilot. The cars eased forward, and I caught the faint sound of shouting. The closer I got the more it sounded like chanting.

Great. Protesters. Not everyone believed Border Patrol performed a public service. Okay, quite a few people thought we ran around the desert ripping children from the arms of loving parents. Or picked off immigrants as they climbed the border fence, like the black-and-white film footage of the horrors at the Berlin Wall.

As I crept closer, the general melee solidified into discernable phrases:

"Death Patrol! Go home."

"Stop killing children."

"Care is not a crime."

"Free Lacy."

They meant Dr. Lacy Hollander. She'd been arrested last year for aiding and abetting illegal aliens and her trial was due to begin today. She was a member of No Desert Deaths, and an outspoken leader making pleas to the government to disband the Border Patrol. She made videos that had gone viral showing No Desert Death volunteers hauling gallons of water into the desert north of the border. They trekked in cans of beans, blankets, and basic medical supplies and left them on well-traveled immigrant routes. Lacy's case had been a hot topic at work.

A small but loud group crowded around the gate. They could be members of any number of organized groups, from humanitarian aid to religious to concerned citizens. They knew not to block the driveway, but they waved their signs and shouted at the vehicles turning in. Someone had strategically planned to be here at shift change. A larger group was likely stationed at the courthouse with only a few protesting here to make a point.

I wore my BP tux—green uniform pants, boots, and a green V-neck T-shirt. I'd change into my uniform shirt and add my utility belt in the locker room when I got inside the station.

"Free Lacy!" Signs bearing that message with a headshot of a grinning Lacy Hollander in her iconic Tilley hat bounced up and down while the protesters chanted. Other signs showed pictures of gallon plastic water jugs with "Care is never a crime!" printed underneath.

I tapped on my blinker and slowed to wade into their midst. Someone slapped the back of the Pilot.

A gray-haired woman bared her teeth just opposite my window and screamed, "Death patrol!"

Someone else banged on the passenger window. "Free Lacy!"

After a hung jury in Lacy's first trial, the government had dropped one of the charges and was back at it. The arrests had been made prior to my joining the Border Patrol so I had nothing to do with the incident, but if you lived in Tucson, you couldn't miss the media coverage.

Just as I nosed through most of the protesters, something too familiar caught my eye. I snapped my head around.

Oh no. It was like someone dropped an anvil on my chest. That stupid red plaid. The wool jacket that was way too expensive, but I'd bought anyway because I wanted to see her smile for once. I thought she'd feel conspicuous and quit wearing it.

Josie.

She stared at me as if willing my attention to her. Her gloved hands clutched one of the water jug signs, which she thrust at me as if daring me to respond. Along with most of the other protesters, she wore a Tilley hat like Lacy's.

A glance in my rearview mirror showed three vehicles behind me trying to get into the parking lot for their shift so I goosed the gas pedal and pulled ahead, directing the Pilot to the curb. My heart pounded with the seconds ticking away, eating my way to being late. I slammed it into park and jumped out, nearly in the path of another agent in an F150. I backed off to let him pass, held up my hand to stop the next car long enough for me to slip through, and stomped toward Josie.

She waited for me, defiant. Her long dark hair swung under the hat and her eyes snapped with fire. She planted her feet and set her mouth.

"What do you think you're doing?" Good start.

She waved her sign and answered with a snide, "Being a decent global citizen." She turned her head to the next driver. "Free Lacy!"

I grabbed her arm. "You should be in school."

She pulled away. "People are dying on the desert, Mom. I think that's more important than music theory."

A young man approached us. Blond and certainly not old enough to vote, he stepped in front of me. "You okay, Josie?"

She planted a hand on his shoulder and moved him aside. "Fine. She's my mother."

His shock showed. "Your mother is the enemy?"

Double damn it. I didn't have the time to deal with Mr. Wide Eyes. I glared at Josie. "You've proven your point. You got my attention. Now go back to school."

She let out a chuckle. "Where's all that follow-your-heart crap you've been spouting? I guess that's only if I'm doing what you approve of, huh?"

I've never believed in corporal punishment but maybe I'd need to rethink that stand. "We will talk about this when I get home. My shift starts in ten minutes and I can't be late."

"Oh no, you don't want to be late to destroy the food and water No Desert Deaths is leaving out to save lives." She raised her chin and glared at me. "Murderer."

I knew better than to let her hyperbole hurt, but it still stung. Teenagers. Deon and I had braced for a certain amount of rebellion. It's normal for a four-teen-year-old daughter to butt heads with her mother. This was all natural.

Just not on my last shift with a jerk of a journeyman. Not now. "Josie…"

She flipped her hair, as only a beautiful young girl can do, and stomped away, shouting, "Free Lacy!"

Damn it. Skirting protesters yelling at me and other agents driving into the lot, I made it back to the Pilot, parked, and hurried toward the station.

I pulled out my phone and dialed. Deon picked up just before it went to voicemail. He sounded breathless and maybe a little irritated. "Hi. I'm about to walk in to take a deposition. What's up?"

"Josie."

He interrupted before I took a breath. "What's wrong?"

"She's here at the station."

Now he was alarmed. "What station?"

"Border Patrol. She's protesting at the gate and I have to start my shift. Can you come get her?"

I knew his full-on lawyer mode. Daddy and husband were completely different than competitive, professional, take-no-prisoners Deon Sanchez, attorney at law. "No. I can't. Is she in any danger?"

"Not unless someone runs them over. But she shouldn't be here. This is where I work. She needs to be in school."

He lowered his voice as if someone walked close to him. "If you can't take her back to school, I say we let her go and talk to her later."

That didn't sit well with me, but neither of us had the time to debate. "Okay. See you later." I tried not to sound resentful.

I punched him off and hit speed dial for my brother, Chris. I explained the situation to him.

He sounded amused. "Ah, our little Josie is flexing her civic muscle."

"Come on, Chris. Can you come get her and take her to school?"

"I've got my case law class in twenty minutes. It's a three-hour class so by the time I got there, she'd be gone anyway." After almost twenty years on the Border Patrol, Chris had gone back to law school. My joining now, on the heels of his disenchantment, smacked of irony.

Chris and I knew better.

He switched the topic. "Going solo soon." It wasn't a question, but I knew what he was asking.

I made sure no one could hear me. "Yeah. I thought I might have seen or heard something before now."

He probably wore that resigned smile. "I told you it'd take time to get to know everyone and for them to be easy around you."

That old impatience nagged at me. "I didn't spend two years to now sit on my thumbs."

"No one knows you're my sister, right?"

"Of course not."

"Good. Someone will tip their hand. The important thing is for you to keep out of trouble. No confrontation. Intel only."

Right.

Josie made eye contact with me and shouted along with her friends. I checked my watch, frustration boiling over. "Why is she doing this?"

Chris laughed. "You're asking me? I raised one teenager. And the only time she skipped school was to go skinny dipping in Romero Pools."

I'd normally smile at the memory of my rebellion. I paid for it in sunburn, an extra term paper, and making dinner for three months straight, but it had been worth it. Today, I wasn't amused. "She's doing her best to make my life miserable."

"I hate to break it to you, but being Border Patrol comes with a lot of misunderstanding and hate. I doubt Josie's protest is as personal as you're taking it."

"Oh, it's personal. She hates me these days."

Clearly, this situation tickled Chris as only a big brother could enjoy it. "With the trial starting today, I'd guess you're going to get a lot of flak. If I were you, I wouldn't wear my uniform in public for a while."

With no other alternative but to leave Josie to do her thing, I hurried into the station to finish changing.

I rushed into the meeting room with less than five minutes to spare before muster. Luke stood at the back and I pushed next to him. "Move over."

He slid a little way so I could lean against the back wall.

Brody sat at a table in front of us. "Free Lacy Hollander. Jesus Christ. She knew what she was doing was against the law."

Luke leaned over before I could tug on his arm to shut him up. Engaging Brody was never a good idea. "You were in on the raid that caught her, right?"

Brody puffed up. "Damn right. She's a real piece of work. Had those two tonks making dinner. They were all cozy as bugs in a rug."

"You didn't have a warrant, though. Is that going to be a problem?" Oh man, Luke. Now I knew why he'd asked Brody about the bust. He wanted to prove that Brody was an ass.

It wouldn't make a difference to anyone in this room. Brody had good friends and not-so-good friends. If you were Border Patrol, you had no enemies because you counted on everyone to have your back. Luke didn't need to get Brody all worked up about Lacy when I had to spend the next eight hours alone in a pickup with him.

"Warrant? What are you, a goddamned lawyer? I didn't need a warrant. I suspected there were illegals in that barn."

"Seems like you'd have a hard time proving your suspicion wasn't based on racial profiling." Luke's expression reflected that innocence he carried so naturally. I knew better.

Brody's face flashed bright red. "Who the hell else would be in that barn if it wasn't damned tonks?"

The duty supervisor strode to the front of the room. "Okay, let's settle it down."

A few people finished up conversations and the room grew quiet.

The duty supervisor began muster by giving an update on the night's activities. A fence had been cut on a ranch in the southwest sector, a tripped sensor led to a group of six mules getting jumped east of the POE—

point of entry. Vigilantes called in the location of a cartel scout but the scout fled before agents arrived. Mostly a quiet night.

"Got a hit on a couple of kids we rolled early this morning." Fingerprinting kids was a new development. Coyotes were using kids to help illegals gain sympathy if they were caught. These kids crossed in sometimes brutal circumstances and were left alone on the desert after the crossers made it through safely. If we didn't capture them and get them into the system of child care, their best case was being picked up by the cartels, returned across the border, and used again. It wasn't unheard of for these kids to end up in a cornfield in Nebraska. Abandoned, alone, not speaking the language.

"Good job on the crew intercepting the smugglers yesterday. This is the way it's supposed to go down. Let's see if we can get that done again."

He located me against the back wall and grinned. "I hear Sanchez is quite the trapeze artist."

My face burned as several agents turned around. There were a few chuckles, an "atta boy" and a "good job" thrown into it, and thankfully the duty supervisor moved on to assignments.

Brody murmured loud enough for me to hear, "Not bad for the geriatric crowd."

I ignored Brody and concentrated on the duty supervisor as he read down the list of assignments. Luke and his journeyman were sent to a checkpoint on Ajo Highway. Luke's mouth turned down in disappointment.

The shift supervisor kept reading his list. "Sanchez and Brody, Avra west." I wouldn't mind trading places with Luke. Even though no one wanted to work checkpoint because you were either on your feet all shift searching vehicles passing along the highway or bored senseless at a checkpoint on a lonely stretch of road. But spending eight hours in a pickup listening to Brody's wisdom or his godawful country music while watching him pack away all the food in his sizable cooler didn't sound like fun.

Suck it up, Sanchez. Tomorrow I'd be on my own. I could deal with one more shift of Brody.

The supervisor inhaled and looked us over. "Don't suppose anyone missed the circus going on out front. Who knows how long the trial will last and whether our friends out there will get bored. But you know the drill.

No engagement. Ignore them. If one of them gets aggressive, let your supervisor know and we'll deal with it."

He took another breath. "None of this is making it easier to do our jobs. The militias and vigilantes seem to be escalating their mischief with the humanitarian aid stations. Lacy Hollander's supporters are doing some retaliating with slashed tires and disrupted camps."

He scanned the room, maybe speaking to specific agents. "Here's the deal: we need to stay out of it as much as possible. We're here to protect the borders, not get involved in a turf war between American citizens. Leave the humanitarian caches alone and don't share intel with the vigilantes. We're Switzerland, people."

He raised his hands and sent us away with his usual, "That's it. Be careful out there. Come home to your families."

Luke and I walked out of muster together. "Brody's an asshole. Sorry you have to hang with him all day."

"I hoped maybe he'd have to be at court."

Luke looked down at me from his lofty, lanky height. "It's jury selection today. I doubt even Lacy Hollander is there."

We waited in line at the armory. I needed to check out an M4. Luke bent over, his mouth close to my ear. "I hope Hollander gets off."

He shouldn't be saying that in the station or anywhere he could be overheard by agents. Our job was keeping undocumented people out of the United States. Supporting those making it easier for aliens to get in wasn't consistent with our mission.

I kept my voice low. "Me, too."

Someone whacked my elbow, making me stumble into Luke. Brody glared at us. "Whenever you feel like joining me, Grandma, I'll be waiting in the truck."

4

Brody had me drive. Our AOR, area of responsibility, took us west and south. In twenty miles I pulled off the highway, drifted through a small settlement of dusty houses. We passed a grade school with the swings still moving from the students recently called in from recess. The nicer schools in Tucson sported coverings to keep the kids safe from the desert sun. But out here, the kids were on their own. I hoped the school at least had heat. November in southern Arizona could be chilly in the day and below freezing at night.

Not far south of town the road gave way to gravel, then sand. Brody stirred from where he'd been slouched in the passenger seat singing along to the country tunes blasting on his Bluetooth speaker. "Turn on this road."

The sandy trail road cut through thick brush and disappeared over a slight rise. When we got about a mile from the gravel, Brody pointed to a tall mesquite. "Park under that tree and we'll have lunch."

I cut the engine. "It's only ten o'clock."

He popped the top off a cooler big enough to hold a picnic for twelve. "What's your point?" He peeled back the plastic cover on a tray of cheese and meat.

I watched while he polished off his snack, scrolling through my phone and checking on the kids' school portals. It looked like they'd both turned in all their assignments and kept their grades up. We had that going for us, at least. I worried about Josie and how to handle her skipping school and showing up at the station to protest.

Brody pulled out his iPad. "Need to catch up on *Swamp People*."

Of course. "I think we ought to do some patrolling," I said.

He gave me a look as if I'd suggested jumping in a Minnesota lake. In January. "We're fine. If anything happens we'll get a call. It's a big desert out there and driving around is a waste of gas."

I tried another tactic. "It's my last shift before I go solo. Maybe you can do some more training." I was bored. More than bored. Like thinking about slitting my wrists bored. Or worse, writing my sister a letter of reconciliation bored.

Dear Ann,

You were right. I never should have joined the Border Patrol. I gave up five months of my life with my husband and family to end up sitting in a pickup on the desert with a lazy man who listens to country music and won't stop eating.

Love,
    Michaela

Brody propped his iPad on the dash and settled in.

I grabbed my coat from the back of my seat. "I'll be out cutting for sign on the trail." It was a random and probably useless exercise but sitting in the cab with Brody was not an option.

Without turning from his iPad, he said, "Knock yourself out."

I wandered away from the pickup, studying the brush on the side of the trail for burlap fibers, rock kicks, or any sign someone had crossed through here. I followed vague animal trails, not finding a sign. It didn't take more than a couple of hours of not seeing anything suspicious for me to think about heading back. I checked my blood sugar monitor and pulled out a protein bar, dreaming of a real meal with my family after Josie's game.

The day-to-day of the Border Patrol was like this. I knew it going in from the time Chris had been an agent. It reminded me of my years at Tucson PD. The job is ninety-five percent boredom and five percent "oh shit."

I probably shouldn't admit to loving the "oh shit" part so much. Maybe that five percent saved me, letting me experience the adrenaline high without causing me PTSD.

I hadn't gone much farther toward the pickup and was still worrying about Josie and her attitude when my phone rang. It made me jump and brought me back into focus. I hadn't expected much of a signal, let alone any calls.

When I reached for it and saw Ann's name on the caller ID, I hesitated. She hadn't called me in nearly two years. She spoke to me when she couldn't help it, and then, only as necessary for her to maintain a close relationship with Sami and Josie.

This wouldn't be good. I punched connect. "Ann? What's up?"

She paused, long enough for me to understand how difficult it was for her to call. "I need your help."

Had she fallen? Was hurt? Needed money? It could be anything. "What do you need?" I tried to make it sound as casual as it used to be when she'd call and ask me to pick up supplies for Mi Casa, or tell me to bring dessert to our family dinner.

Her voice cut me like a razor. "I wouldn't have called you if there had been any other way."

Okay. Well, this wasn't reconciliation, I guess. I waited, not wanting to let her hear my disappointment.

"You're at work, right? On the desert."

"Yes."

"Good. I need you to find someone missing around Sasabe."

"What? From Mi Casa?" The immigrant services non-profit my sister ran occupied an old office complex in the south side of Tucson.

"Of course not." That big sister arrogance steeped her tone. "The Missing Migrant Hotline got a call that said someone is lost."

"Who reported it?"

She sounded irritated. "It's an anonymous tip."

I tried to sort this out. "First of all, I'm not close to Sasabe. And secondly, you need to call the station and report this as an emergency. They'll send out agents who are closer."

She hung up. No argument. No explanation. Nothing. Just a dead line.

I stared at the dried pods hanging from a mesquite tree and fumed for thirty seconds. Then I dialed her back, as I'm sure she knew I would.

"Okay. You think someone is missing on the desert but you don't think calling it in would be helpful." I purposely didn't apologize.

She sounded measured. "If your agency would respond to emergencies from migrants, I wouldn't be calling you. I'm desperate."

"Do you know anything about this person? Age, gender, time they've been missing?"

"I think it's a woman, out overnight. All I have is a general location, and right now, I'm worried."

She should be worried. The desert was no place to traipse around on your own, especially on the border. The list of dangers is long. Cartels, rattlesnakes, heat exhaustion, dehydration, mountain lions, scorpions, cliffs to fall off, washes and sand to twist ankles, and this time of year the cold could lead to exposure. "Do you know where she went missing?"

"I've got some coordinates."

"Sasabe is clear on the other side of Tucson from where I'm patrolling. I can radio it in and have someone check it out."

"Never mind." She hung up again. Damn Ann. If there's such a thing as Big Sister Syndrome, she suffered long and hard.

This time I waited a full minute and a half before I gave in and called her back. "Okay. If you've got the coordinates, why not send out someone from one of the immigrant agencies?"

I pictured her sitting behind her desk at Mi Casa with her wheelchair next to her. Her face intense and uncompromising. She'd found the old office complex, jumped through all the hoops city, state, and federal governments could throw at her. She'd converted it and set up shop. Who knows how many immigrants she'd assisted in the twelve years since she'd opened the doors? She might be the bossiest, most annoying big sister on the planet, but I was in awe of how many mountains she managed to move, most of them from her wheelchair.

"If you don't want to help, that's fine. I'll find someone else."

"I thought you said you wouldn't ask me if you had anyone else." *Score one for Michaela.*

Silence. More silence. Then, "Are you going to help me?"

"I can't just leave my area and run over to another. I'm in my last day of training with a journeyman."

"That's typical."

"What's that mean?"

"It means you give your job top priority. I get it. No problem. I also give my job top priority. The difference is, my job is saving people. I'm not sure what your job is."

Let's just get right down into the slop. "You know what I do." She didn't know everything I planned on doing on the Border Patrol. Chris and his old friend Manuel Ortiz had been trying to discover a network of corrupt agents working with the cartels. The dirty agents were getting paid to allow certain vehicles across the checkpoints or misdirect desert chases. After Manuel's murder, Chris decided he'd do more good by getting his law degree. He hadn't recruited me to take his place and hadn't been pleased with my insistence on continuing their investigation. But he accepted my determination—what he called stubbornness.

Ann took a shot at me. "And what you don't do is help your family when they really need you."

I was tempted to play her game and hang up. But that wouldn't get me anywhere. I missed Ann in my life. The old Ann, of my youth. Why I longed for a relationship with her now, when this kind of situation wasn't uncommon, I didn't know.

Okay, I did know. Since our parents had died when I was twelve, Ann was mother, sister, friend, and anchor to me. "Okay. Give me the coordinates and I'll check it out." I didn't know how I'd get Brody to go along with it. Whether it was guilt or concern for the missing woman, I felt compelled to try. Doing Ann this favor might help us find our way to being a family again.

Ann gave me the coordinates and I jotted them down.

"Thanks for doing this." Her words and tone didn't quite match, but maybe it was a first step.

By the time I made it back to the pickup the sun looked down on Baboquivari Peak, casting rays through the windshield to warm the cab. Though the bright light radiated across the valley, ricocheting from the sand, casting shadows from the mesquite and barrel cactus, the November temperatures felt brisk.

Brody's music blared through the cracked window. As I climbed in he cast me a disdainful look. "Find anything?"

"Nope." How was I going to talk him into patrolling toward Sasabe?

He brushed the top from his blue cooler on the bench seat between us and reached inside.

I ground my teeth while he fumbled his plastic ice packs around as the incessant wail of another country song slithered from the speaker. He finally leaned in and mumbled to himself, moving trash and empty food storage containers around until he fished out a Snickers bar. He gave me a triumphant smile I tried to absorb politely when I really wanted to slap him. "I'd offer you one, but this is the last I've got." He smelled more than musty after his four hours of dozing and snacking in the warm pickup cab.

I waved it away. "I already ate." He didn't need to know that eating for me wasn't a matter of whim but one of managing my diabetes. "How about we do a little driving? I didn't see any sign of crossers out there."

He patted his pot belly, the green of his Border Patrol uniform faded from many washings. "You'll learn soon enough not to waste energy wandering the trails."

It would take an hour to drive to the coordinates Ann gave me. "I thought it might be a good way to pass the time on a slow shift."

"Let me give you some good advice, rookie."

I'd had enough of this jerk's "good advice." He recommended things like making sure I kept my phone battery charged in case I had to lay in wait for a group of smugglers. You wanted to be able to play your games to pass the time. Or this gem: if someone calls for backup and you know there are other units close by, pretend you're too far away to be of any use. I rested my arm on the steering wheel and gazed out at the sun's play on the desert.

"Be sure you keep hydrated and your belly full. If you take an emergency call, you don't want to run out of energy chasing down runners. And if you end up laying up for a long time, you don't want to get hungry."

As if Brody ever chased smugglers or border crossers. His big concern was having to lay up somewhere away from his vehicle. Although he seemed to jump more than his share of groups in the desert. Maybe he did have a few tips I could use.

When I'd tapped the location into my GPS I found we could head cross-country before turning up Highway 86 to Three Points. Inspiration struck. "There's a great ice cream place in Three Points. I'm buying."

Brody lifted his eyebrows. "That sounds like a good plan." He waved me on and I started the pickup.

I was surprised Brody fell for it and noted to not underestimate the power of a sweet tooth.

It took another hour over rough terrain to get close to Ann's coordinates. By that time the sun had reached its zenith and was heading toward the western mountain range. Only three more hours left in our shift. With the long drive back to the station in Tucson, Brody wouldn't allow me a lot of time to mess around.

On this road there were tire tracks and lots of footprints in the sand. That would be aid workers, hikers, or ATV recreationists. Smugglers and immigrants were usually adept at covering their tracks. Sometimes the last person in line carried a broom and swept the signs away, more often they all wore carpet shoes: chunks of carpet sown onto booties that hid shoe prints in dirt.

I drove past the tire tracks and leaned forward, sweeping my gaze back and forth from the windshield out the side window, cutting for sign.

Brody didn't like that. "What the...? Let's get going."

"It doesn't hurt to take a look. We've got time to kill before the end of the shift."

He sniffed. "Not much."

I spotted a broken twig on a creosote bush. A sliver of a path, not even wide enough to be called a trail, wound through the brush. I stopped the truck and tried for a sheepish smile. "Gotta water the cactus."

Brody sighed. "Guess I will, too." He climbed out while I dropped from the driver's side and scurried through the bushes.

"Jesus, Sanchez. You don't have to take a hike. I'm not gonna peek."

He probably would peek but that wasn't my concern. I trotted down to where the trail dropped into a dry wash. Not long after I left the pickup and picked my way through the brush, an overturned rock in the obscure trail told me someone had been through here.

Maybe it was Ann's missing person. I hollered for Brody. "There's sign of people here." Now that I had a trail, my progress slowed.

Brody caught up to me in a matter of minutes, about as happy as I'd expected. "What's going on? I don't feel like going on a wild goose chase."

The sun shone brightly but the breeze bit. Cat's claw, creosote, and other thick brush closed on the trail. The clean air carried no hints of civilization or much of anything. "I can't tell how long since someone was on this trail, but I think it's recent."

Brody grumbled, "Thinks she's Sacagawea."

The signs on the trail seemed slight, and I questioned if I really tracked someone or if I followed a series of coincidences, maybe simply a coyote on the hunt. I should call it off and head back to the pickup. Take my lumps with Brody. Tell Ann I couldn't find her missing person and have her report the disappearance through official channels.

I kept following the animal trail but it didn't look promising. Brody complained about my misguided and naïve mission, but he didn't stop. If I didn't see something definitive in the next five minutes, I'd quit, get my butt back to where I belonged, and make it home in time to enjoy Josie's game and dinner with the family. I'd suffer Ann's wrath later.

The packed sand in the dry wash looked disturbed a few feet ahead of me. Almost like a herd of cattle had crossed it. I hurried to the spot. Distinctive footprints came down one side of the wash and up the other. At least one set of hiking boots, several from cheap tennis shoes with light tread, and maybe even children.

Brody folded his arms. "Now we have a real trail."

He studied it a moment longer. "These tracks must belong to a group of immigrants, maybe without a coyote or with one who didn't know jack about his destination." He grabbed his radio and called it in.

The sun slipped lower, getting closer to the top of the Baboquivari mountain range. Its angle sent cool shadows playing among the thick desert growth. Up ahead a lighter spot showed open sand. Trees outlined a small clearing. The ground was churned up and an empty can of beans lay on its side next to a crushed gallon water jug. As I approached, the scrub brush on the opposite side of the clearing rustled and the tail end of a couple of coyotes disappeared. Not being picky eaters, the coyotes probably thought licking the bean cans tasted fine.

I took a few more steps into the clearing to find more empty cans and water jugs. We'd found a humanitarian aid cache. A threadbare backpack, like Sami's bookbag, lay discarded along with a black gallon jug, the kind immigrants carried from Mexico. More trash and a few worn clothing items were left in piles here and there. This stopping point looked like it had been used by several groups over time.

"Ain't this nice," Brody said, surveying the area. "They can't wait to get to America and trash it like they do their own countries. No need for backup now. These freeloaders are long gone."

Ann's missing person must have been part of a group that had stopped here. For some reason, she got separated and the rest of the group made it out. Someone had called for help. I couldn't tell Brody any of this.

I gazed away from the area, wondering where the migrant had gone and how to track her down. My attention caught on something, and I stopped to focus on what I'd thought was a pile of clothing slung across the roots of an old mesquite. The dark shadows of the afternoon had masked what obviously was not a discarded pile of clothes.

Hairs on my neck rose and heat flashed across my skin. Maybe a small groan escaped as I rushed over to what I now identified as a person. Some of her ash-blonde hair was captured in a ponytail, but most of it straggled on the back of her head and on her cheek, motionless in the still desert chill. She lay on her stomach with her feet tangled in the tree roots, her arms outstretched on the sand. What used to be hands looked like a plate of barbecue ribs after the meal ended. Damn coyotes.

The back of her T-shirt showed the logo of a woman with open hands and the words *No Desert Deaths*.

Brody stood behind me. He let out a whistle. "I'll be damned."

I twisted to look up at him. "What?"

"That's Lacy Hollander."

5

Brody could have taken charge but clearly wanted to avoid responsibility for something this large. Still in training, I had no authority. So we stayed with the body while we waited for Liz Hinkin, senior shift agent, to arrive and take command. Brody sat under a mesquite and lounged on its tangled roots, playing a game on his phone. Even relaxed, his face still had that sour, pinched look. I perched on a log across the clearing from him to get the last sliver of sunshine. The sheriff's office had been contacted and would come process the scene as a homicide.

I didn't touch the body, and kept all my movements to a minimum so I wouldn't compromise the scene any more than it was already. As a cop I'd seen dead bodies before. It's not something a person gets used to; at least I didn't. I'd seen Lacy Hollander on the front page of the Tucson paper and watched her on the evening news. She'd usually worn that trademark Tilley hat and spoken with such passion about the plight of immigrants crossing the desert. She led the fight against separating children from parents and cited horrifying accounts about people dying of thirst and exposure.

Now she lay silent and pale, her hat nowhere to be seen. She wouldn't be fighting for those in need any longer. When Ann said someone was missing, I hadn't imagined I'd find the woman at the center of controversy in Tucson. Had Ann suspected this? Who had really given her the tip that sent me to this location?

It made sense Ann would know Lacy Hollander. They both advocated for immigrant safety and human rights on the border. But Ann's non-profit helped legal residents with services like shelter, food, jobs, and travel arrangements. No Desert Deaths operated at the edges of the law. Getting involved with No Desert Deaths, even peripherally, could jeopardize grant funding or even taint Mi Casa's reputation within the donor community.

I'd take Ann's information about the missing person at face value. She'd been forwarded an anonymous tip from the hotline. I didn't need to know who informed her.

Brody didn't look up when we heard an engine rumbling. Hinkin's voice came on the radio, and I answered and directed her to our location. Without much concern for her pickup's suspension or paint job, she powered the four-wheel drive close to the clearing and cut the engine. In moments she stood with hands on her hips, surveying the body.

Brody had stowed his phone and posed proudly beside her. "This is gonna cause a real stir, don't ya think?"

Hinkin ignored him and kept looking at the body. "What the hell, Sanchez? Are you part bloodhound?"

My face grew warm. "Phone's dumped in that slashed water jug."

Liz glanced at the drowned phone and back at the body.

I spoke again. "Gunshot is my guess. Looks like an exit wound on her back. The damned coyotes started on her fingers but maybe not a lot of other damage. I don't suppose she's been here for more than twenty-four hours."

Hinkin glanced at me with a hint of surprise.

I hurried to excuse my comments, deciding not to inform Hinkin about the tip I'd received. Ann didn't need to get dragged into an investigation. "Just a guess. From my time on the PD."

"Good work finding her," Hinkin said, letting the rest go.

Brody shot a hostile look my way. "Pretty good coincidence. Sanchez got out to take a piss, wandered off and got lost. When I finally found her there was this trail across the wash, looked like a herd of buffalo crossed. A two-year-old couldn't have missed it."

Hinkin got out a grunt before two sheriff's deputies pulled up. In short order they were followed by an ambulance, and then a couple more BP agents. In no time, the whole clearing seemed like a small town.

While the crime scene investigators set up, I stood with Luke.

Brody sauntered over, face puckered up. "I hate to say it." He sounded anything but sorry. "But she deserved it."

He was not going to do that. I closed my eyes for a beat to calm down.

Luke turned an outraged face toward him. "What?"

Brody, getting the reaction he sought, waved his arms in front of himself. "Yeah. I mean, she's got no business being out here on the desert. It's not a place for women." He smirked at me. "Present company excluded."

I focused on Hinkin, who was speaking to a deputy. Ignoring a bully is the best response.

Brody continued baiting Luke. "She was breaking the law. Aiding and abetting. She and all her No More Deaths buddies should be thrown in jail. She harbored criminals."

Luke jumped in. "One of the deputies said they're pretty sure it's a cartel thing. They think Lacy probably came to resupply the aid station and surprised coyotes bringing in illegals."

Brody laughed. "Of course they say that. They're lazy."

I raised my eyebrows at Luke to telegraph the irony of Brody calling someone lazy.

Brody didn't see and kept on. "If they blame it on cartels they're done. But this, son, this is the work of the militia who are sick and tired of people like Lacy Hollander coddling criminals who are out to harm America."

Luke didn't know when to quit. "Lacy Hollander wasn't a threat to United States security. She took a group of nine people to a barn on a private ranch because it was freezing outside and they had small kids."

Brody pointed at Luke. "Right. She didn't call us. She didn't report illegal aliens to the authorities. Instead, she gave them succor. These people were breaking the law. They're a danger to our country."

Luke shook his head. I could have told him to save his breath. "She had no legal obligation to call Border Patrol," he said.

"Guess the courts aren't gonna get a chance to debate that now, are they?" Brody taunted.

Luke snapped his head to the body and appeared to be fighting back tears.

I was about to come out swinging at Brody for picking on Luke when Hinkin walked over. "County's got this handled. They want us to secure the perimeter." She sent us in different directions.

As Luke crossed behind Brody on his way from the clearing, Brody spoke under his breath. "If I was one of those humanitarians, I'd be watching my back. With Lacy gone, the militias are going to need a new target."

Before I started my search, I texted Deon that I'd probably be late and would meet him at the game. I reminded him to make sure Sami had her heavy coat. He gave me a thumbs up and I thought a moment before texting back, *We need to talk to Josie about the protest.*

A few seconds later my phone vibrated with, *You and I need to discuss it first.*

He was right, of course. We always tried to present a united front with the kids. Probably a good idea in this case since her protesting at my job still made me mad.

I trudged through the thick brush swinging my flashlight back and forth for a half hour, looking for anything out of the ordinary and not finding it. The soccer game would start in a couple of hours. If I left right now, I might be able to make it for the start of the game. But I wasn't leaving right now.

Hinkin hollered at me from the clearing, "Sanchez. Come on back."

She didn't need to ask twice and I hurried to her.

"Shift ended an hour ago. I think Brody's at your pickup already. You guys take off, and when the next shift gets here, I'll let the others go." Typical Hinkin, she hadn't shown any emotion about Brody slacking off and heading to the vehicle. I'm not sure I had that kind of restraint.

Even though I didn't feel good about being linked with Brody and seen as the weakest team on the mission, I was relieved to be going. There might still be a chance to see most of Josie's game. I trotted down the trail, now well-worn by the agents and deputies.

Arguing voices became clear the closer I got to the road where we'd left the pickup. I rounded the last curve and stopped to see Brody in a heated discussion with a thin man.

In the dark, the man had his back to me and Brody faced him. He stood a head taller than Brody and seemed determined to confront him. His gravelly voice didn't carry far enough for me to understand his words.

Brody held his hand out and braced it against the man's chest. "Go away. The last thing you need is to let anyone see you here."

The man backed off, then spun around and poked a finger into Brody's chest. Whatever he said was lost in a tone of anger and threat. He stomped off and jumped on an ATV, cranking the engine and shooting sand as he tore off into the darkness.

Brody stared after him before walking back to the driver's side and sliding into the pickup.

I waited a moment, then trod to the truck and opened the passenger door. "Hinkin relieved us of duty." I climbed in. "Been waiting long?"

I wasn't surprised he never mentioned the man on the ATV.

6

I didn't change from my uniform. Josie's game would start soon and I didn't have time to spare. Tucson traffic offered the usual rush hour frustrations. Backed-up interstate and long lines at every light in the city. I tapped at the steering wheel, imagining Josie dribbling down the field and kicking a goal.

Until almost two years ago, I hadn't missed more than a couple of her or Sami's games, recitals, school plays, or the usual run of activities. I'd hung up my Tucson Police Department uniform when Sami was a toddler and took on the role of full-time mom. It felt weird to not be the hub of the wheel of their lives. Hard to admit to the slight feeling of freedom.

Lights shone from the large windows at the front of Mi Casa, though shades kept the view from the street. I pulled up in front, taking the chance Ann was at the center instead of her house. Josie, who spent more time with Ann than anyone else in our family, said Ann avoided being home alone as much as possible.

I was grateful for Josie and Ann's relationship. When I'd told Ann my plan to attend the Border Patrol Academy two years ago, she'd blown up. She'd cursed and railed at me, trying every argument to keep me from joining.

"Chris finally came to his senses and quit, and I thought this family was owning up to our responsibility. And then you jump in. What's wrong with you?"

"I think I can make a difference." Especially if Chris and I uncovered the dirty agents.

That hadn't gone over well. After an hour of back and forth, with raised voices and tears, Ann hadn't been able to agree to disagree. Having Josie and Sami spending some time with her let me keep some tabs on Ann's health and attitude.

In his last year of law school, Chris didn't have the time to do more than stop in occasionally to say hello to Ann. He frustrated me by not asking the right questions or looking for tell-tale signs of her deteriorating health.

I whipped into the lot and hopped out of the Pilot. Hopefully this stop wouldn't take long. I didn't relish telling Ann the news about Lacy Hollander, but since she'd sent me out looking, I owed it to tell her in person.

The sounds of rapid Spanish broke into a loud song as a radio station seeped through the façade of the old office complex. The building ran along the street, recessed enough for a narrow parking lot. Two wings jutted back, creating a courtyard. The offices had been converted to dorms, a communal kitchen/dining room. A large gathering room occupied what used to be a lobby area. Ann's office sat directly off the common space, her door almost always wide open.

The glass front door was locked. I knocked, then had to bang again before someone heard me over the radio. The shade on the door slid to the side and a round face appeared. The shade slid back. I heard a sudden rustle of activity and anxious voices.

I waited for a few minutes. The radio stopped abruptly, and someone pulled the shade aside again and squinted at me. The shade fell back in place and the lock clicked.

A young woman a few inches shorter than me and half as wide burst out and folded her arms over her chest. "What do you want?"

Oh yeah, uniform. Border Patrol might not be a reassuring sight for people who'd entered the country so recently. I held up my hands in surrender. "Just looking for Ann. I'm her sister."

The door opened again and a young man popped out, pulling the door closed behind him. He rested a hand on the woman's shoulder and gave me a friendly smile. "What's the problem, Serena?"

Serena didn't take her eyes off me. "Says she's Ann's sister. Ann ever tell you she had a sister in Border Patrol?"

The guy sported a light-colored buzz cut and looked like a college ROTC recruit, not someone I'd expect to see volunteering at Mi Casa. He thrust out his hand. "Derrick Fowler. You must be Josie and Sami's mom."

Serena leaned back with an appalled expression as if he shook hands with a giant slug.

I matched his friendly tone. "Michaela Sanchez. You volunteer here?"

Serena lifted her chin, showing me how unwelcome I was.

If this woman had met Josie here and enlisted her help at the protest, I already disliked her way more than she could ever dislike me.

Derrick seemed relaxed. "I stop in most days for an hour or two between classes to help Ann if she needs some errands run or heavy lifting done."

An awkward pause followed this before I said, "Is Ann here?"

Derrick laughed. "Oh, sorry. No. I dropped her off at the high school for Josie's soccer game." He cocked his head. "Aren't you going?"

I backed away. "I'll talk to her there. Nice to meet you."

Derrick and Serena stood in front of the glass door looking like a weird version of *American Gothic*, guarding Mi Casa until I drove away.

Wondering how I'd break the bad news to Ann in a public place, I finally made my way to the high school parking lot. Of course it was full, and I wasted another several minutes cruising until I found a place. There must be some other activity going on, since soccer never drew a full crowd, just dedicated parents and family. They'd all been there for the initial kick-off, I was sure.

I trotted toward the ticket counter, my heart sinking to see it closed up, along with the concession stand. Not much time, if any, would be left of the game. I heard some cheering from the stands, nothing like the roar of a football or baseball game, but enough from the soccer crowd to tell me a battle waged. I zoomed through the opening in the stands and glanced at the scoreboard lit up against the night sky. Tied, just under a minute left.

Not caring if I offended anyone, I nudged my way between fans at the edge of the field and scanned the blue uniforms for Josie's number. I spotted her as the whistle blew, possibly signaling an injury timeout. Along with her teammates she ran to the sidelines. Ignoring the glare of the woman next to me, I turned to scan the bleachers.

Deon sat about halfway up the stands behind Josie's team bench. I didn't see Sami but she could be hanging with her friends somewhere. Everyone in the bleachers seemed to be shouting.

I didn't bother climbing up to join Deon. Somehow he seemed to know I had arrived and found me. His smile of welcome gave my heart a little hitch.

That feeling of someone watching me tingled up my neck and I turned, not sure what to expect. A few yards away, sitting in her wheelchair at the designated spot in the first row of the bleachers, my sister pinned me with her glare. Her eyes lingered on me long enough to convey her contempt and I remembered my uniform.

Sami leaned on the back of Ann's chair looking about as bored as a preteen can look. She raised her head, caught sight of me, and sent a smile my way. Just that greeting seemed to lighten the heavy cloud that had gathered around me and I waved, maybe at both of them.

Ann's face turned from me to the field as the teams ran back out. Cheers erupted.

Tension tightened the crowd sparsely distributed in the bleachers. So many times I'd been wrapped up in the outcome of a child's ball game. It had seemed so important. But today, I'd seen life and death play out on the desert and didn't feel the same pull to the field.

Controlling the ball, the white team passed skillfully, moving up the field as they mounted an attack on the blue goal. Josie tracked back from midfield to help her team's defenders, her own blue jersey momentarily disappearing in the crush of bodies. When a blue defender went down under a forceful challenge from the white team's tall striker, parents howled in protest but the referee kept his whistle in his hand and waved to play on.

Suddenly Josie won the ball with a clean slide tackle and sprang to her feet. Finding herself in space, she dribbled at top speed toward the white goal and cleared the halfway line before several white jerseys closed in.

Spotting a teammate on the opposite side of the field, Josie played a long diagonal pass but continued running toward the goal without the ball.

Each and every one of the fifty-odd spectators were screaming as the scoreboard on the opposite sideline ticked down the final seconds remaining in the game with the score still tied 1-1.

Everything disappeared except my daughter's sprinting form on the green field in front of me. The bright lights of the field accentuated the vivid blues and greens of their uniforms, making the grass look like a lush park. The flash of the ball as Josie's teammate sent it in a high arc toward the goal—what looked like a terrible, hopeless shot that would miss by several yards.

But it wasn't a shot. It was a pass.

Timing it perfectly, Josie jumped impossibly high and hammered the ball with her forehead, past the flailing arms of the onrushing goalkeeper and into the corner of the net.

My heart broke open and clogged my throat, sending tears to my eyes. My beautiful, spirited, smart girl must feel the thrill of success all the way deep into her bones. Part of me soared with her. Pride that she was mine, sure, but full of happiness at her elation. I took off with the rest of the fans to flood the infield.

Since I was standing at the fence, I had the advantage over those plunging down the stands. Amid the gathering crowd, I made my way to where Josie was already surrounded by teammates and fans, hugging and screaming. She looked up and our eyes connected. I couldn't wait to grab her in a bear hug.

Her smile slipped a little, then she shifted her gaze beyond me and it brightened again. The whole stadium seemed to have made it to the center of the field, jostling and shouting. Josie pushed her way toward me and I tried to open my arms. She dodged to the left of me, her grin wide, her eyes shining. With all the adrenaline of her win, she launched herself into Deon's arms. He caught her and bounced her up and down before letting her go.

Their embrace, their wide grins, their total focus on each other both thrilled and crushed me. I missed being a part of the club. Missed it a lot.

The crowd thinned and I joined them. Deon stood with his arm around Josie's shoulders as they spoke to another teammate. With their voices loud and high-pitched, the girls relived the game with such excitement it was impossible to interpret their exact words. You couldn't mistake that Josie belonged to Deon. She had his dark hair, skin, and eyes. He was a handsome man and she took that attractiveness and made it feminine. My blonde, blue-eyed coloring didn't surface in Josie. Maybe the only physical trait she inherited from me was my height and thin frame.

As far as personality, well, we were probably more alike than she'd ever admit.

Deon caught sight of me and his grin widened. He held out his other arm and hugged all three of us together. "Did you see the game-winning goal from our MVP?"

"I did." I rubbed my hand across her shoulders.

Josie ducked away from my touch. "You don't get a medal for that." She threw her arm around her teammate's shoulder, almost to demonstrate the substitution for us, well, for me. They skipped off to throw themselves in with other teammates.

Deon shrugged. "It was an awesome goal. Glad you got to see it." He stepped back and took in my uniform, almost as dirty as Josie's. "Hard day?"

I hadn't thought about Lacy Hollander for the last ten minutes. The memory landed heavy and cold in my gut. I needed to find Ann.

"At least it ended on a high note, huh?" Deon said.

"We need to talk about Josie being at the demonstration this morning." I hadn't meant to be so abrupt.

Deon winced. "Not now, okay? She just won the game. Let her live it a little before we come down on her."

"We can't ignore that she was at the station this morning."

He looked surprised. "She's following her conscience. Like we taught her to do."

While people streamed toward the parking lot, I geared up to make a point about age-appropriate behavior. "But—"

He held up his hand. "Later, okay?"

I clamped my mouth and took a breath to switch gears, searching the infield. "Where's Sami?"

His eyebrows dipped. "Ann's ride showed up, so Sami took her to the parking lot. She's mad at me. Who knows what I did wrong this time."

What had happened to our sweet little family? We used to be giggles and inside jokes, dancing and playing. Now it seemed we had crossed arms, slammed doors, and annoyed silences.

Deon hugged me once more then dropped his arm. "Maybe we can all make up over dinner."

As we started walking toward the parking lot, I said, "What do you suppose that will be tonight?"

"Whatever it is, you need to pick it up. We don't have anything at home. I'll go wrangle Sami. She needs poster board and probably glitter and stickers and glue and whatever else she can talk me into for a poster for social studies. Due tomorrow. She told me about it on the way to the ball game."

Back in the old days, I unpacked their bookbags when they came home from school. I knew the homework assignments. I had a handle on when we needed snacks and what dress-up costumes were looming. It felt a little like my world was slipping through my hands. But this was okay. Everyone should take responsibility for themselves. Me continuing to be Control Central wasn't necessarily good for them. I believed this.

It didn't take away the guilt. "Okay, I'll wait for Josie and we'll get dinner and meet you at home."

Less than an hour later Josie emerged, showered and buzzing with the win. She approached the driver's window and I rolled it down.

As if issuing an order, she said, "A bunch of us are going for pizza. I'll be home later."

The wave of our next fight built on the horizon. "Not tonight. You've got school tomorrow."

"But practically the whole team is going. Why can't I?"

I could make some comment about how tired she probably was since she'd started her day with a protest. Or I could explain that neither Deon nor I wanted to have to go out again and pick her up. Though all of that was true, I really just wanted everyone home, under the same roof. "I'm the mom. That's why."

"Oh, right. So now you're the mom. Convenient."

I ignored the cut as she huffed into the car, tossing her athletic bag in back.

"I thought we'd stop at Whole Foods and get dinner," I said when she'd settled in.

"Of course."

I waited my turn to back into the flow of traffic exiting the lot. "I don't want to cook tonight, do you?"

She crossed her arms. "It's not my job."

Teenagers. You can't live with them. You can't surrender them to the nearest firehouse. Or could you? I mulled that over instead of fighting with her about whose job she supposed it was to cook dinner.

"Lasagna or rotisserie chicken?"

"I could be having pizza with my friends."

"I'm thinking the chicken. Maybe they'll have roasted Brussels sprouts."

She kept her face turned toward her window. "Could you please not wear your uniform to my games?" The disdain dripped from her words. I guess nobody liked my uniform.

How much of this crap should I put up with before I called her on her attitude? "I was running late and didn't want to miss your game."

"You missed it. Okay? One play doesn't count."

"But it was a rockin' play, right?"

She let out a sigh. "I'd rather you not show up at all instead of showing up in uniform."

We made it through the first stop light. The businesses lining the busy street looked cheery, even if the atmosphere in the car absolutely was not. "I'm proud of being Border Patrol. Yesterday we stopped drug smugglers in the desert." I purposely avoided today's grisly discovery. Josie would be devastated by the news, but I couldn't tell her until it was released to the media. "We tracked them and had a wild chase. They all had big packs—"

"Yeah, so how many kids did you rip from their parents' arms today?"

I flipped my turn signal and pulled into Whole Foods. "We've talked about this. The Border Patrol does not separate—"

"Right. That's the official line. I don't believe it and neither does anyone with half a brain. So, yeah, just please stay away from my games."

I found a parking place and stopped the car. Without taking off my seatbelt or moving, I said, "Okay. That's enough. You're a smart girl. You've got lots of friends, you're popular at school, you're pretty. But let's just come down from that holy place you think you inhabit."

She gave me a side eye, showing how little that meant to her.

"I'm going in to get dinner. Are you coming with me?"

She looked me up and down with all the disgust a teen can muster. "Not when you're dressed like that."

7

Morning came way too early. Deon's phone started singing his latest pop favorite and panic zinged through me before I opened my eyes. He rolled over and tapped off the alarm.

"What's wrong with playing a sweet ballad for wake-up?" I said, pushing myself to sit up so I wouldn't be tempted to go back to sleep.

Deon bounced up, all smiles and energy. "I like to get up to inspiration. Get the blood pumping."

"You shouldn't need a jump start after I got your blood hot last night."

He kissed me on the way to the shower. "It's a new day."

The girls rushed into their morning routines without badgering. Maybe my working really did make them more self-reliant. I could hope.

I wanted to head out early so I could stop to talk to Ann. So far, news of Lacy Hollander's death hadn't hit the media. Maybe since the call had come from Border Patrol to the sheriff's office, the beat journalists hadn't picked up on it yet. That would change quickly, I was sure, and Lacy Hollander would be making headlines again.

Josie and Sami had both been out of sorts last night. They'd eaten the chicken and Brussels sprouts mostly in silence. We used to be able to count on Sami for incessant chatter, but even she was silent.

Before the end of dinner, I'd ventured a topic. "I saw Ann at your game."

Josie didn't look up from her plate. "She's always there." It seemed obvious she'd meant to say, "You're never there anymore."

I swallowed the salty goodness of a roasted Brussels sprout, not at all guilty that I hadn't stood in my kitchen preparing it myself. "She looked pale. Is everything okay with her?"

Deon watched the girls.

Sami looked up. "She asked if I can come over on Saturday and help her clean her house."

"Do you want to?" I asked.

She tilted her head. "Yeah. I guess. I mean, she can't do a lot of the stuff she used to."

"With Uncle Fritz in jail and Efrain deported, no one is there all the time to help." Josie raised her eyes to me, as if all of it was somehow my fault.

Sami piped up, "She's got Derrick. He helps her."

Josie looked at her plate but didn't say anything.

I urged her. "Is Derrick good help, do you think?"

She let her fork clatter onto her plate. "Why are you pumping me for information. If you want to know how your own sister is doing, why don't you go see her?"

Telling Ann about Lacy didn't seem like a great opportunity to fix things between us.

I'd splurged on peach pie and ice cream in hopes it would sweeten up the girls, but that didn't work. Josie refused it with heaps of condemnation that I didn't know she hated peach pie. Which was a new development since she'd eaten it last summer. She stomped upstairs, not quite slamming her door.

Sami had slurped down dessert, then taken off in a huff at something Deon said.

Alone in our room, I'd told Deon about discovering Lacy Hollander. His comforting embrace led from one thing to another. At least I'd been relaxed and satisfied enough to get a few good hours of sleep before stress woke me up.

I spent the rest of the night in fitful sleep. Much of it due to thinking about Lacy Hollander's death, but a great deal worrying about how to heal the rift between me and Josie and bring harmony back to our home.

With barely more than a see-you-tonight to each other, all four of us thundered out of the house and blew in four directions. Mine took me south with fifteen minutes to spare to talk to Ann. My Pilot was the lone vehicle in the parking lot, but the shades were up on the glass front door and it opened easily when I tugged.

No one occupied the front lobby, but voices of adults and children competed with a Spanish radio station coming from the kitchen. I heard the squeak of Ann's crutches on the linoleum before I saw her emerge from the kitchen hallway.

She hesitated when she saw me. "I wish you wouldn't show up here in your uniform. It terrifies the residents."

I patted my olive-green T-shirt. "No uniform. I'll change at the station."

Ann started working her way toward her office. Maybe she knew the news wouldn't be good. I wanted her safely in a chair before I told her about Lacy. Her look of disdain settled on me for a moment before she started moving again. "Please. You don't need the patches to be obvious Border Patrol."

She made slow progress. I hadn't been inside Mi Casa much since I'd enrolled at the academy. It hadn't changed a great deal. Two long tables took up space on the tiled floor. Low shelves filled one corner, stuffed with colorful baskets of Legos and blocks. Picture books lined one section. A kids' table with small chairs held a basket of Crayons and piles of coloring books and paper.

Large cardboard boxes of clothes sat next to one of the tables, and piles of folded tops and pants filled the surface. It appeared as though someone had been sorting donation items.

Ann made it to her chair and dropped into it. She inhaled and let it out in a whoosh, as if she'd just run a marathon. "Tell me."

Dark circles drooped under her eyes and I swear she had double the wrinkles since the last time I'd seen her up close. Worry knotted in my stomach as I stood in front of her desk. "Are you okay?"

She gave me that slow-burn stare she'd perfected when we were kids. It worked to send me out of her room when her friends came over, as well as compel me to hand over the last dinner roll at Thanksgiving. "I'm fine."

"Sami said you asked her to come help out on Saturday. Do you want me to come on my day off? I'd be happy—"

She waved a hand. "Tell me what's going on."

How to begin? "We checked out the area you sent me to."

I stopped and she waited a beat. She sounded nervous and annoyed at the same time. "And? Did you find the missing person?"

"We found Lacy Hollander."

Ann paled and looked like she lost her breath. "Is she...? Did you...?" She trailed off.

This kind of news is never easy and I was not doing a good job of delivering it. "I'm sorry. She's dead."

Ann's eyes filled and her lips pressed into themselves. She drew in a long breath through her nose and let it out. "What happened?"

"She was shot. At an aid station. The sheriff's department is pretty sure she accidentally crossed paths with traffickers."

Ann propped her arms on her desk and lowered her face into her hands. Her shoulders didn't shake with sobs. She sat motionless for a minute and I waited.

When she looked up, her eyes were wet, but no tears had fallen. "You need to find who killed her."

I stepped closer. "The sheriff's deputies will handle the investigation. We aren't involved in that."

Ann leaned back in her chair, looking spent. "It sounds like they'll label it cartels and that's that."

"What else would it be?"

Her voice was harsh. "Think about who hates the people helping immigrants? Cartels don't care as long as they get their money. No. It's Border Patrol who wants to round up the innocent and send them back."

Even though she basically called me a murderer, I managed to keep my response clipped instead of lashing back. "Border Patrol didn't kill Lacy Hollander."

She raised her eyebrows. "And who works for Border Patrol?"

I raised my hands in surrender. "I don't know what you're talking about."

"Oh, come on. The militias. They want to scare us out of the desert. But they won't do it."

This conversation had no end. I let it sit there for a second or two before changing the subject. "Let me help you to your house." She lived in a bungalow behind Mi Casa, joined by a wooden fence with a gate wide enough to accommodate her wheelchair. It had been a perfect arrangement when she lived with her husband, Fritz. Now she lived there alone.

"I'm fine."

"Look, I'm here. It's not a problem."

She swiveled to her computer and started tapping keys. "You're not here every day. I get along on my own, thank you very much."

"Why don't you call Derrick? Sami says he's good help."

"You know Derrick?" She looked surprised.

"He and Serena greeted me when I stopped by last night to tell you about Lacy. Serena was a whole lot less than welcoming."

Ann gave me a pointed stare. "Serena is committed to helping those less fortunate than us. She gives so much time and effort to the immigrant cause. She's a hero."

"So maybe she can give you a hand today."

Eyes on the screen, she said, "Even if I wanted to, I can't call them. They're taking a day off."

"Then call someone else."

That dark stare came out again and I knew I'd lost. I dropped into the chair opposite her. "Right. So. Let's talk about No Desert Deaths."

She lost her rhythm on the keys, then picked up again. "Let's not."

"You're working with them, aren't you?"

She ignored me, kept typing. "Why would you think that?"

My gaze wasn't as compelling as hers, though I tried. "Lacy was shot in the most rugged, isolated area of southern Arizona and you happened to have an anonymous tip that sent me to the exact area."

She didn't stop working.

I leaned forward. "Come on, Ann. Talk to me. You can't be involved with them."

She didn't look up. "I can't?"

"Lacy was on trial for harboring felons. It's possible she would have ended up in jail. Now that she's gone, the same people who targeted her will want to find another poster child against illegal immigration. You could get in trouble. Lose Mi Casa. Is that what you want?"

"What I want"—tap, tap, tap—"is for this country to wake up and understand people are dying on the border. Families are being ripped apart. This needs to stop."

I took a deep breath. "If you're in jail you can't help immigrants, like you do every day."

She reached for a pen and made a note on a pad. "Don't worry about me."

Even though I tried not to, I raised my voice. "I do worry. What if the same person who came for Lacy Hollander comes for you?"

Her hands landed on the keyboard again. "I thought you said it was cartels. They aren't likely to show up at Mi Casa looking for a crippled lady."

Yes, Lacy probably had surprised drug smugglers at the aid station. But I remembered the duty supervisor briefing us on escalating tension between vigilantes and humanitarian workers.

And I thought of the rage in the voice of the man Brody confronted yesterday.

8

I left Ann's place feeling like nothing had improved between us, and stewed as I battled traffic on my way to the station. Even though a few protesters clustered around the gates, thankfully, Josie wasn't among them.

Clutching my venti Starbucks cup, I hurried down the corridor to muster. The room was already crowded. When I slipped through the doorway, someone called out, "There she is. Bloodhound."

Liz slapped me on the back. "Hell, yeah."

I found a place next to Luke at the back wall. He leaned over and, under his breath, said, "How are you doing? You know, after finding Lacy Hollander?"

Her death had been right under my skin since I'd found her and I thought it might be there for quite a while. Meantime, I had kids, a husband, a sister, and a bucket of life to deal with. "Hanging in there," I said to Luke.

The duty supervisor nodded at me. "Okay, kiddies, let's settle down." He walked us through the status of the night shift. "We got a call from Ford and his crew around 0200. A group of six carrying bundles. They dispersed before we got there. We recovered two bundles of heroin."

He ran through a few other incidents without mentioning Lacy Hollander. My guess was that they wanted to keep the news close until the details were released to the media and the shit storm began. After the briefing, the supervisor gave out vehicles and assignments. When he got to me, he said, "Sanchez. Since I can't keep you out of east Sasabe, that's where you're going today. Keep that nose to the ground."

Someone let out a Bloodhound bay and a few people laughed on their way out of the room.

Luke and I made our way out to the parking lot lugging our lunch coolers. He stopped with me when I reached my assigned pickup and gave me a cute grin like a kindergartner on his first day when he eyes the water table. "Are you excited?"

For almost two years I'd been thinking of this. Deciding to be Border Patrol had been a tough family decision. Back then, both the kids had been all for it. It might have seemed exciting and romantic to them. But after me having to attend the academy in New Mexico for five months, and then the on-the-job training here, they were pretty much over the thrill.

I'd agonized over the decision. But once made, I was all in. Well, except for the waves of guilt. But pretty much all in. So yeah, I was excited. "I don't suppose every day can be as exciting as yesterday."

"Maybe," he said, not sounding convinced. "But there's stuff going on out there and we're here to stop it."

Brody strutted out to the parking lot. "You got lucky yesterday, Grandma. Don't let it go to your head."

I ignored Brody and flashed Luke a conspiratorial wink before turning to my pickup.

Clouds hung low and spit some moisture from time to time as I drove west of town and turned south. I finished my coffee on the way to my AOR. The supervisor was right. The site of Lacy's murder drew me like a bat to a mosquito. Because of all the activity surrounding the murder scene, the road was churned up and dust rose behind me.

I parked my pickup at the animal trail I'd followed yesterday and retraced my steps. Trucks and ATVs from the sheriff's department and Border Patrol had torn up the trail, but I preferred walking back to the site so I could study the surrounding landscape. The walk warmed me, and despite the cool air and gray day, I unzipped my jacket.

Yellow crime scene tape flapped in the slight breeze. One end was tied to a mesquite branch, the other loose. Some of the other tape had broken free altogether and had been snagged by cholla and cat's claw bushes. The area of the aid station had been worked over by so many agents and officers it looked more like well-used picnic grounds with scuffed dirt and footprints covering every inch of ground.

I hadn't been paying much attention to stealth so I was surprised to see someone in the clearing. He stood in front of the spot where Lacy had fallen, his head down. He was tall and lanky, and not an ounce of fat seemed to hide under his faded khaki T-shirt and camo pants. This looked like the same guy Brody had the heated conversation with last night. He gave the impression of being part of the desert. Alive in the way a cactus lives, without impulse and exuberance.

I placed a hand on my gun. "Hello." I tried to sound casual.

The man spun around so quickly I jumped. Alarm flashed up my spine to see the pistol he aimed at me. Even from across the clearing his eyes shone with a blue so vivid it rivaled a Caribbean sea.

As if I'd woken him, he seemed to come back to himself but not slowly. After two seconds, he shoved his gun into his belt at the small of his back. "Border Patrol."

I nodded, hand still ready to claim my weapon. "Agent Sanchez."

He turned back to the spot where Lacy had bled into the sand. "Checking the scene of the crime?"

Who was this spook? "Did you know the victim?"

"Victim." He snorted, then stepped back and looked at me. "She's no victim. She walked into this with her eyes wide open." Violence rippled just under his skin, his eyes blazed.

I concentrated on sounding calm. "Are you working with No Desert Deaths?"

He scoffed. "Me? Ma'am, beg your pardon, but I swore an oath to the Army to protect and defend America. It would be treason to work with people helping the enemy."

Okay, that meant he was part of the citizen militia patrolling the border. Play soldiers creating malicious mischief. As the cliché says, consider them armed and dangerous. "You didn't answer me. Did you know the victim?"

He swiveled his head toward the blood-darkened sand. "Yeah. I knew

Lacy. I warned her to stay away from the border. But it wasn't enough for her to be prosecuted and locked up. No, the moment she's out on bail she's on the desert again. Doing exactly what she shouldn't be doing."

"When was the last time you spoke to her?"

He squinted at me. His eyes were the kind of blue that seemed to have been faded by the desert. Beautiful and somehow damaged. "She was aiding and abetting the enemy. Breaking the law of the United States."

"Do you think she accidentally came across traffickers and they killed her?"

He focused on me and sniffed. "What do you think?"

"The sheriff's department is investigating. I'm only checking out the scene."

He flashed me a disgusted look and gave me his back, stepping toward the mesquite on the north edge of the clearing.

"Where are you going?" I thought I should stop him but didn't have any legitimate reason for doing so.

"Maybe you don't have any real work, but I do. Crime won't take a break to mourn one do-gooder gunned down because she was sticking her nose where it damned well shouldn't have been stuck."

"Sounds like you knew her pretty well."

"Who didn't know Lacy Hollander. It was only a matter of time before she couldn't be allowed to live."

This guy gave off creepy vibes in all the rainbow colors. "Who do you think killed her?"

He spun around, the rage I'd detected under the surface suddenly bursting out. "She's dead. That's all. But let me tell you something. All these people out here aiding and abetting or harboring, or whatever else they call breaking the law, are in danger. Maybe she's the first one lying face down in the sand, but she's not going to be the last. War is declared."

That sounded like a threat. Maybe enough for me to detain him. Bring him in for questioning. "War with who?"

He glanced away from me, head tilted toward Baboquivari Peak. I doubted he was admiring the scenery. "The border is a dangerous place. Not only does everything in the desert want to hurt you, there are people out here who kill for fun."

"What people?"

He exhaled in exasperation, as if I'd asked a stupid question. "You're obviously new. You've got drug smugglers, scouts, coyotes, scared immigrants, angry ranchers." He pointed to the dried blood stains in the sand. "These humanitarians who claim to speak for the voiceless, defend the defenseless, and talk about the dignity of human lives and ending human suffering are some of the worst." He spouted as if he'd said these things many times.

"Which group do you belong to?" I asked.

He narrowed his focus to me, making the hairs on the back of my neck rise. "I told you. I took an oath to defend and protect this country. I belong to the patriots."

Patriots. Was that a militia group? I recalled other organized groups such as Arizona Border Recon or Minute Men. "Is that the name of your unit?"

He scoffed again. "Unit." He shook his head. "Go ahead and investigate this scene or whatever you need to do. I'll get back to work."

I raised my hand. "Wait." I pulled my phone from my pocket. "I need your name and address. Some way to contact you."

He laughed and shook his head again.

My radio came to life. "All agents in the area. 10-15 by twelve. Arieta Wash. They've grenaded. Requesting air support."

Like translating Spanish to English, I had no trouble understanding a family group of about twelve people had been spotted but they'd scattered. I pulled the receiver from my belt. "Tango 721 responding. I'm ten minutes away." I wouldn't have time to haul this guy in even if I had something to tag him for, but I'd get his contact info at least. I clipped the radio on my belt and looked up.

The clearing was empty. The spook had vanished in the short time I'd shifted my attention to the call.

Creepy.

9

Ten minutes later I pulled up behind two other units on a sandy trail road. Bright sunshine burned away the last of the clouds, giving us a brilliant afternoon. The *wooft* of a chopper sounded in the distance. Fresh footprints and broken twigs created an obvious trail and I ran along it. The tracks broke up and I picked a set to follow. My first shouts were met with a response from Liz.

"Over here." Her voice directed me to the northeast, and in no time I came across eight people sitting cross-legged in a semi-circle. Two women, one who seemed not even twenty and one middle-aged, sandwiched between two middle-aged men and two adolescent boys. A family group, maybe. Maybe one of the men was solo.

Two little girls, obviously twins, sat close together but away from the others. They didn't look scared as much as tired. In one hand they both held a small stuffed animal that looked brand new and in their other hand they clutched a granola bar. They looked to be about eight years old.

I raised my eyebrows at Liz to ask about the girls.

She shrugged, her face tight. "They say they crossed with their father. We don't know where he ran off to but he's not their father. We captured these girls with a group last month. Different dad."

At least Liz had given them something to eat and a toy to focus on. Situations like this must be why Liz had built that hard shell around her emotions. I'd need to learn how she did that.

Squatting in front of the girls, I placed a hand on each fragile shoulder. "Hola," I said. Both girls ignored me. I patted them lightly and, not knowing what else to offer them, backed away.

Brody stood between the two groups, his back to the twins and facing the family with his automatic rifle held like a storm trooper. He glowered at them and I wanted to punch him. "Welcome to the party, Grandma."

A tall cliff rimmed the clearing behind Brody. Unlike the desert around Tucson, down here, thick grass, now dry and dead, covered much of the ground. The clearing was hard-packed dirt. It was a well-used camping site for recreationists. It even had a stone-lined fire pit and smattering of grass where the cliff provided shade most of the day. Mesquite and thick under-growth gave the place a private feel. There wasn't a spring in the cliff, but it felt as if there could be.

Liz roamed the periphery of the clearing. "There are some runners. Maybe coyotes. These guys aren't talking." She nodded to the group.

Brody gloated. "The chopper will locate them, don't worry. We aren't letting these *tonks* get free." He emphasized the word and grinned at me, probably knowing how much I detested it.

The official explanation is that tonk is an acronym for True Origin Unknown. Others believe it refers to the sound when a flashlight is banged onto the head of an illegal immigrant.

"I can take over here if you want to go after the runners," I said to him.

He pulled his gun close, as if ready to aim. "I'm fine here."

I knelt in front of the group and spoke in slow Spanish. For many Central Americans, Spanish wasn't their first language and it definitely wasn't mine. "Did you pay someone to bring you across the border?"

The older woman lowered her eyes. A couple of the others turned their gaze to one of the middle-aged men. I focused on him. "Is this your family?" I indicated the people sitting with him.

"Si." He spoke quietly and I leaned in to hear him.

Brody paced behind me. "Of course they had a goddamned coyote. That's who took off."

Someone on the chopper radioed Liz and she stepped back to confer.

Luke and another veteran agent trotted into the clearing. "What've you got?" the agent said to Liz.

"They scattered when we spotted them. Maybe half a dozen more out there. This is what we caught." She pointed to the dismal family sitting in the dirt. "The guys in the chopper said a couple took off east and another few north."

The agent tapped Luke's shoulder. "Let's take this set of tracks."

Ben Rodriguez, an agent I'd worked with, entered the clearing from the trail. Liz pointed to Brody. "Come with me." To Rodriguez she said, "Stay here with Sanchez."

Brody frowned. He didn't make an immediate move toward Liz.

Rodriguez laughed. "Bet you wish you hadn't had that diablo burrito this morning. Gonna make humping in the desert hard."

Brody sneered at him. "I can run you under a table."

Rodriguez cracked up. "The saying is drink you under a table, dude. And I doubt you could do that either."

"Just don't let Grandma release the prisoners," Brody said.

Liz's radio came to life with a report from the helicopter. "We have visual. The ridge to your right. Halfway up in some rocks."

"Let's go, Brody." She slipped through creosote and prickly pear. Without her sense of urgency, Brody shouldered his gun and trooped after her.

Rodriguez pulled his gun but held it pointing down.

The little girls kept their heads close together and their eyes in their laps. I continued to question the family. "Who ran away?"

The man shrugged as if he didn't understand.

"Is it the people you paid to bring you across?"

Still nothing.

Rodriguez leaned against the side of a rock. "They won't tell you. If the cartel finds out they said anything, they'll be killed. Besides, their trip is probably guaranteed. If they don't make it this time, the next try is free."

I knew he was right. The revolving door shot the immigrants back to Mexico and most of them would try to cross again. The unlucky would die in the desert. Too many. The lucky would eventually make it in. Only a small percentage gave up and went home. In many cases, these immigrants sold everything they owned and borrowed from family and friends to pay the coyotes to get them across.

If they made it, they'd find a job, and we knew those opportunities were something grand, like cutting chickens in a packing plant, working for less than minimum wage in restaurants or hotels, or landscaping beautiful yards in suburban America. They'd begin sending money back to pay their loans and help finance the next family member's immigration attempt. They couldn't quit and go home. They had nothing to go back to.

In a few minutes the chopper's rotors sent waves of percussion over us, directing the agents on their hunt. Another agent arrived and joined the search. I hated having to stand guard on a family clearly traumatized and two little girls caught in an endless nightmare. The woman cried softly. The two young men looked confused and upset. The group's spokesman seemed defeated, while the other man seemed to be taking it all in stride. Maybe he'd been through this before.

"We're going to have to take them back to the station and process them, you know," Rodriguez said.

I didn't know much about Rodriguez. He'd been my journeyman for a month's rotation. He had a wife and two grade school-aged sons, so we'd spoken a little about raising kids. Tall, dark, and kind of handsome, he didn't offer a lot of Border Patrol gossip or advice. I got the impression he preferred to keep his opinions to himself, do the job, and go home to his family. Since Chris and I didn't know who the dirty agents were, I started off suspecting everyone. But I couldn't believe Rodriquez was one of the bad ones.

"This is a nice spot," I said, when I'd given up trying to pry information from the immigrants. "I'm surprised it isn't a supply stop for No Desert Deaths."

Rodriguez looked around. "It probably was. They rotate around so the vigilantes and the patrol don't keep destroying supplies."

Luke made his way into the clearing. A tough-looking Latino man cuffed with plastic restraints behind his back walked in front of him.

Rodriguez grinned. "Good hunting."

Luke directed the man to the edge of the group and put his hand on the man's shoulder to let him know to sit. "Had to run over the top of Brody to get to him."

Rodriguez laughed. "Not surprised."

None of the others looked at the newcomer, and I assumed he must be the coyote.

A half hour dragged by and the chopper took off, maybe called away to another mission. Standing with the immigrants instead of chasing the runners made me jumpy, and I considered leaving them to Luke and Rodriguez and randomly searching the brush. That probably wouldn't help anything so I tried to be patient.

Liz crashed through the brush at the edge of the clearing.

We heard Brody before we saw him. "I had the greaser if you hadn't interfered." He stumbled behind her.

Liz's face showed uncharacteristic irritation, but she didn't say a word. She stopped in front of the group seated on the ground and stared at them a moment. Without comment she pulled her radio from her belt and cued it. "Need transport for 10-15 by seven."

The good news was that the company the Border Patrol contracted for transport had a vehicle available. The bad news was that it would take forty-five minutes to an hour before we'd be relieved. We set to work filling out the field forms to send to processing.

With time to wait after that was finished, I said, "There was a weird guy at the scene of Lacy Hollander's murder when I checked it out earlier today."

Rodriguez raised one eyebrow. "What guy?"

"Maybe a vigilante."

"What makes you think so?" he asked.

"He was talking about taking an oath and protecting the border."

Liz perked up. "What did he look like?"

"He had really blue eyes and—"

Several of the agents laughed or made noise. "So, you met old blue eyes," Liz said.

"You know him?"

Brody said, "Everybody knows Ford Dewlinski. He's a legend."

I gave Liz a questioning look, hoping to hear her version.

She answered, "Dewlinski's been down here about six or seven years. He's 'commander'"—she gave the word air quotes—"of Recon to Reclaim the Desert."

Rodriguez inserted his comment. "It's not a catchy name, but he's got about a half-dozen or so regulars to take his orders. Few more on weekends and holidays."

Liz continued. "Ford is mostly harmless..."

Rodriguez pushed in again. "If you don't count killing a guy two years ago."

Brody's loud voice broke in. "He was acquitted. Rightly so. That wetback was a bad man and he needed to go."

Liz didn't acknowledge either man. "He shot a known coyote. This guy had a reputation for raping every woman or girl he brought across. He stole their money. He left more than one group on the desert without water or food. So, yeah, not a quality person."

"But Ford is a stand-up guy." Brody seemed intense. "He demands discipline from his soldiers; most of them are retired military. Ford knows how to find those slippery cartel scouts and he's captured more smugglers than most of the agents on Border Patrol."

That time Liz rolled her eyes, a rare show of emotion. "He's a volcano ready to explode. You can feel it. We hope he's been honest and called us whenever he's tracked and detained someone, but we don't know that. Some of those skeletons people find out there could be from Ford as easily as the cartels."

"You say that like it's a bad thing," Brody said.

A rumble of an engine sounded close.

Rodriguez cast a confused look. "Did anyone else respond to your call?"

"Nope." Liz scowled.

"I'll go check it out," I said, more than anxious to get away from Brody.

Liz flicked her chin at me in a go-ahead motion. That's all the permission I needed, and I hurried toward the trail road.

The Border Patrol vehicles left little space for another to get around us in the sandy strip that served as a road. But the pickup we'd heard apparently hadn't intended to pass, because it was parked and empty behind Rodriguez's vehicle.

Without hesitating, I took off, following footprints. If the people from the pickup were recreationists, I'd need to steer them away from the area. We didn't want them adding to the confusion.

Clouds milled about overhead, dimming the sun and keeping the air cool. Maybe we'd get another bout of rain or sprinkles. Despite the temperatures in the fifties, by the time I'd climbed the ridge following the trail, my face pounded with heat and exertion.

The footprints and other sign I followed led me toward the edge of the cliff, about a quarter mile from where Liz and the others held the immigrants. They might be gathering everyone up to move them toward the road where the transport could drive up and load them.

I thought again of the little girls. My children lived in a clean house without threat of rain, heat, or freezing temperatures. They had enough food to fill their bellies and slept in a comfortable bed every night. Maybe immigration services couldn't offer those two girls much, but it had to improve their lives over this constant walking on the desert.

The scramble up the cliff took me over rock piles. I studied each surface before placing my hand on the rocks to pull myself up. That wasn't a technique I'd learned at the Border Patrol Academy but one I'd picked up from growing up in the desert. It only takes one scorpion sting to learn that lesson.

By the time I reached the rocky summit of the ridge I was covered in sweat and dirt, yet I felt more alive and engaged than when I'd sat guard with the immigrants. The hilltop opened into a narrow passage with steep drops on either side. Rocks and scrub made moving slow, with many opportunities to stumble or be scratched by cactus and thorns. The thick grass obscured footprints, but broken twigs on the bushes made trailing them fairly easy. A slight breeze ruffled the brush but didn't bring much relief from the heat.

Hushed voices ahead alerted me to keep my breathing soft, though the climb had been exerting. I kept trailing the mumble of conversation. A woman and a man.

They stopped moving and I crept closer. They crouched behind a large rock as they looked into the valley. I assumed they'd pinpointed the group of immigrants and agents.

I cleared my throat to let them know of my presence. "Border Patrol," I said by way of introduction.

I figured they were hikers who came across the vehicles and got curious. I'd round them up and send them on their way in short order.

When they startled and turned around, I realized the situation was a bit more complicated. I searched my memory for their names. Serena and Derrick. Volunteers at Mi Casa.

With the sun behind my back, it took them a second to recognize me. When she did, Serena cocked her head at a belligerent angle. "Ann's sister. What's-her-name."

Derrick looked nervously over his shoulder. "Agent Sanchez."

Two large backpacks sat on the ground along with six plastic gallon jugs of water. I inclined my head toward them. "Is that yours?"

Serena thrust out a hip. "No. Not anymore. It's for the desperate people you're persecuting down there. We're here to help."

I knew it. If these people were "volunteering" at Mi Casa, it could only mean Ann was involved with No Desert Deaths. Damn it. Did she want to end up in jail? Did she want to lose Mi Casa?

Serena took a step toward me. "Our timing couldn't be better. It's good to leave them food and water, but it's even better to free them from the American Nazis."

This woman belonged in a melodrama. "Whatever you plan to do, you'd better think twice," I said.

Derrick bent his head toward Serena. "We need to take off. Nothing we can do for them now."

Serena stepped toward me. "Those people aren't hurting anyone. They're victims. All they want is to start a new life. They'll get jobs, pay taxes, send their kids to school. Just let them go."

"First of all, it's not up to me to let them go. Secondly, they broke the law. If you're into fairness, tell me how that's fair to everyone else immigrating through the proper channels? And thirdly, not everyone down there is a good guy. There's at least one coyote. I'm sure even you can appreciate the coyotes are not performing a valued service out of the goodness of their hearts."

Serena twisted her head over her shoulder. "Take a look. There's a family. Mother, father, daughter, two sons. They want to work. I'd rather err on the side of kindness and giving people second chances than worrying they're somehow bad people."

"There are also two little girls who need help getting away from the cartels who are using them."

"And you're going to help them? Please."

Serena clearly hadn't listened to anything I'd said. She seemed A-okay with turning cartel employees loose to rape, extort, murder, and ruin people's lives. "Why don't you leave this to the professionals. Head back to your truck and drive away. Leave your water and beans someplace new."

Derrick took Serena by the arm. "Come on. We should get out of here."

Serena yanked her arm from Derrick's grasp. "Go back to the truck. I'm not going to let these gorillas haul those poor people away."

Derrick looked uncertain.

"Whatever you think you want to do, I'm warning you not to do it." I made my voice as authoritative as possible.

"Or what? You'll turn me in? Do you really want to shine a light on me, someone closely associated with Mi Casa?"

There it was. I bluffed. "Ann isn't the one out here interfering with an arrest."

Serena raised her eyebrows. "No. But she's the one at Mi Casa taking in undocumented immigrants and hiding them from authorities. You mention my name and you can be sure Ann's will be shouted from the mountaintops."

Blackmail. This woman had *cojones*, that's for sure. The sound of an engine made us all turn to squint toward the road. All we could see from where we stood was a line of dust highlighting a vehicle heading our way. That would be the transport.

Derrick tilted his chin toward the road. "That's more of them. We need to go."

Serena didn't look at him. She kept eye contact with me. "I'm not leaving as long as those poor people are being held."

I tried to reason with her. "Don't get involved. Save your energy for politicians and votes. Bring water and food out if you want, but don't mess around doing anything else. You could get arrested or end up hurt. This isn't a playground."

Serena stared at me, narrowing her eyes in calculation. Her hand slipped into her pants pocket and she shifted her attention to the side of the ridge. Whatever sifted through her mind, she gave it due consideration.

Derrick put a hand on her shoulder. "Come on, Serena. We need to leave now."

Serena's mouth turned up in a cagey smile. She pulled her hand from her pocket and held up a disposable cigarette lighter.

Oh, no. I realized I'd smelled a whiff of something burning. Not an overpowering campfire, but just a hint. I hadn't paid attention but now I understood. I followed her line of vision to where a cloud of dense smoke rose on the side of the ridge.

Dead grass, thick as a carpet, and November dry.

"You didn't." The words slipped out as I ran past Serena and Derrick to look over the side.

Serena laughed. "Let's see if you can hold your prisoners and fight a wildfire at the same time."

I shouted down, hoping the other agents would hear me. "Fire!"

10

Luke was the first to climb up the hillside. I already had my coat off, beating the ankle-high flames. He slipped out of his jacket and joined me. Within seconds more agents arrived. The grass was thick and dead but the morning sprinkles had dampened it and the flames didn't take off as they might have.

The smell of burning weeds filled my head and my eyes stung. Even if the flames weren't raging, smoke accumulated in the still air, choking us and clogging our throats. We succeeded in smothering most of the fire and I squinted through the smoke to locate Derrick and Serena.

No surprise they were long gone.

The croak of Brody's voice made me turn. He finished his conversation by stating our location and stashed his phone back in his pocket.

The flames had been quashed and only a few spots smoldered. The clouds moved back in and light drizzle started.

I glanced at Liz and our eyes connected for a split second before she turned away. She'd seen Brody's call but didn't comment. Instead she pointed to me and Luke. "You stay here and make sure the fire's out."

She raised her voice. "The rest of you..." She broke off to cough. "Let's see if we can find the runners."

Luke and I patrolled the ridge, stomping on anything that looked as if it might ignite. What could Serena be thinking? Reckless, thoughtless, just plain stupid. And she had access to Mi Casa, seemed to be in charge when Ann was out. And Derrick. Mr. Helpful. Maybe he didn't light the fire but he and Serena were a pair.

What was Ann involved in? A few fat raindrops hit my cap.

Luke walked over to where I monitored the hillside for any hotspots. "Who'd have thought of starting a fire to distract us? That coyote must be important."

Still unsettled by Serena's willingness to do damage and her threats to expose Ann, I only paid half attention to Luke. "Huh?"

He kept his eyes on the hillside. "I suppose the coyote's partner started the fire. I mean, who else would it be?"

The supposed good guys. "Oh, right." A green uniform flitted in and out of the brush below us. "Looks like Rodriguez caught someone. I think we're good here. Let's go down."

I followed Luke as we hurried to the road where the transport vehicle waited. We arrived in time to see Rodriguez help the middle-aged woman in the back and onto a bench. Her husband and the younger woman already sat inside.

"Did you get the boys?" Luke asked.

Rodriguez shook his head. "They were fast. I hope they stay together."

The cold rain dripped down my neck and soaked the collar of my T-shirt. "It could get below freezing tonight." Those two little girls were out there somewhere.

While the rain battered down, more agents returned. We had four seated inside the transport. The rest of us stood in the rain until Hinkin called on her radio.

"I spotted a couple of runners due north of the road. Could use some help out here."

Rodriguez and another agent stayed with the transport truck. The rest of us separated and headed north.

I'd only gone about twenty yards from the trail before I lost sight of the other agents. Through the patter of rain the buzzing of an ATV grew close. I watched the trail until the nose of a four-wheeler edged to the road and stopped. The man behind the handlebars wore a camo hoodie that didn't give much protection from the rain. Behind him on the cargo basket huddled two small lumps shrouded in an Army-green rain slicker.

Brody emerged from the trail behind the ATV. He unzipped his coat and peeled it from his shoulders. The bundles in the basket moved and separated, one staying under the slicker, the other quickly getting swathed in Brody's jacket. He lifted the first down and she stood on skinny legs while he unloaded her sister.

Brody reached up to shake hands with the ATV driver. The driver tilted his head up and his hood dropped back enough for me to see the thin face and a glimpse of those startling blue eyes.

Brody took the hand of each little girl and walked them toward the truck. Ford cranked the handlebars of his ATV and sped back the way he'd come.

Had Brody called Ford to help track the prisoners? Had they specifically targeted the twins? Unlikely. They were probably the easiest to find. What mattered was that the girls had been located and would soon be dry, warm, and fed.

We searched through the rain for another hour before Liz called us back in.

I'd never heard her curse before but she could rival any sailor with the words she spewed. "We had them. Two coyotes for sure. And now they're free." She seasoned her outrage with a few more delightful phrases. "They raped that girl." She pointed to the truck. "God knows what they did to those little girls." She punched the air. "Now we're going to let them do it all again."

Turning in Serena and Derrick wouldn't recapture the criminals. It wouldn't give the little girls a better history or a brighter future. But it could end up sending my sister to jail. It could shut down one of the few resources for new immigrants in Tucson.

Maybe I couldn't get justice for this act, but I'd do what I could to make sure it didn't happen again.

That calm mask slipped over Liz's face. She checked her watch. "Shift is over."

I kept my phone busy on my way back to Tucson. Deon's call went to voicemail. He might be in a late meeting. Sami answered right away and chattered nonstop about her classroom art project where they were constructing a life-size ocean panorama.

I let her go on for several minutes, then jumped in when she took a breath. "Is Josie there?"

"Yeah. She's in her room." I waited while Sami climbed the stairs and told me about how Liam fell into the paper mache stingray and broke it. After a quick bang on the door, she said, "Mom wants to talk to you."

In a supremely annoyed voice, Josie answered, "I'm doing my homework."

"She's doing her homework," Sami said.

I gritted my teeth. "Give her the phone." This kid.

"What?" Josie said.

I knew she didn't want to hear from me so I made my voice all sunshine and light. "Wanted to say hi. See how it's going."

"I'm starving. When are you coming home?"

I kept up my cheery tone just to torque her off. "It'll be a couple of hours. You can get dinner started if you want."

"Or I can get a snack."

A short pause and Sami came back on. "Can I have a snack?"

"A small one. Love you both."

"Love ya."

Ah. The sweetness of motherhood.

Next up: Chris. He didn't bother with hello. "I'm on my way to class. What's up?"

I cut to the chase. "Do you know Steve Brody?"

Chris laughed. "I know he likes to eat, talk big, and avoid work."

"That's the one. Do you think he might be involved in the network?"

Chris's breath huffed a little, as if he was jogging up steps. "Nope. I can see where you'd like to pin something on him. But he's not a total jerk."

"Oh, I think he's a total jerk and more."

Chris let out a ha. "I get it. He'll surprise you sometime, though. Hey, I gotta go." And he did. Without a good-bye.

Even with all the smoochy warmth from my daughter and brother, I knew the worst of my family confrontations was yet to come.

11

My uniform was still damp by the time I returned to the station in Tucson and I smelled like a doused campfire. The rain had tapered off but I shivered in the cold air. Winter in Tucson didn't bring blizzards and icy roads, but we didn't get swimsuit weather year-round.

I stood under a warm spray for a long time, knowing I had to stop at Mi Casa before going home and needed to brace for confronting Ann. That big sister thing hung over our relationship. I'd never stopped wanting her approval and friendship, and standing up to her took more out of me than facing down an army of drug smugglers.

The sky had cleared and the first stars punched the indigo sky. Deon would be getting home soon and I hoped he'd find the groceries I'd set in the fridge for a pasta and sausage dish we all liked. Cooking seemed like a gargantuan chore on top of everything else. First, I'd talk to Ann. Then on to Josie and the protest. Tonight was my night for dealing with all the things.

This time I donned street clothes before going to Mi Casa. In jeans and a fleece, looking like any ordinary volunteer, I tried to open the front door. I was surprised to find it already locked and the curtains drawn for the night.

The ritual of knocking and waiting and the shade being drawn back and falling over the door started again. I half-hoped Serena would appear.

Knocking her into next week might feel pretty good. Someone yanked the shade back and squinted at me, let it drop. Ann unlocked the front door.

I pulled it open, waiting for Ann to maneuver her crutches and stand back to let me in. I strode into the lobby. No one occupied the room, but a big crowd was gathered in the courtyard. Through the glass on the back door, I saw a group of about twenty-five people of all ages, from young kids to middle-aged. For so many people, they made very little noise.

Ann made a point of watching me take in the group, then she turned her back and slow-thumped her way to her office. I stayed in the lobby and waited for her to drop into the desk chair and prop her crutches against the wall. Her face disappeared behind her computer monitor.

I stomped into her office and shut the door in a not-so-gentle way.

Her wheelchair sat beside the desk as usual. The paintings on the walls hadn't changed. Neither had the two long tables I'd bought from Costco and donated, still piled high with papers, folders, and a sippy cup no doubt left by a toddler. It felt the same as it had for years. Nothing new, except I was no longer welcome.

All the love and loss I felt for her came out in a rush of anger. "What are you involved in?"

She didn't glance up from her screen and started typing. "Right now, I'm filling out a form for a grant for single mothers."

I slapped my hand on the desk and was rewarded when she flinched. She sighed and leaned back. "Thank you for not wearing your uniform. But, honestly, I'd just as soon you didn't come inside at all. You bring bad vibes."

"Oh? Bad vibes. Well, bad vibe this." I realized my finger was jutting in her direction, if not exactly in her face. "That woman I met last time I was here, Serena. The volunteer you praised for being the face of kindness and caring? Well, she just set fire to the desert. She put seven agents in danger. Not to mention scattering immigrants across the desert."

A small spark of surprise flashed in Ann's eyes before she shut down and produced a fake yawn. "I don't know what you're talking about."

I pushed some straggling hairs off my forehead to give me a moment to gain self-control. "This isn't like you."

She looked at me. "What do you mean?"

I plopped into a chair, tired, sad, not wanting to fight. "The political battles wage all around you but you created this safe place. Mi Casa was conceived in kindness. You've done an amazing service. And you've done it within the bounds of the law."

She didn't seem affected by my speech. "Is someone saying I've broken the law?"

I gripped the chair rails and didn't answer.

She let that sit for a second. "So, Serena set a fire? Why?"

"We caught a group of immigrants and were waiting for transport to take them to processing. Serena decided the best way to distract agents and free the immigrants was to start a fire. She succeeded. It took us an hour to douse the flames, and in the meantime, all the immigrants ran off."

She seemed satisfied. "May they all make it to freedom without being rounded up like stray cattle."

"Scared, abandoned, hungry people are out there on the desert tonight where temperatures are going to dip below freezing. It's raining. Two little girls, twins about eight or nine, were in that group. Left to figure it out on their own. In the winter. And you think Serena did a good thing?"

Now I had her attention. "Did you find the girls?"

"Luckily someone got them to safety. It was a vigilante. One of those evil-doers you accused of killing Lacy Hollander. You know, just your everyday bad guy out saving kids." Actually, that seemed like a pretty apt description of Brody.

Ann fired back at me, ignoring the good deed. "Are you kidding me? Are you talking about Ford Dewlinski?"

I didn't answer.

"Of course you are. Because he's the face of the militia. Did you talk to him? What was he doing out there?"

Since I could remember, Ann always acted like the authority on everything. I couldn't help but tell her this time she was wrong. "It wasn't Ford who turned them in."

"How do you know?"

"Because I was with him when I got the call."

Her jaw dropped. "You can't be around Ford Dewlinski. He's dangerous. Stay as far from him as possible."

No one fired me up like Ann. "In case you don't remember, I'm trained law enforcement. I can take care of myself. Anyway, I was trying to do something for you. I thought maybe I could find some answers about Lacy Hollander and went back to the murder site."

She lasered me with her eyes. "What was Ford Dewlinski doing at Lacy's murder site?"

Damn. I'd fallen into that hole all by myself. "Never mind."

She wouldn't drop it. "He shouldn't be there. It's not right."

"He wasn't Lacy's killer. The sheriff's department is sure it was a cartel killing." As if I knew anything about the investigation at the sheriff's department.

Ann's lip turned up in a snarl. "Company line. We don't know who killed Lacy but it wasn't the cartels."

I felt compelled to defend Ford. "He recovered two little girls from the desert. He saved their lives. Even if they hadn't been scattered by Serena's fire or apprehended by Border Patrol, those people were facing a brutal night out there. It's possible they might not have survived if we hadn't brought them in."

Without pause she unleashed a torrent. "This is what those poor people have been reduced to. Families with young children fleeing from violence and poverty. And you've closed up all the routes with checkpoints and walls. They have no choice but to cross the most rugged and dangerous sections of the desert on foot. You're causing hundreds of deaths and destroying families."

"Jesus, Ann. I'm not here to debate with you. Those girls weren't with their parents."

"They weren't traveling on their own."

I leaned forward. "We've seen them before. The coyote uses them over and over. The myth is that if they're caught, the immigrants will be treated better if they have kids. Once the coyotes get their cargo through safely, the kids are either abandoned or picked up and hauled back to do it again."

Ann's eyes rounded. "Oh my god."

"Right. Those little girls have been caught before. That means they've made that trip, walking at night, risking snake bites and injury, going thirsty and hungry, sleeping on the ground in the heat and the cold, over and over again."

Ann's eyes misted.

"And your good friend, Serena, set a fire that sent them out on the desert alone. Do you think the coyote was going to look for them? More likely he's already in Mexico and those people are on their own."

"That's why we put out water and food."

We weren't getting anywhere.

She hesitated, not wanting to ask. "Did you arrest Serena?"

I stood and paced to the back of her office. "What she did was reckless and stupid. She could have burned the whole desert. She could have killed people."

Ann waited.

"No. I didn't arrest her."

"Why not?"

"Because she said you were involved."

Ann scoffed and indicated the wheelchair. "I didn't set fire to the desert."

"She said you're hiding immigrants here. And if I arrested her, she'd reveal it all."

Ann's face paled. "She said that?"

I nodded. "Those people outside." I pointed beyond her to the court-yard window. "Are they here illegally?"

Ann acted as though I hadn't spoken. "Was Derrick with her?"

That seemed like an abrupt change of subject. "Yeah. Why?"

She pushed back from her desk. "He told me Serena is getting more radical and that Lacy's death really messed her up. He promised me he'd keep an eye on her and try to calm her down."

I stared at Ann, the heat rising. "She knows about Lacy Hollander?"

Ann waved it away. "It's all over the news now, but I told her this morning."

"I thought you said she had the day off?"

Ann gave me a look of challenge. "I called her." After she'd told me she couldn't call Derrick.

"Listen to me: you can't be involved with these people. They're going to destroy everything you've created."

Ann's face hardened. "It's war. Don't you see that? I can't only dole out resources to those few who make it into this country legally. There are so many more people who need help. They're dying on the desert."

It was like arguing with water. "It's illegal to keep them here."

"I'm under no legal obligation to inform law enforcement or Border Patrol."

I knew that already. But it sounded as if she'd studied the laws and was hoping to get around them. "It is if you're actively hiding them from agents. And you are."

"You aren't going to turn me in, are you?" She challenged me in the same way as when I'd caught her sneaking out at night in high school.

I stood in front of her desk. My job was protecting the border. What about protecting my sister? She'd given me an impossible choice. "No. I'm not going to turn you in."

"Thank you." She sounded as if she took my compliance in stride.

My chest constricted at what I had to do next. I'd protect Ann as much as possible. But there was something more important than my love for her. "Do what you need to do."

She gave me that sanctimonious big sister smirk. "I don't have a choice. People need help."

I walked toward the door believing I might never be allowed to return. "I also have to do what I need to." I couldn't hate this more. "As long as you're involved with No Desert Deaths, I can't allow Sami and Josie to come here."

She gasped and stared at me. "No," she whispered. "You can't do that. They're the only family I've got."

My heart felt crushed and a lump hardened in my throat at the sound of her desperation. I wanted her to understand. "It's too dangerous. You could get raided at any moment. You've got angry, unpredictable people like Serena ready to explode. And you don't know the lengths some of these undocumented people might go to if they were threatened."

Anger flashed in her eyes. She braced her hands on her desk and rose.

"You're being cruel and manipulative. Why are you hurting Sami and Josie so you can hurt me?"

"I'm not"

She leaned on her desk, her face rigid and commanding. "You'll destroy any love Josie has left for you."

"They'll be in danger—"

She pointed at the door. "Get the hell out of here. Now."

12

I drove through evening traffic, barely noting that full darkness had taken over. I couldn't begin to balance the day on any kind of scale. I'd come face to face with one scary dude, then saw him deliver two little girls to safety. I'd protected my sister only to lose her. Chances were, the day had another burp waiting when I confronted Josie about her participation in the protest.

At least I had Deon in my corner. Since he and Josie seemed on solid ground, maybe he could back me up.

I finally made it home. I'd ended yesterday too late and started today too early. In the meantime, I'd seen too much. What I really wanted was a glass of wine and a soak in the hot tub. What I needed was to get some kind of healthy dinner into all of us, but especially me. My diabetes wouldn't react well to exhaustion and poor eating choices.

Josie's music thundered through the ceiling and Sami cranked the volume on the TV. She was watching some reality show with a bunch of young adults fighting over everything. It bounced on my brain, making me want to throw the pasta bowl at them.

My phone buzzed and Deon's face appeared on the screen. It was one of my favorite photos of him, holding baby Sami in one arm, his electric razor in the other hand and a big grin into the mirror. "Hi. I hope you're telling me you're on your way. Can you stop at Fry's and pick up ice cream?"

He sighed. "I'm going to be late tonight. Sorry. Probably another two hours."

A lead weight dropped into my stomach. How could I complain? He'd taken the brunt of parenting while I went to the academy. We were a team, right? But I'd hoped he'd be here to help me with Josie. "I'm sorry. I'll save some dinner for you."

"But sadly, no ice cream."

"Maybe we can figure out some other sweet?" I used that husky voice he liked, though I felt anything but playful.

"Now that's motivation to get out of here quicker."

I punched the phone off. My job might be kicking my butt, my relationship with my sister might be in the toilet, I might be losing touch with my brother, and I definitely had issues with my daughter, but for right now, my marriage seemed to be okay. I knocked my knuckles on the wooden cutting board.

Sami wandered away from the family room and climbed a bar stool opposite me.

"Are you done watching that?" I asked, and when she nodded, I grabbed the remote off the back of the couch and killed it mid-fight.

I came back to the kitchen and started chopping sweet peppers. "How's it going at school?"

She twisted her stool back and forth. "I made it into the top reading group. Brian Standage is a total jerk. And I need black knee socks for spirit week."

That about summed up her life. "I made appointments for pedicures. Did you check the movie times?"

"Oh. I forgot to tell you. I can't hang out with you. I'm going to Nikki's party. They were talking about it at lunch yesterday and when I got up to move to another table, she asked me why. I told her because she didn't invite me and she was all like, 'I did, too,' and I was like, 'No, you didn't.' And then I started to cry and then she started to cry and all the kids at lunch made fun of us."

I dumped the peppers into the sauté pan along with the onions I'd already chopped and started the flame. "So, it's all okay now?" I still didn't trust that little narcissist.

She brightened. "Yeah. But tomorrow can we go shopping to get her birthday present?"

Josie sulked into the kitchen, her eyes red and swollen. "When's Dad coming home?"

"He's going to be late." I stirred the vegetables and tried to sound kind. "Did you hear about Lacy Hollander?"

She glared at me as if I'd shot Lacy. "Yeah. I heard."

"I'm really sorry, Josie."

She looked at the saucepan on the stove. "Are you making that sausage stuff again? With canned sauce? Can we order something with Uber Eats?"

This stage better run its course soon or I'd end up strangling this kid. "We're going to sit down as a family and have the dinner I'm preparing for us."

"That's a hard pass for me. Without Dad it's not really the whole family, now is it?"

I crumbled Italian sausage into another pan. "We need to talk."

She gave me her back and headed toward the hallway. "I've got homework."

I shot my steely mom voice at her. "Sit. Down."

She stopped walking, and even if I couldn't see her face, I knew she was debating her options. "Right. Now," I added for effect.

With the overinflated disdain of an affronted teen, she spun around, flounced back, and threw herself onto a bar stool next to Sami.

Sami kept still, her eyes bouncing between me and Josie. I could send her away but maybe this would be an object lesson.

Josie turned her head toward me, tilted it in disgust, and stared beyond me to avoid any sign of respect.

I'd brought this helpless baby into the world. I'd rocked her, nursed her at my breast. Picked her up when she tripped, soothed her through tummy aches and heart aches. I'd throw myself in front of a speeding truck for her. But right now, I really wanted to punch that attitude off her face.

I'd agreed to wait until after Deon and I discussed it, but he was gone and now seemed the time. "What were you doing at the station yesterday morning?"

Her eyes shifted but not to me, just to another meaningless object behind me. "If you'd paid attention to anything outside your own little world, you'd know there was this trial going on? It's a totally bogus charge against a courageous woman trying to save lives."

"This is exactly what I'm talking about. Lacy Hollander was doing illegal and dangerous things and now she's dead."

Damn. That last word seemed to echo in the kitchen.

Josie's eyes teared up. "Whoever killed her is trying to scare those of us working to help immigrants. We won't let that happen."

She sounded like that lunatic, Serena. "Lacy Hollander was shot because she tangled with a coyote who works for the cartels. Her murder is no warning, it's the way the cartels operate. At any rate, none of it means you can skip school and wander around on the streets."

She flicked her eyes to me and blew a contemptuous breath. "I wasn't wandering the streets. I was protesting injustice. I am not going to do nothing while this fascist government takes away our right to save lives and reduce suffering."

Sami didn't move. Obviously, she thought I might not remember she was sitting there and didn't want to draw attention to herself.

"Wow," I said. "You've really bought into the whole line. Did Serena and Ann drill that into you?" I knew I shouldn't condescend. *You're the parent. Don't let her push your buttons.*

"You're the one who taught me to be kind to people no matter who they were. Remember in kindergarten when Mark Bennet pushed Tasha because he said black kids couldn't use the swings? I do. I hit Mark in the mouth and even though I got in trouble you told me I did the right thing."

I didn't remember the incident. "I can't believe I condoned using physical force."

She flipped the tilt of her head from left to right and let out another hot breath. "You said I should have tried talking to him first, but in the end, the most important thing was to protect someone who needed me."

"That sounds more like me."

She leaned forward. "Right? So, like, ten years ago you were all about protecting the weak and being kind. And now you're all about attacking poor people on the desert and throwing them in jail or deporting them back to countries where they're going to get killed."

I held up my hand. "Hey, that's not what the Border Patrol does."

"What about ripping children away from their parents and putting them in jail? How kind and protective is that?"

"Okay, that's enough. We don't do that." I thought of the twins. Prying them out of the cartel's grasp and getting them into foster care seemed an improvement in their lives. But this wasn't the time to explain that to Josie.

She sniffed and tossed her head back. "Sure. You don't do that. I believe you."

Sami raised her hand a few inches off the counter. "Um, Mom."

I tried to keep my voice calm. "The Border Patrol is there to protect the country from some bad people. Drug smugglers, human traffickers, terrorists."

"Immigrants are none of those things."

I was losing the battle with keeping my temper. "But it's those immigrants who are dying out there, abandoned by the coyotes they've mortgaged themselves to."

She slammed her hand on the counter at the same time Sami said, "Mom."

Josie shouted, "That's why people like Lacy Hollander are leaving water and food and blankets on the desert. To help those people and keep them from dying. And now she's dead, too." She burst into tears and I desperately wanted to pull her to me.

"That's why I'm out there, too. To create a deterrence so they won't attempt that dangerous trip, and if they do, to find them and get them to safety."

Josie swiped at her eyes. "You're the problem and you don't see it. Just because your job is to hurt people doesn't mean I can't try to make the world a better place. I believe the lessons you taught me about kindness and caring and I'm going to do what I can to live them, even if you lied to me about believing them."

My logic wasn't getting through, and in frustration, I pulled out my last card. "You can't skip school to go protest without getting permission from me or Dad."

She gave me a satisfied smile. "Dad gave me permission, so I don't need you." She slid off the stool and sauntered toward the stairs.

"Mom," Sami said.

I raised my eyes to her and saw her pointing to the stove behind me. That's when I smelled burned vegetables and sausage.

13

I'd meant to talk to Deon when he got home from work last night. He'd never mentioned he'd given Josie permission to skip school for the protest, even though we'd skimmed over the topic a couple of times. He'd asked me not to broach the subject with Josie until he'd talked to me. That meant he probably intended to explain his position. I tried not to feel undermined and betrayed, but it wasn't easy.

The problem was that I fell asleep before he came home. When he slid into bed, I snuggled next to him, no thought of conversation. And once the alarm clocks sounded and forced us out of bed and on the run, it didn't seem like a good time for a heart-to-heart.

Muster had progressed as usual. I was assigned an area north of Sasabe and Luke drew checkpoint duty along the same highway. I didn't blame him for being disappointed, but I'd be doing the same duty soon, I was sure.

I spent the breezy morning patrolling my area, stopping every little while to get out and walk some trails, cutting for sign. Nothing happened, giving me all kinds of time to worry and churn about Ann and Josie and Deon. Even though Sami's world had smoothed out, I even spared a concern or two for her. I left Chris alone on this treadmill of anxiety; he could stress about his law school career without my help.

Wherever my thoughts wandered, they kept returning to Ford Dewlinski. One intense son of a gun. Creepy the way he seemed to appear and disappear. Ann's words of warning came back to me. Did he kill Lacy? Is that why he was at the scene that night when Brody sent him away? And why he returned the next day?

I was only fifteen miles from Sasabe. It couldn't hurt to pay a visit to Ford, see what kind of pulse I got from the guy. Other than scary and weird.

The desert out here was choked with Joshua trees, cholla, and ocotillo. I drove south along the highway, passing through the checkpoint and waving at Luke. He looked miserable and bored.

I continued along the rolling hills until the port of entry's huge canopy loomed over the next hill. A few abandoned adobes with shattered windows and gaping holes where doors used to swing bunched along the roadside. The Border Patrol station on the left was shrouded in fencing and concertina wire. Around a curve a bright yellow adobe declared itself the grocery store with a post office waving an American flag next to it. A few more abandoned buildings rounded out the rest of the town.

The highway curved, one way heading to the border checkpoint, the other running parallel to the metal border fence.

A good-sized adobe house that appeared intact sat on a slight rise. It seemed like the one decent place around and I slowed to take a dirt road heading toward it. Across the road from the house, three or four other dwellings hunkered. One looked like a double-wide trailer sided with chipped adobe. The others were small and uninteresting, mostly hidden by an ancient sycamore and the ubiquitous mesquite.

Identifying Ford's house wasn't difficult, mainly because of the three flags flying from the pole in front. The American flag, the Arizona state flag, and another. Black with a white scorpion, it identified itself as Recon to Reclaim the Desert. A craggy wood fence encircled a sparse yard that led to a well-kept old adobe house.

Now that the sun had climbed higher, I unzipped my jacket, though I kept it on. Not quite shirtsleeve temps yet. A firepit full of blackened ashes and surrounded by planks propped on rocks for benches took up one corner of the yard. The smell of campfire rose as I walked through the yard and up the concrete steps. It ignited my temper about yesterday's arson.

Ford may be an intense vigilante with the reputation of a rebel but he had a definite sense of order. The porch had been swept and the front door recently painted. Two windows faced the front porch, reflecting the afternoon sun without a desert home's usual thick film of dust.

I banged on the door. "Border Patrol."

Nothing moved inside the house. I banged again. "Border Patrol," I shouted louder.

Still no answer. From the edge of the porch a maze of corrals stretched, the alleyways filled with tumbleweeds. Clearly, Ford wasn't a rancher. I cupped my hands to peer into a window. A sofa and a couple of chairs, a rug on a wood floor. A long kitchen table with a few items. Wait. I squinted to see more detail.

"No one home," a woman shouted from behind me.

I turned to an ancient brown-skinned woman standing on the dirt road in front of the house. She wore purple sweatpants and a black hoodie and cradled something in her arms. She waved her hand at me. "Ford and his bunch. They're gone."

I dropped off the porch and walked toward her, my boots crunching on the yard. "How long have they been gone?"

She stepped away from me. "Probably off on some shenanigans. Don't know. Just know they left and I didn't want you to keep making so much noise. It upsets my dogs." A ceramic chihuahua rested in one arm. A deep beige with brown ears and lifelike sweet eyes, it almost looked real. She ran her hand from the little head to the tail and then scratched behind its shiny ears.

I glanced up and down the road in front of Ford's house. The only dog around was the one in her arms. I pointed to the brown wreck of a shack a few hundred feet away. "Is that your house?"

She checked as if seeing it for the first time. "No." With that, she turned and started to walk away.

I caught up to her. Since she'd been so forthcoming with my other questions, I didn't expect much, but I asked anyway. "Do you have any idea where they might have gone?"

She kept a surprisingly quick pace, her hand stroking the back of the little ceramic chihuahua. "The usual place probably."

Progress. "Where's the usual place?"

She didn't look at me, just kept making time down the dusty road. "You ask a lot of questions."

"If you tell me where to find Ford, I'll ask him the questions and leave you alone."

A tick of a smile at the corner of her mouth. She stopped and lowered her chin to her chest, then raised her eyes to me. "I'm Edna. Who are you?"

With a dip to my chin, like a truncated bow, I smiled and said, "Agent Sanchez." Then, "Michaela."

"Okay, Michaela. What do you want from Ford?"

Might as well go straight at it. I liked Edna and didn't think she'd tolerate beating around the bush. "A woman was killed in the desert and I want to ask him about it."

Edna started walking again and, without hesitating, said, "He didn't have anything to do with that."

"How do you know?"

She waved a hand in the air between us as if shooing me off. "I know lots of things."

"Do you know who the woman is?"

She nodded. "That blonde one, I imagine. Like you."

"Lacy Hollander. Have you seen her around here before? With Ford?"

Edna turned her head up at me and shielded her eyes. "I don't spy. I only pay attention when my dogs get upset. Unless she was making noise or up to shenanigans, I wouldn't see her."

She'd failed to answer the question. "How well do you know Ford?"

"He's a good man. He hauls firewood for me and brings me groceries."

"You're friends?"

She shuffled along the dirt road. "I already told you Ford didn't hurt that woman. What else do you want to know?"

"I appreciate your faith in him. But I'd like to check him out myself. You seem like the kind of person who likes to form her own opinion so I'm sure you understand. You said you know where to find Ford?"

"He has a camp north of El Mirador and La Osa roads. Out on the flat. Likes to train his recruits out there. I like when he takes them there. They upset my dogs."

We continued to the last house, a little wood shack no bigger than my master bedroom. "I'm busy. You should go."

"Because I upset your dogs?"

She pointed at me. "No. There's other people I'm going to see who won't like you. So you need to go." She pivoted toward a dilapidated chain-link fence about waist-high. The aluminum gate Edna slipped through had curlicues at the top but the welds had broken and hung at wacky angles. She hurried up the broken cement to a wood porch lined with an array of ceramic dogs. Those big dogs you see in people's yards that make you look twice because you don't know if they're real. A German shepherd, dalmatian, Irish setter, and several others stared out at the road under the cover of a ramshackle porch.

She turned around and grinned at me. "See? They like you." She ran a hand down the dalmatian's head and spoke in a Native American language, the consonants sticking low in the back of her throat, before dropping into a folding lawn chair with nylon weaving. She settled the chihuahua into her lap.

"Thank you, Edna." Maybe I'd make it a point of stopping in from time to time.

She waved. "You bring to mind that other blonde. The one that died."

Edna might know more than she let on. "Why is that?"

"You mean well but you're probably gonna get into trouble."

I started into her yard to prod her into giving me more.

She shooed me. "You get along now."

Before climbing into my pickup, I tromped back to Ford's front porch. With one glance to make sure Edna hadn't followed me, I put my hands back on the window and leaned in to see. I'd been right.

A floppy Tilley hat lay on the table. Exactly like Lacy Hollander wore.

14

A thousand Lacy Hollander hats were floating around Tucson. Since Josie had worn one the day of the protest, there was probably one in my house. But Josie's didn't have blood on it.

Maybe the one on Ford's table wasn't stained with blood, either. It could be mud, or sauce from a spilled can of beans. Or anything.

Driving slowly on the dirt road, I considered what to do. Ford was a good friend of the Border Patrol. I didn't think I should burst onto the scene, a rookie on my second day of solo patrol, and insist on searching his home. Border Patrol wasn't in the business of murder investigations. Before I made any decisions I needed more facts.

Driving by the huge border facility, I felt a sudden fatigue and glanced at my watch. Wow. Several hours had passed and I'd forgotten to eat or even check my blood sugar. This close to where Luke worked the checkpoint, I'd stop and eat with him. Wouldn't hurt to take a break.

Luke stood at the side of the road watching for vehicles, holding his M4. Two other agents milled around a small shed that acted as a checkpoint. Their pickups were parked on a gravel clearing next to the shed. Clouds hung low and heavy. Chance of rain today hovered at fifty percent, pretty high for the desert, but it hadn't started yet so we could enjoy some time outside.

Luke watched as I pulled next to the other pickups. I grabbed my lunch cooler and stepped out. "Have you got time for lunch?"

Luke tipped his head toward the building. "Mind if I take a break?"

One of the other agents waved him on and stepped out of the shed to take Luke's place.

Luke hurried to his vehicle and grabbed his cooler. He met me at my truck and I unlatched the tailgate. "Glad you came by. Those two are watching movies and I'm staring down the road thinking I've made a big career mistake."

I jumped up and planted my rear on the tailgate. "My morning hasn't been quite as boring but nothing to write home about."

The agent who'd replaced Luke slipped back to the doorway of the shed, clearly watching the movie again.

With his long legs, he easily sat next to me and dug into his cooler. He brought out a thick Subway sandwich, which smelled of pepperoni and ham and all things glorious. "I've only seen a few lonely ranchers all day. This is killing me."

I pulled out my thin sandwich. The first bite sent my stomach in a riot of hunger that surprised me. I chomped another bite almost immediately.

Luke grimaced. "You couldn't do any better than peanut butter?"

I reached for a bottle of juice, cracked the lid, and washed down the sandwich. "I haven't had time to hit the grocery store. It's good, though. I like peanut butter."

A beat-up pickup topped the hill to the south, heading our way. Luke stood up to meet them at the road and the other two agents let him take it. I kept eating as the pickup slowed to a stop and Luke leaned in and spoke a few words, then listened to their response and waved them through.

He returned and sat back down. "All day. More of the same."

I munched on an apple. "We knew there wouldn't be excitement every day."

He sighed. "I've had my share of checkpoint duty."

"Beats processing," I said.

A white Border Patrol Tahoe approached from the north. It eased up to the checkpoint and rolled down the driver's window. A cascade of country music poured out. "The hits just keep coming," I said.

The other two agents bantered with Brody for a moment and then went back to their movie.

Brody pulled up and leaned out the window, his country music spewing out. "Hi, kiddies. What's happening?"

Luke lifted his hand to show the empty road. "This."

Brody raised his voice over the idling engine and the wailing cowboy. "One of the sensors was tripped and I'm heading down to check it out. Let's go, Grandma."

What excuse could I use? "I'm getting a bite to eat."

He waved his arm in a come-on motion. "Me, too. Bring it and get in. You might learn something."

No way around this. I placed my juice bottle and the empty sandwich bag in my cooler. "My day is officially worse than yours," I muttered to Luke.

Luke faced me with his back to Brody. "Might be the only time I'm grateful for checkpoint duty."

After I deposited my cooler in my pickup and grabbed my M4 and rain gear, I climbed in with Brody. I'd taken a rash of crap for the rain poncho. Border Patrol doesn't supply a generous uniform allowance and not many agents opt to spend hard-earned money on luxuries such as rain gear. Being a little older, more settled, and married to a high-earning attorney, I felt entitled to the poncho. Call me a princess if you want to, but I'd do what I could to stay dry.

Brody blew a kiss to Luke, rolled up his window, and gunned the engine. "Thought you were bringing your lunch."

"I wasn't hungry anymore."

I'd prefer to drive with the windows down so I could better study the roadside for sign. Brody had the heater raging and his country music blaring. I hoped for a short mission with this stellar example of compassion and courage.

He munched on a granola bar, probably his version of healthy. Though his face still looked sour, it held the hint of humor. Not a good sign. "Okay, look. We got off to a bad start but I'm willing to let bygones be bygones."

I offered a half-hearted smile of acceptance and watched the Joshua trees speed by outside my window.

He pulled off the highway to a sandy road. We followed a winding trail, twisting between tall ocotillo cactus and the ever-present sage and mesquite. I rolled down my window and watched for sign but he kept the pace too fast to really see much.

Brody had to nearly shout to be heard over his music. "… Grandma?"

Since my head hung partway out of the window to avoid that racket, I only heard the last word and had to ask, "What?"

"I said"—he leaned over and turned the radio down—"are you finding anything interesting out there?"

Maybe if I had my own vehicle and could travel a slower speed. "Not yet. Whatever tracks are out here will be washed away if it rains."

"Oh, it's not gonna rain." He said it with such confidence, and yet I smelled the possibility in the air. "I think, so far, I've taught you well, even if I do say so myself. You're doing better than most of our trainees. Probably because of your experience and"—he paused to emphasize the point—"*maturity.*"

"Thanks." What else should I say?

"I think you've earned the right to know some of the real intel only I can impart to you."

I perked up. He couldn't mean he was letting me in on the crew working with the cartels. Absolutely not. But he was up to something. "I'm here to learn."

"If you keep your eyes open, maybe you'll end up being a decent agent."

I tried for a friendly and deferential smile. Chris said maybe Brody would surprise me. I couldn't deny at least a little curiosity about what that meant.

He stopped the pickup in a brushy area and climbed out. "Come on, Grandma. I've got something to show you."

I reached into the Tahoe for my rain slicker.

"You won't need that," he said. "I told you, it's not going to rain. I've been doing this job long enough to learn the signs. It's damn-sure going to rain somewhere, but not here."

I didn't argue but also didn't put my jacket back. I rolled it up and snapped it onto my utility belt. "I thought you said a sensor was tripped."

"Someone else will check it out."

That had been an excuse to get me out here. What would he show me? I didn't trust him and couldn't imagine he trusted me. Maybe this was some kind of trap or even rookie hazing. "Where are we going?"

He slammed the door and I met him on his side of the Tahoe. He grinned and pointed two fingers at his eyes, then at mine. "Watch and learn, Grasshopper."

I didn't tell him his hand signals were all wrong and kept the sigh to myself. He slid his M4 onto his shoulder. "You'll want your weapon."

I took my M4, draped the strap across my body, and plodded after him.

He sauntered to the front of the Tahoe and started on what appeared to be an animal trail. His fist pulled a Snickers from his pocket like a hidden treasure and he unwrapped it, shoving half of it in his mouth. When he'd swallowed most of that, he spoke. "There's no hurry. I figure we've got a ten-hour shift. Might as well take our time."

Sure. The United States was paying us to stroll along the desert. It wasn't my idea of patrol. I'd spent a month each with Rodriguez and Liz. Both of them kept moving during their shifts. Driving roads, hiking ridges, taking calls for backup. Even the shifts I'd completed at processing or checkpoints held more action than Brody's habit of doing as little as possible.

We walked for about a half hour, approaching a string of rough mountains that rose from the desert floor as if dropped from space. The range created the Altar Valley between where we stood and Tucson. One of the roughest and most remote areas in the country. We followed the trail that switch-backed up a hill and descended a narrow valley.

"What are we looking for?" Brody wouldn't wander in such rugged country without a reason. And I doubted it would be good.

"You'll see." He almost chortled, a sound that unsettled me.

The mountain on the west towered above us, strewn with rocks and a ton of cactus varieties just waiting to hurt us. We made our way through a sandy wash that during monsoon season would be another easy way to get killed. The smaller hill we'd topped to get into this slot canyon shaded us on the east. This gully felt isolated and private.

The last thing I wanted was to be alone with Brody this far from anything and anyone. I couldn't imagine Brody would be stupid enough to hurt me. Probably. But if knowing his secret could lead to discovering the corrupt network, then this would be worth it.

Making conversation with Brody held no interest for me so I turned my attention to listening to the quail and their wow-wowing. Their song was accompanied by the trill of a cactus wren and the varied tunes of a mockingbird. The mesquite, manzanita, cholla, and usual suspects poked at us, but keeping such a slow pace, I was able to avoid any damage.

Too bad Brody didn't feel the same as I did about talking. "You're new to Border Patrol but already you're making friends and maybe even some enemies."

"I don't feel that I've made enemies." *Except maybe you.*

He waved his hand. "You don't know they're enemies because you aren't plugged in, like I am. But if you're accepted by our group, you'll have all the friends you need."

Who else was in his group? "So why are we here?"

"This will give you an advantage over all those other rookies. You're the oldest in your class and one of the few women starting at this section. So, the more help you get, the better."

"If this is something helpful to the patrol, then you really should let everyone in on it."

"Not everyone thinks it's a good thing."

Brody couldn't care if I was his friend, and there's no way he'd let me into a secret cabal in cahoots with the cartels. He must be pulling some kind of prank. "I appreciate you trying to help me out, but I'm feeling uncomfortable with this whole mission."

Brody's mouth fell open. "Uncomfortable? Honey, this isn't college where they give you a napping room and bring in puppies to make you feel loved. This is the border. There are bad hombres out here and we need to use whatever we can to defeat them."

Honey? "I'm not looking for a safe space, sweetie. I'm a Border Patrol agent. If you've got something to teach me about protecting the border and the people out here, then I'm here to learn it."

His eyes widened in mock surprise. "Oh, Grandma's full of spit and vinegar today. If you don't want to know my secret, that's okay with me. Just wanted to give you a leg up."

Time to make my exit. "Thanks for thinking of me, but I'm okay playing on a level field with everyone else."

He skirted around me, heading back the way we'd come. "Have it your way. Trust me, you want to know what I brought you here to see."

"I think I felt a drop. Those clouds look ready to let loose."

"I told you, it's not going to rain." He kept treading down the wash but couldn't seem to shut up.

Brody held up his hand in a signal for me to stay quiet, then slowed even further. At the edge of a narrow wash he stopped. I looked over his shoulder into a roughly circular area with some scraggly grass. A large mesquite grew from the side of the wash, its roots twisting along the ground. A few logs lay on their sides and a jumble of large rocks gave the area spots of shade from every angle of the sun.

Brody relaxed and stepped into the clearing.

About a dozen plastic gallon jugs lined the roots of the tree. In a crag between two rocks a cache of canned beans tumbled. I don't know what I expected. A meeting of cartel scouts? A gathering of the corrupt Border Patrol network?

"This is a regular stash." Brody pulled his M4 from his shoulder and took aim at the beans. Without waiting he squeezed off several rounds.

I felt like they smashed into my chest. "What the hell?" I hollered at him.

He turned to me, surprise on his face. "It's a crime to leave trash on the desert."

That was his argument for destroying food? So many things I could say to him. Starting with the obvious that shooting the cans would create more trash than leaving them alone. And ending with the fact that those cans of food might save someone's life.

He snickered. "Oh, Rookie Bleeding Heart Syndrome. I get it. You feel sorry for those poor people crossing the desert."

He walked over to the water jugs. "Give it a month or two. Maybe less. You'll see who those poor people really are."

He flipped the snap off the sheath on his utility belt and pulled out his knife.

"Come on, Brody. Leave the water." This was his big plan. Because he considered me soft on immigration, he wanted to show me the ropes. Teach me to be as mean as him. What a peach.

He raised his arm and brought it down, slashing through a jug. The water splashed into the sand. "I'm initiating you into the hard, cruel world of the desert, baby."

"Stop it!"

He slit another jug.

That was too much for me. When he raised his arm again, I blocked his wrist and he missed the mark. He turned on me, his knife coming up as if he considered slicing me as well as the water jugs.

I braced, ready to pivot away, already wondering how I would get out of this without hurting him and ending my Border Patrol career before it started.

A scream, like something from a Dracula film, burst from a stand of manzanita north of the clearing. A chill raced from my scalp down my spine and I drew in a breath.

Brody raised his M4 and spun around, but I dived for the gun, sending the round into the dirt and the bullet ricocheting harmlessly into the wilderness.

The screaming animal took shape in the form of a little brown woman wearing a clear plastic rain poncho overtop a black hoodie and purple sweatpants. She dropped a colorful bundle that looked like yarn on the ground and placed her ceramic chihuahua on top. With the force of a hurricane, she ran at Brody and jettisoned herself into his round belly. I'd bet the words screeching from her were curses in her native tongue.

Brody stepped back at her impact. That prune face puckered with animosity and he braced himself as if to attack. His gaze flicked to me.

Edna screamed again and flailed at him.

He gave me a sly sneer and turned back to her. It didn't take much for him to latch onto her wrists and shove her to the side. Another sidelong look to me, and he strode across the clearing to the bundle Edna had dropped. Brody picked up the dog.

She let out a howl. "Don't hurt him!"

Brody laughed. "Oh, is this your precious?" He held it aloft as if he meant to drop it on the hard ground.

This was enough bullying. "Cut it out." I stalked toward him and held out my hand for the chihuahua, as I'd do if Josie and Sami quarreled. "Leave her alone."

Brody glowered at me and slammed the dog into my palm. I scrambled to grab it with two hands. "Spoilsport," he said.

Without comment I returned the dog to Edna. She clasped it to her chest, shooting Brody a murderous look.

"Oh, quit looking so high and mighty. I know about you. Your husband took off and half your kids are in jail and the other half are living on the streets of Tucson begging for a drink."

Edna's face drained of life.

The nasty grin that split his face worried me. With a swift movement, he bent over and plucked up the bundle. Now I saw it was a crocheted blanket, maybe pieced together from leftover yarn of various projects.

Edna's fingers massaged the chihuahua's ears with frantic movements. "Leave that alone. Get out of this place. You don't belong here."

Brody held the ugly blanket in his fist. "This is my country. It's you who doesn't belong. Go back to your own country."

Jesus. I ground out a reply. "Her family was probably here long before anyone thought about slapping a border on the map."

Brody's furious eyes turned to me. "Is that so? Well, there's a border now and she's on the wrong side."

Before I could stop him, Brody whipped his knife from his sheath and stabbed at the blanket.

Edna yelled, "No!"

Brody sliced the knife through the yarn with jerky motions. Then he did it again, leaving the blanket a pile of useless yarn.

A few fat raindrops plopped on the sand at our feet.

Edna's dark eyes glittered and the guttural words falling from her mouth had to be a dire curse.

Brody stuck the knife into his sheath. "If I see you again, I'll arrest you and I'll make sure you're deported."

He was behaving worse than Sami's friend Nikki. "Stop acting like a total jerk."

Brody strode past me. "Get your ass in gear or walk back to your rig."

15

It might not have been the smartest choice, but I opted to stay and help Edna, passing up my ride back to my pickup. I pulled my poncho from my belt and shook it out.

Edna knelt under the mesquite. Small rivulets of tears joined the rain to stream into the deep wrinkles of her cheeks.

Once I draped my poncho over myself, I crouched beside her. "I'm sorry."

"I loved them and now they're gone." She wiped her face with the sleeve of her hoodie. "He's a mean man."

I couldn't argue with that. "Can I help you back to your house?"

She stood up, showing no sign of creaking joints or age-weakened muscles, and hoofed it across the clearing, following in Brody's footsteps. "You park on the road?"

I took a few steps after her. "No. I came with the other agent."

She abruptly spun around. "You let him go without having a ride back?"

"I thought you might need some help." I pulled out my phone and checked it, not surprised but disappointed to discover I had no phone signal.

With quick strides she passed me, heading toward the manzanita she'd jumped out of earlier. "That wasn't very smart. I can take care of myself. Now you're stuck."

"How did you get here?"

She scrambled up the incline, maybe on a narrow animal trail. "How I get everywhere. I walked."

Fantastic. I trotted after her. "How far is it to Sasabe?" The rain kept up a steady drip.

"It's a ways. You could have stayed here but there's no food or water anymore." Like a little desert mouse, she scampered along the trail.

I had no choice but to fall in line behind her, keeping her quick pace. "Does Ford know about that place?"

She didn't turn. "I don't know what Ford knows or doesn't know."

"Do you think he'd approve?"

She didn't sound at all winded. "It's a war out here. That mean man, he chose his side. Ford's got his. I know mine. You gotta choose your side."

"It's not that black and white."

Edna marched on. "Hmph." She increased her pace.

I must have insulted her because she resisted all my efforts at conversation. After a time, I quit asking questions and trusted she'd eventually get me back to civilization.

The rain eased off after a time and the sun took on the task of drying everything out. We trudged along in silence for about an hour. I was surprised when the sun bounced on the roof of the port of entry not far away. Apparently, Brody's route to the cache had taken about two-thirds of a circle. Edna and I had walked the last third back to Sasabe.

She turned her face up to look me in the eye. "Go there. Your people." She pointed to the border facility and darted down the road to her house without another word.

Of course, I caught some ribbing when I walked to the checkpoint. I made it sound like Brody was playing a joke, some kind of hazing for a rookie. They bought it, probably knowing what a dick Brody was. A bored agent was happy to drive me back to my pickup at the checkpoint.

Luke jumped all over me when I slipped out the passenger side of the agent's pickup. "What happened? Where's Brody?"

I gave Luke the same story I'd told the others. He didn't need a reason to dislike Brody any more than he already did.

I climbed into my pickup, rolled down the windows, and drove south. My shift would be over in a couple of hours. Without a clear plan I turned off on a wide dirt road, noting the name La Osa Road. I slowed and tried to concentrate on cutting for sign along the side of the road, but my gut churned and I wasn't focusing.

Seeing Brody be so cruel to Edna made me question the concept of good guy and bad guy on the desert. Edna's view didn't hold a lot of wiggle room. She obviously thought of Ford as a good guy. I wasn't so sure.

What about me and Ann? Was there a definite line between good and bad there? I didn't want my relationship with Ann to be over. Since I was twelve years old and our parents died, it had been Chris, Ann, and me, not always in harmony but always together. She loved my daughters almost as much as Deon and I did. They loved her. We were family.

I couldn't sever that tie. But I had to protect my kids. Didn't I have to protect Ann, too? If she was involved with Lacy and No Desert Deaths, would the same person who killed Lacy go after Ann?

What if that person was Ford?

The Border Patrol didn't investigate. I'd said that before. But if this was war, as Edna said, as Brody said, and as Ford said, I owed it to my family to find out.

My choice to turn on La Osa wasn't as random as I'd told myself. Edna had given me the location of Ford's training camp, and when I came to El Mirador Road, I turned north. It wasn't difficult to see the tire tracks in the dust veering off the road and disappearing behind a thicket of Joshua trees and low mesquite.

The sun warmed the desert. November in southern Arizona is a magical time, bright sunshine and milder temperatures. The morning chill was now only a memory. This might be my favorite time of year. Shirt sleeves and shorts for the afternoon, or in my case, a uniform now thankfully dry.

I followed the tracks west, and in a matter of five minutes I came upon a rain-splattered red pickup sitting at a whacky angle from the two flat front tires. I parked and inspected them. Obviously, they'd been slashed.

War.

I followed the narrow but well-trudged trail about a quarter mile through the brush. This time of year, the color sprang primarily from the red buds of Christmas cactus and the occasional yellow or pink flowers on the barrel cactus. The recent rains caused tiny grasses to sprout all along the desert floor, giving it a look of fluffy carpeting.

In no time I came upon a well-used camp. Two men and one woman surveyed the area. All of them seemed to be in their mid-thirties and they each wore at least one visible handgun. Outfitted in desert camo from their shirts and jackets to their hiking boots, they looked G.I. Joe official.

A ton of gear jumbled in the center of the camp. Camo packs with food packages tossed around, some of them slit open and spilling into the dirt. Sleeping bags, water bottles, collapsible shovels, fire starting equipment, cooking gear, rifles, scopes, and knives. Expensive backpacks had been slashed and a pile of warm clothes smoldered in the center of camp. Aluminum camp chairs lay in twisted heaps. Everything a squad would need to conquer a small country, and it looked as if Bigfoot had thrown the ultimate frat party.

The three soldiers grumbled and cursed, picking up items and discarding them. One man with a thin face and straight dark hair that fell across his forehead said, "The bastards broke my binoculars. I just bought them for this trip."

The other guy leaned over a pile of sleeping bags and sniffed. "I think they pissed on our bags."

"Animals," the woman said.

I agreed, though I'd seen BP officers do the same to humanitarian supplies left for migrants.

"Going hunting?" I asked, and stepped into their camp.

They all spun toward me. The dark-haired guy reached for his sidearm. When they took note of my uniform, they relaxed a little. At least they no longer seemed ready to shoot.

The other guy, in my opinion a little pale and soft to be running around on the desert at night in November, gave a disgusted snort. "Look at this. They actually do show up when you need them."

I surveyed their scattered camp. "Are you having problems?"

The woman, clearly upset, raised her arms for emphasis. "What do you think?"

I nodded in sympathy. "It gets worse, I'm afraid."

All three looked at me. I gave them the bad news. "They slit your tires."

"Are you kidding me?" the pudgy guy yelled.

I held up my hand. "It's okay. I'll give you a ride back to town and you can get help."

"That's the least you can do. We're out here humping our asses to do your job." This from the out-of-shape guy.

I raised my eyebrows. "Thank you?"

The woman shot him a warning look. "We appreciate your help. Thanks."

"Agent Sanchez," I said, and reached out a hand to the dark-haired man.

He gave it a brief, firm shake. "Tim Lewis."

I rounded the circle and collected the others' names. Marcy Downs and Dell Bosworth.

The three of them seemed comfortable together. "How did you all end up down here?"

A trace of a smile softened Marcy's face. "We were in the Army together in Iraq. When you take the oath, it's for life." Isn't that exactly what Ford said?

Dell said, "Our buddy told us about this group protecting the border. He got us all to come down here for a week every November."

They fell silent. Then Tim said, "Now we come down here to honor him."

Marcy lifted her gaze from the sand and focused on me. "Suicide."

Their pain felt solid in the afternoon breeze. "I'm sorry." What other words could I offer?

"Yeah, well, we're doing what we swore to do: protect the United States." Dell's voice was strong and defiant.

Tim kept his focus on the woman, clearly marking her as their spokesperson. I turned to her. "Are you Recon to Reclaim the Desert?"

She pointed to the patch on her shoulder. "Yep."

A slight breeze ruffled the creosote bushes and the tip of my nose tingled with the cooling afternoon air. Clouds ruffled the sky like a trail of lace.

"Who do you think did this?" I asked.

Marcy paced away a few steps. "No Desert Deaths. Obviously."

Dell agreed. "It's right up their alley. They talk about being caring and ending suffering and look what they did to our stuff."

"Where were you when this happened?" I asked.

Tim tilted his head to the left. "We got a call to patrol toward Brown Peak."

"Did Ford call you?"

Marcy stood with her hands on her hips surveying the damage. "We haven't heard from Ford for days."

Dell continued. "It was John."

That was a new name. "John who?"

Tim and Dell looked at each other before Dell said, "I don't know his last name. He's just this guy who volunteers with Recon to Reclaim the Desert."

Marcy walked back over to us and flung herself to sit, somehow folding her legs with her military boots on. "We all thought he was out of the organization. But here he is, in charge now."

"Not the commander. Ford's still commander," Dell said.

"Sure," Tim said. "But maybe the operation is getting bigger or he's recruiting or working someplace else. We don't know. But John's giving the orders for Ford."

They spoke rapidly and I tried to keep up. "Why did you think he was out of the organization?" I asked.

Marcy said, "He kept doing stuff without Ford's okay. John was all like, 'Let's kill the smugglers instead of call the Border Patrol.'"

Dell said, "He told me it would save the government something like fifty thousand dollars if we killed them instead of sending them through the courts."

That sent my nerves to tingling. "Did he ever kill anyone?"

Tim and Marcy gave each other a meaningful look, but I didn't know what it meant. Marcy said, "Not that we witnessed."

"But you think he might have?"

Again, they exchanged looks. Tim broke it off and stared at the ground. After a moment, Marcy started again. "One night we were patrolling a mountain range. We'd found some scouts and had engaged with them and subdued them. Tim and me and John got three of them. I think Dell was with Ford on another mission. But one of the guys slipped away."

Tim hadn't moved.

"John took off after him and left me and Tim with the other guys. We heard a couple of shots and pretty soon John came back to join us. He said he shot at the guy but he'd got away."

"You think he killed the scout?" I asked.

She snapped back at me. "I never looked. We took him at his word."

Tim raised his chin and gave Marcy a look before turning to me. "But the day before we were due to head back we were out in that area again. I swear I smelled something dead."

"You don't know that," Marcy said.

Dell poked at a pile of hamburger buns crumbling in the dirt. "I smelled it."

"But you didn't go check it out so you don't know. None of us do."

Dell tapped the bun and it broke apart. "You didn't let us go near it. You were afraid John had killed the guy and you didn't want us to get involved."

Marcy stood up again and walked away. "We didn't see it. We don't know anything."

"Did you talk to Ford about it?"

Tim shook his head. "No. But John and Ford went at it a couple of times. Some other volunteers told us Ford finally had enough of John's insubordination and kicked him out."

"But he's back," I urged them.

"I just told you that," Marcy said. "He called and sent us to the mountain. He said it was on Ford's orders."

Tim stood up suddenly. "This is it. I'm done with this. I came out here to protect the border from illegals and criminals. I didn't come out here to get involved with this petty fight."

"What do you mean a petty fight?" I asked.

Dell answered for Tim. "According to some other volunteers it started a couple of months ago and it's gotten worse. No Desert Deaths accused

Recon to Reclaim the Desert of destroying their aid drops. Which we've done sometimes but they said we were tracking them like the smugglers and destroying stuff as soon as it was dropped. So they started retaliating by vandalizing our stuff. Nothing like this." He pointed to the camp. "Just let air out of a tire or something. This"—he swept his arm around again—"could kill someone. Out here without water and no way to get help."

"But you have phones," I pointed out.

Dell gave me an annoyed look. "Sure. But they don't always work out here."

I couldn't argue with that. "How long has the trouble between you and the aid workers been going on?"

Tim looked worried. "We ought to tell her."

Marcy frowned at him, and when no one spoke, I did. "Tell me what?"

Tim eyed his companions. "The last couple of years when we've come out here, it's been good. Ford had a plan and we executed it. Our job was tracking and observing. We patrolled the desert, mostly at night. When we found something, we'd contain it and then call Border Patrol."

"This year it's all gone to shit," Dell said.

Marcy waited a second before saying, "Seems like Ford got soft."

I pictured those icy blue eyes and his set mouth in the tanned crags of his face. "Soft?"

Dell snorted and I fought the urge to tell him to knock it off. "When we first started coming out here, we really patrolled the border. I mean, if anyone crossed, we went after them."

"But not now?"

Tim unexpectedly joined in. "Ford doesn't want us going after the migrants anymore."

"Illegal aliens." Dell picked a weed stalk and shredded it.

Marcy added, "He wants us to focus on the drug smugglers and human traffickers. So, yeah, we can go after illegals if we run across them, just not focus on them."

A civilian using force to detain or capture anyone is kidnapping, even on the desert. If we caught vigilantes holding people against their will, we'd arrest them. Or, some of us would arrest them. Others, like Brody, would gladly accept the prisoners and take credit for the apprehension.

"Why did he change his attitude?" I asked.

Marcy punched a sleeping bag into a stuff sack. "We don't know. Maybe he feels sorry for them."

"Seems reasonable," I said, earning another snort from Dell.

Tim bit his lip. "Sure. I mean, we don't want anyone to die out here. But if they know there's supplies and stuff, it'll only encourage them to keep coming across."

"And when they do," Marcy continued for him, "they take our jobs, don't pay taxes, put their kids in our schools, burden our health care system and welfare."

Of course, Dell had to add his snort. "They're not coming here to better our country, they're only in it for themselves."

Marcy leaned in. "Right. And we're not saying we don't feel sorry for them. But they have their own country. If they don't like it, they should stay home and fix it."

Tim agreed. "But it's not only the migrants. Ford used to be clear that leaving the supplies out on the desert encouraged the cartels and also the terrorists. I mean, we heard that last month they caught five Palestinians sneaking through near Sasabe. We can't allow that."

Dell threw a bit of weed into the wind. "Ford doesn't feel sorry for them. He's trying to keep the peace. The humanitarians are getting violent and trying to engage us to get us into trouble. Ford wants us to back off. So, yeah, let them have their little water stations."

"Maybe," Marcy said. "I know Ford was worried about the trial. Thought it might make people more sympathetic to the illegals."

"What trial?" Dell said.

Marcy said. "You know, that Lacy Hollander chick."

Dell sneered. "I hope they lock her up. She's a traitor."

"Would Ford have any reason to dislike Lacy Hollander?" I asked.

Marcy said, "Well, yeah. She was a traitor, putting our country at risk."

Tim said, "Besides that, you mean?"

I didn't know how long they'd been out on their adventure, but they might not have heard the news. "Lacy Hollander was found murdered two days ago. About five miles from here."

They were silent for a while. Then Dell said, "Look, we're not happy she's dead. But maybe she shouldn't have been out here, you know?"

"What do you mean?"

He pointed to the gear strung out on the ground. "Those humanitarians. They aren't trained. They have no business running around out here. They aren't armed. Anything could happen."

"Did Ford ever talk about the aid workers? Lacy in particular?"

Marcy cocked an eyebrow. "There is that one thing."

"What thing?" I asked.

Tim gave her a puzzled look but Dell seemed to suddenly recall. "Yeah, that thing with the IED."

Improvised Explosive Device? That sounded more serious than dumping water in the sand.

Tim snapped his fingers at the memory. "That's right. Ford was really pissed at that."

I focused on Marcy with a look to invite her to tell me about it.

She hesitated.

"What happened with the IED?" I prompted

Marcy's irritation flared. "There was no IED. Purely fabricated. Fake news."

Tim nodded. "Yeah, Lacy accused Ford of having IEDs and the Border Patrol raided his house."

"And they didn't find any?" I said.

She blew a raspberry. "Obviously. Or he'd be in jail. No, one of the militias by El Paso was setting them out on the border roads and ended up killing a few crossers. Like Ford always says, we're not militia. We're vigilantes."

I gave her a questioning look.

She shot a glance to Dell. "Recon to Reclaim the Desert is not out to overthrow any government or take the law into our own hands. We're here to be vigilant."

She paused and a silent signal seemed to pass between them, though I didn't see it. Together they recited as if rehearsed, "Recon to Reclaim the Desert focuses on obtaining intelligence through reconnaissance operations. We take on the challenge of locating and documenting the smuggling activities and players within our borders." They grinned at each other as if it was an inside joke.

Tim's mouth turned up in an embarrassed grin. "We had to memorize that before they gave us our Recon patch."

Dell said, "We're not a militia. We're vigilantes. We don't shoot people. Don't even round them up. We just find them and tell you guys where they are."

"That's on Ford's directives?" I wanted to make sure.

Tim pulled a camera out of the smoldering campfire. "I paid six hundred dollars for this." He dropped it, then let his eyes travel over the campsite before glaring at Marcy. "That's it. I'm outta here." Tim headed toward the path.

Marcy scoffed. "How are you gonna leave? We've got two flat tires and no water."

Tim pointed to me. "Agent Sanchez is here to help us."

I agreed. "If you've got one spare, I can help you with the other until we get to Tucson and you can get another tire."

Marcy considered this. "That'll work. I've had enough of this too." She passed Tim on the path. "Agent Sanchez and I will take care of the tires. You guys pick up the camp and load it into the back of the pickup."

Tim's jaw dropped as I followed Marcy. He didn't say anything as he turned back to camp.

16

I followed the three of them on a sandy trail road, then gravel, to a two-lane paved road, and finally onto Ajo Highway. They pulled off at the first gas station by Three Points. It took less than an hour to get the tire traded off and for me to be back in business. By then my shift was nearing an end so I headed back to the station, thankful for a day completed on time. I wasted no time heading home.

When I walked into the house the comforting spicy smell of chilis, onions, and cheese, along with Deon's special refried beans, enfolded me. My stomach growled and my mouth flooded with anticipation.

Deon stood behind the kitchen island dishing Spanish rice onto the four plates lined up in front of him. He flashed me a smile. "Perfect timing."

Sami swiveled on a stool across from Deon, leaning on her forearms. "Dinner with all of us. And Dad made enchiladas!"

"God bless you," I said to Deon, and hurried over to plant a kiss on his lips.

"Yuck," Sami said.

I slipped around the counter and gave her a smacking kiss on her forehead.

She rubbed it off. "So slobbery."

"Where's your sister?" I asked as I deposited my gun and belt in the safe and spun the lock. I pulled my ice packs from my lunch cooler and slipped them in the freezer. Home. Sigh.

"Upstairs in her room, like always." Sami swung her chair from side to side.

No time like the present. I squeezed Sami on the shoulder. "Go upstairs for a little bit. I'll let you know when dinner is ready."

She stopped spinning. "It's ready. Dad's got it on the plates already."

Deon eyed me, then turned to Sami. "Mom says go upstairs. Don't argue."

She popped off the chair and landed on the tiled floor. "Oh, man. That's not fair."

"Sami," Deon warned, and she huffed again, performed a pirouette, and trotted away. Her feet thudded on the stairs as I washed my hands at the kitchen sink.

"Okay," Deon said, wiping his hands on a towel. "What did I do wrong?"

I leaned against the sink. "What makes you think you've done something wrong?"

"Obviously, you wanted to be alone with me. If you'd wanted to have sex, you'd have dragged me upstairs. Sending Sami upstairs means I'm in trouble."

I folded my arms across my chest. "Okay. Well, I'm not happy that you gave Josie permission to skip class and protest outside the station."

His eyebrows shot up. "I did what now?"

That's what I thought. I reached into the fridge for a seltzer water. "I know you asked me to wait to talk to her until you and I had a chance to discuss it. But she pushed my buttons—well, we pushed each other's buttons. And when I questioned her about it, she said you okayed it."

He smiled. "She asked me to sign her out for a field trip to Davis-Monthan Airfield."

Clever girl. "Well, technically, that's right. The station is at the entrance."

"I didn't think too much about it. I was getting ready for the depositions and she handed me the phone to call the school. I told them she was going to the air base and that was it."

"She's in so much trouble." I walked to the doorway and unlaced my boots.

"I shouldn't have let her trick me."

One boot dropped to the floor. "There's that. But she shouldn't have been out there in the first place."

"Why not?"

I dropped the other boot and padded back to the kitchen. "That's where I work. I'm the barest of a rookie. It's bad to have my kid protesting."

He pulled the enchiladas from the oven. "Did it cause you any problems?"

"Well, no. Not yet."

He considered me. "She's got a right to her own opinions."

This wasn't going the way I'd thought it would. "Of course. But we're a family and we support each other."

Deon spooned beans onto the plates. "I don't see that Josie protesting for human rights is not supporting you."

This didn't seem like a fight I should have in my own home. "It's my job."

He glanced over his shoulder at me. "Your job is to take away human rights?"

I gulped my seltzer, feeling the burning fizz in my throat. "My job is Border Patrol and she was protesting outside."

"She's really torn up about Lacy Hollander's death. Maybe we can go a little easy on her?"

"And maybe she could be a little more considerate of my position."

He turned to me and put his hands on my hips, drawing me close. "We raised her to be compassionate and to stand up for what she believes. Do you think we should have raised her to only stand up for what we believe?"

God, he sounded just like her. Don't the marriage vows state that parents are always on the same side? They should. "Can't she protest somewhere else?"

He kissed me. "Come on, be proud of her. She's a good kid."

"Who tricked you into giving her an excuse to skip school."

He turned back to the plates. "We'll talk about that."

The thudding of kids' feet on the stairs stopped our discussion.

"Thanks for making dinner. I'm starving." I pulled out the silverware drawer and counted out forks, knives, and spoons. Before I started with Border Patrol, we ate together most evenings. I cooked and we gathered at the fully-set dinner table. These days, even if we miraculously ended up eating at the same time, we usually sat at the counter bar, gobbled dinner, and flew away in a rush.

"In honor of a homecooked meal, let's eat at the table like civilized people," I said.

Sami and Josie appeared. I smiled at them. "I thought I told you I'd call you to dinner."

Josie frowned. "Can we eat now? I only have a couple of minutes."

Again, I felt outside the fence. "What's going on?"

Josie planted a Tilley hat on her head. "The candlelight vigil for Lacy Hollander?"

I turned to Deon. "Do you know about this?"

He shrugged in an effort to dismiss it. "Josie asked if she could go to it with a few friends. I said yes."

A vigil for a young woman murdered on the desert. We didn't know who killed Lacy and if it might happen again. A man roamed at large with frigid blue eyes and a rage hot enough to singe the desert. And we were letting our daughter loose in the world? "Where is this taking place?"

She exhaled. "Jacome Plaza."

Downtown, after dark. I didn't like that. "Who are you going with?"

She thrust out a hip and pleaded with Deon. "You already said I could go. We're not doing anything bad. Just lighting candles and honoring Lacy. Come on. You said yes."

Deon gave me a look that after all our years of marriage I interpreted with no problem. He'd taken care of it and I should trust him.

Josie's phone blipped in her hand. She glanced at it. "They're here. Gotta go." She spun around.

"Hey," Deon said, stopping her immediately.

She turned to look at him.

He opened his palms to the plates on the counter. "I made enchiladas because you requested them."

Was that the slightest shadow of remorse on her face? "I know. But they're here and I've gotta go." She gave him a charming smile. "Save me some?"

He gave her those sad, soulful eyes that got me every time. "Be careful. Wear your coat. Be home by nine." He shot the conditions at her.

Apparently, my daughter had a stronger will than I did. "Nine?" she whined.

He lowered his eyebrows. "Nine."

"Fine." She took off.

"Coat!" Deon yelled.

The closet by the front door opened and slammed closed, followed by the same with the front door.

Sami climbed up to a bar stool and slid a plate in front of herself. "Can we eat now?"

I settled next to her and drew my own plate in front of me. "It looks delicious."

Deon pulled his plate over and passed forks down the line. "Dig in."

The three of us chatted, but Josie's leaving seemed to put a weight on us. Even Sami didn't rattle on. That might not have as much to do with Josie as it did with Sami getting older and learning that not every thought needed to shoot out of her mouth. Or maybe she and Deon were still on the outs.

Deon's enchiladas were perfect and the traditional sides filled me until I thought my skin might split. I got up to take care of the dishes. Sami helped me, then moved into the family room to watch TV, and Deon retreated upstairs to read a brief.

I wandered into the family room where Sami was staring at the TV. "Hey, want to practice self-defense?"

Self-defense was really an excuse for us to wrestle. It had started out as a game when the girls were little. They'd attack me and I'd show them how to defend themselves and eventually we'd all roll around the floor in giggle fits. The older they got, the more real moves I threw in. Now they often accompanied me to community workshops where I taught self-defense. It had always been a way to defuse tension in our home.

Sami didn't look at me. "Naw. It's not fun without Josie."

After trying to engage Sami and being shunted off for a ridiculous sitcom, I climbed the stairs to our bedroom. In his stocking feet, Deon propped himself on the bed, a volume-muted football game flashing on the TV. Papers spread all around him. He gathered those next to him. "Want to sit here? You can change the channel."

I walked into the closet and started taking off my uniform. "I think I'll go to the vigil."

His surprised voice wound into the closet. "Now? Downtown?"

I pulled on jeans. "It's a tragedy Lacy Hollander was killed. I kind of want to be there." A dark hoodie hung on a hook and I slipped it over my head and walked out of the closet.

Deon studied me. "You're going to check up on Josie."

"Is that so bad?" I found warm socks and sat on the side of the bed to put them on.

He scanned the pages in his hand. "Do you want me to go with you?"

"Nope. I won't be long. You stay here with Sami."

He looked relieved. "Good. You two keep out of trouble." He grinned. "Make good choices." His nose was already buried in his work before I walked out of the bedroom.

What kind of trouble could we get into at a candlelight vigil?

17

I ended up having to park a half mile away. The sound of a woman's voice over a loudspeaker floated through the area as I walked from the neighborhood north of downtown. Small adobe and wood cottages snugged together, most of them remodeled from early last century. They weren't fancy even in their youth and had seen some hard times over the years. Recently, gentrification had turned this neighborhood into one of the most sought-after in Tucson.

I dodged orange trees reaching across front fences and hanging over the sidewalk. The cracked cement required some attention to keep from tripping. But the sounds of a crowd cheering occasionally and the continued sound of a speaker kept me moving forward.

The air felt brisk, probably in the lower fifties. Wintertime in Tucson. I flipped my hoodie over my head and buried my hands in my jacket pockets. About a block from the park smatterings of people appeared.

Most of them carried signs but didn't hold them up. I assumed people passionate about the vigil were already at the plaza, so I was surprised to see so many hanging around.

Jacome Plaza stretched in front of the main library. A concrete area half the size of a football field accommodated everything from the annual jazz festival to AU pep rallies. Now it was filled with people in Lacy Hollander Tilley hats holding candles.

The closer I got to the park, the denser the crowd. I nearly turned around and headed home when I recognized the speaker as Serena. She stood on a stage behind a microphone. Her voice held earnestness and fire.

"Lacy Hollander was a hero. She gave tirelessly to the cause of ending human suffering and death. For that, she was arrested by her own government. Undaunted, she didn't give up. Even to the hour of her death she was caring and doing what she could to help the migrants risking everything for a new life."

I didn't know how long she'd been at it but it sounded as if she could keep going for a while. I let her words wash over me as I scanned the crowd for Josie. The beauty of a university town is the social and political awareness and the energy to participate publicly. Tucson had its share of rallies, protests, demonstrations, and marches. This vigil had drawn a huge crowd, even by Tucson standards.

Finding Josie might be more of a challenge than I'd expected. Especially since so many wore Tilley hats. I pushed through, my eyes searching. Many people held candles with little cardboard circles to keep hot wax from their hands. The delicacy of the flames emphasized the tragedy of a young and passionate woman cut down too early.

An abrupt moment of silence forced me to stop moving and lower my head in honor of Lacy. Then everyone, including an off-key Serena, began to sing "Amazing Grace." She turned the mic over to another woman with a much better voice. Interesting choice for a song, but it had lots of verses and I guess even someone as passionate as Serena needed to take a break every now and then.

I worked my way toward the back of the plaza where a row of stone benches created a demarcation from the pavement to a grassy area. If I could climb on a bench, I might get a better view.

I waded into the thick of those gathered, slipping through small crevices between bodies. Lots of young people focused on the stage, singing along. Many had glistening eyes, wet cheeks, or were sobbing outright. While Lacy's death was tragic, the drama played large out here. I spotted a knot of kids from Josie's school and kept my eyes on them as I tried to get through the sea of bodies.

Serena started talking again, though I tuned her out for the most part. There was a moment for applause. Maybe she was turning the stage over to someone else. I didn't come to the vigil to hear the speakers. I wanted to connect to my daughter.

The new speaker cleared her throat. "It's time we commit to humanity. To standing up to cruel authority forcing migrants into the most dangerous lands in the whole world."

The sound of that voice took my breath away. I whipped my head around to the stage, my body pinned in the crush of people. I was too far away and too many people stood between us for me to see. Without regard for anyone, I fought my way to the stone bench and shoved my way up.

"Dude," a young man said, irritated.

"Well, excuse me," a thirty-something woman snarked.

Josie stood on the platform, mouth close to the microphone. My brilliant, articulate, angry daughter's voice rang out clear and strong. Fourteen years old. Still a child, yet she spoke with such authority.

I blinked back hot tears, not wanting to miss a single second of her standing in front of hundreds of people. My heart expanded, threatening to crack my ribs. Pride. Oh dear god, yes. Look at her, so wonderful.

Fear. Even more than the pride. Lacy Hollander had been murdered for her beliefs. Josie was exposing herself to danger. "Caring is never criminal," Josie said.

The crowd responded with shouts and applause.

To the side of the platform I spotted Serena standing with several others, adding their applause and shouts to the rest. Ann sat in her wheelchair in the middle of the group, huddled into her coat.

A disturbance toward the back of the crowd caught my attention.

A large blonde woman in a camo canvas jacket started yelling, shoving a placard forward. I couldn't hear her words but her rage rolled off in waves. Several other people behind her surged forward, shouting and brandishing posters like weapons. "Go Home." "Make America Great Again." "Love it or Leave it."

While some people backed away, others shoved forward. Those here for Lacy's vigil and those protesting the gathering clashed. I turned my attention to Josie, who seemed not to have noticed the fight breaking out.

Another group in camo surged from the right, creating a wedge toward the back of the crowd.

"Josie!" Fighting my way through the chaotic crowd to the stage would take too long. If I skirted the edge of the plaza, behind the anti-vigil bunch, maybe I could make it to Josie quicker. My eyes scanned the edge of the well-lit space and I stopped.

Where the surging protesters met the oncoming vigil participants, cold blue eyes drew a sharp bead on Josie. He wore a battered ball cap and an Army field jacket. His eyebrows drew together in a scowl and he started moving through the melee.

She kept speaking into the mic, but with the conflict rising, her words were drowned out. I hurled myself off the stone bench, bouncing into two young men and squeezing through.

"What the hell?" one of them said. The other shouted something but I didn't stop to apologize or care. I started grabbing jacket collars and yanking people out of my way. I needed to get to Josie.

To my left I searched for Ford. He made better progress than I did as he fought his way through the fracas, his eyes focused on the stage.

A water bottle hurtled from the outer edges of the fight, flying straight toward Josie. It nicked her arm, spraying water on her. She jumped back, now realizing the gathering had turned.

"Josie!"

Behind me the volume increased. More people became aware of the skirmish and some of them turned to join the fight. Others seemed to be trying to escape from the plaza. The tide of bodies shifted in random patterns as I fought to get to Josie, feeling like I was struggling in the throes of a nightmare.

The back of Ford's head rose above the crowd a few feet ahead of me. If he'd killed Lacy Hollander for her role in humanitarian efforts, would he hurt Josie, too? I threw an elbow into a young woman's side and ducked under her arm when she reached around.

Now that I was only twenty feet from the stage, Ford was nowhere in sight. My daughter held onto the mic and stared out at the plaza, looking more confused than scared. Another water bottle hurtled toward her and she backed up.

"Josie!" I watched helplessly as she stepped back on the small platform and toppled. She disappeared. I didn't know where Ford was and I'd lost sight of Josie. Had she slammed onto the pavement and hit her head? Was Ford behind the stage and already dragging her away?

I didn't know how I cleared the last stretch. I might have punched and kicked bystanders. All I knew was that I rounded the stage to a relatively bare space.

Ford was perched on one knee, reaching out to Josie, who sat on the cold pavement, her legs straight in front of her.

"Hey! Get away from her!" With both hands I shoved a man out of my path and raced toward Ford and Josie.

He looked up as I barreled into him full speed, knocking him back.

He rolled over his shoulder and ended up in a squat, looking ready to spring to attack. I crouched, ready for him.

"Mom!" Josie yelled, and I couldn't tell if she was scared, relieved, hurt, or agitated.

I forced myself to stay focused on Ford. He wouldn't get to Josie as long as I was alive.

Ford let his gaze drift from me to Josie. I hated those icy eyes studying her.

"Mom," she said, a little less frantic. "I'm okay. It's fine."

Ford rose and relaxed. He nodded to Josie and turned his hard eyes on me. "Your daughter?"

I stayed low, wanting to take him out.

He shook his head. "You, of all people, should know better than to let her be a target."

Risking my ready stance, I reached into my pocket and pulled out my phone. "Get the hell out of here before I call the cops."

Ford sneered at me and ticked his head toward the plaza. "I'm guessing cops are on their way if they aren't already here."

"Mom." Josie touched my shoulder.

I swung my arm out and shoved her behind me.

"Jeez, Mom. It's okay. I fell off the stage and got the wind knocked out of me. This guy was helping me."

Ford glanced around, his eyes narrowing on Ann and the group standing around her.

I stepped forward. "You have no business being here. This is for Lacy Hollander. People came to honor her and mourn. You couldn't respect that?"

His voice rolled like a low growl. "You have no idea why I'm here."

"I know you don't belong here."

He waved his hand at me in an angry dismissal as he turned and slipped around the side of the stage.

Josie stepped beside me. "What's going on with that guy?"

I kept my eyes riveted on him like a deer tracks a wolf. The plaza had emptied, leaving only a few pockets of people talking to cops. Ford maneuvered around them all and disappeared into an alley.

When he was gone, Josie tried again. "Do you know him?"

She looked at me with her deep brown eyes, fearless, curious, determined. For a second I couldn't speak, then I pulled her tight against me. "Thank god you're safe."

She hugged me back. Maybe for the first time in a year. But not nearly long enough. She pulled away and met my eyes. "You're crying."

I felt my face. "Am I? You scared me."

"I'm fine. What are you doing here?"

It took me a minute to remember. I came to the vigil to show Josie I supported her. I wanted her to know that being Border Patrol didn't mean I'd quit caring about people. I still believed in humanitarian efforts. Maybe being here would bridge a gap, show her I was willing to step toward her.

Seeing her speaking on stage sent a wave of pride through me. But knowing the risk she put herself in, and her being so naïve and idealistic, the mother bear in me stirred to life. Lacy Hollander's death was a tragedy, but that didn't give anyone the right to manipulate and use a fourteen-year-old.

I took Josie's hand and started dragging her toward Ann and her entourage. "It doesn't matter why I'm here, but it's a damned good thing I showed up."

Ann sat in her wheelchair, her face pale, lips nearly purple. Serena and a couple of others stood next to her. They spoke rapidly, gesticulated and shouted. All clearly rattled.

The group separated when I broke into their midst.

Serena threw her arms around Josie. "You were awesome. Oh my god. Rocked the house."

Josie, whose hand was clamped into mine, watched me over Serena's shoulder. Whatever she felt, her face held no clue.

I looked down at Ann. An unbridled fury rose into my chest. "What are you thinking?"

Ann blinked at me, as if she didn't hear me.

Josie grabbed my arm. "Leave her alone, Mom. She didn't have anything to do with me being here."

Serena glared at me. "Back it off, Tiger Mom."

Josie pulled her hand from mine. "We need to get Aunt Ann home. She's really tired."

Serena kept her eyes on me. "Josie is amazing. She's got the fire and can really make people take notice. Don't you think?"

"What I think is that you have no right to exploit a child to get attention."

Josie pulled away from Serena's arm. "I'm not a child and no one is forcing me to do anything. I wanted to speak. This is important."

I turned to Ann. "She's a kid. You're brainwashing her for your own purpose."

Ann looked pale and didn't seem ready with a response as usual.

Feeling a little like a bully but not really caring, I shot all my fear straight at Ann. "She's my daughter, not yours. You can't go behind my back and bring her out here. Did you write her speech? What did you hope to gain? Getting sympathy by using children's voices. She's not Greta Thunberg."

Josie yelled at me but I didn't hear what she said. She tugged at my arm, trying to get me to back off.

Ann's mouth moved but she didn't speak. In the shadows from the plaza's bright lights, she looked colorless.

Damn it. I leaned over and wrapped my fingers around her arm, leaning close to her face. "Ann?"

She struggled for a breath and closed her eyes.

"Ann!" I placed my palms against her cold cheeks. "Josie, call 9-1-1!"

18

I held a paper cup half full of cold coffee. The powdered creamer swirled a grease stain on the top. The window reflected the waiting room behind me and Josie sitting ramrod straight on a vinyl couch.

Her face looked drawn and worried. She wouldn't allow me to touch her and hadn't spoken to me since we followed the ambulance here two hours ago.

Serena and Derrick had been here for a while. They'd huddled with Josie until Serena had given her a hug, told her what a good soldier she was, and they'd departed to attend a meeting with No Desert Deaths.

No one gave me an award for not throttling Serena, though I deserved one. I'd talked to Deon and we made the decision for him to stay home with Sami. No need for all of us to suffer this stress.

A shuffle of soft-soled shoes sounded in the hallway, approaching at a fast clip. I swiveled from the window, relieved to hear it. I'd called my brother but the message had gone to voicemail. Deep into case law with his study group, he'd silenced his phone. He'd called me back when he saw the message and when I told him about Ann, he'd promised to be here immediately.

Chris rounded the corner into the waiting room, his eyes searching for us. "What's—?" He didn't get any further before Josie threw herself into his arms.

She clung to him and burst into tears. The first I'd seen her cry since Ann had collapsed in the plaza.

He held her tight and sought my face.

I spoke quickly to give him the most important information. "Ann's going to be okay. She had a reaction to some new pain meds they gave her."

He patted Josie's back. "It's okay," he soothed. "Here, let's sit down."

He led her back to the couch, and she tucked into him when they sat. She didn't look at me but buried her head in Chris's shoulder and continued to cry softly. It hurt to see her turning to Chris instead of me, but she'd held back for so long, I was glad to see her let go a little.

"I'm sorry I didn't get your message sooner. What happened?"

Josie pulled her head up. "Mom attacked her at the candlelight vigil."

Chris gave me a questioning look.

I sat at the edge of my chair. "I did not attack her. I was mad that she'd put you in danger."

"I wasn't in danger. You don't give me any credit for knowing my own mind."

"Hey," Chris said. "What happened to Ann?"

"The doctor said the cold probably weakened her. The new meds made her nauseated and she'd been throwing up. She didn't tell anyone. She had no food in her stomach, probably was in quite a bit of pain, and she had a seizure."

"But she's okay?" He sounded as if he needed a little more reassurance.

Josie glared at me and dropped her head onto his shoulder.

How was I ever going to make it right with Josie? Perhaps this was a teenage phase and we'd grow back together. What if it wasn't? My responsibility as a mother was to keep her safe. But I owed her the room to grow and discover the world and her place in it. Damn it. Part of me longed for those days when a skinned knee was our biggest problem. I focused on Chris. "They're giving her an IV now. We can take her home in a couple of hours."

"Home to Mi Casa? Is that a good idea?" he asked.

I hoped it wouldn't make things worse for Ann. "I'm taking her to our house with me. She can stay in the guest room for a few days. We're going to have to figure something out. She can't stay at Mi Casa alone."

Josie sat up, ready for the fight. "Ann will hate being at our house. With you. You're the reason she passed out in the first place."

Chris squeezed Josie to him in a sort of reprimand. "Your mother didn't change Ann's meds or make her not eat. She's bad, but she's not that evil."

Josie didn't laugh. Neither did I.

Chris took his arm back. "Your house is probably the best place. My extra room doesn't have a bed and I'm never home. She can't stay at Mi Casa."

Josie stood up. "I can stay with her. I can take the city bus to school. Someone else is always at Mi Casa during the day. It's a perfect solution."

"Absolutely not." No way. No how.

Josie backed off the rage and took on a reasonable tone. "Maybe you're not the reason she's in here, but she's not comfortable around you. She won't get better under your roof."

Chris raised his eyebrows at me. "She's got a point."

They were ganging up on me. "You haven't spent any time with Ann since the semester started," I said to Chris. "How would you know what she'd want?"

He held up a hand to stop me. "I'm in my last year of law school. I don't have time to eat or sleep, let alone babysit a stubborn sister."

Josie pushed her advantage. "Both of you are super busy. You have these new careers and all of that. But Ann is doing what she's always been doing. Only now she doesn't have Fritz or Efrain. You know if you don't let her stay at Mi Casa she'll fight you and probably get sicker." Josie was playing us and I knew it. When had she become such a diplomat—or manipulator?

Chris looked at Josie as if seeing a flower bloom. "Wow. You're really growing up."

I didn't need his overwhelming admiration for Josie's sudden maturity. He didn't see her moping, slamming doors, acting as if the world revolved around her. And yet, about this, she wasn't wrong.

"What about Derrick," I said. "Isn't he supposed to be a big help?"

Josie flattened her lips and gave me a strange look.

"What?" I said.

She paused. "There's something about him. I don't know."

Chris and I gave her time to say more. She finally shrugged. "He's not family." She eyed me. "No one is home during the day at our house, either."

By the time we got Ann out of here it would be midnight. We'd have to refight this whole battle with her, and even in her weakened state, her combat skills exceeded Josie's. With only a few hours left of the night, it seemed best to give in for now.

I sighed. "Fine. But I'm staying with you tonight."

Josie leaned back into Chris's side, and he put his arm around her and drew her close. She closed her eyes, safe and content.

For now.

19

We got Ann home and into bed. She seemed relieved to be in her own space and I congratulated myself on at least one good decision. She didn't say much during the process and fell asleep almost immediately. I gave Josie the spare bedroom and I took the couch.

Deon didn't like the idea of Josie staying with Ann for a few days any better than I did but we agreed to take it one night at a time. Neither of us were excited to have my bossy and demanding sister in our guest room, mostly because we knew she'd hate being there and make sure we all suffered for it.

Of course, I didn't sleep much and woke up early. I tiptoed into Josie's room and nudged her.

"Come on. We need to get home and regroup. I've got to go to work and you have school."

She sat up in bed, wearing an old T-shirt of Fritz's she'd taken for the night. "I'm not going to school today."

Guess we were donning our gloves early today. "Oh yes you are. You already skipped one day this week."

"Only morning classes, and Aunt Ann needs me."

"And you need school."

Ann's muffled voice came from her bedroom. "Go to school, Josie. I'll be fine."

I held my hand out to the doorway. "There you have it. God has spoken."

"I heard that," Ann said, sounding stronger than last night, if not completely up to her usual fighting shape.

Josie threw back her covers and climbed out of bed. We both walked into Ann's room. She sat on the edge of her bed, reaching for her crutches. "I promise I won't do anything too strenuous. I'm going to eat some toast. Probably go back to bed."

I picked up the crutches and leaned them against the wall away from her. "We'll get your wheelchair."

She frowned at me but didn't protest.

I nodded at Josie. "You get the chair." To Ann I said, "I'll slip over to Mi Casa and tell them you won't be at work today. I'll see if one of the women can come over and get you breakfast." Wishing I could still meet her in the pick-up line after school and ooh and ah over the picture she drew for me, I mentally clenched my teeth and said, "Josie can grab a bus and come back here after school."

It took a while to get everyone situated at Ann's, rush home to spend a second filling in Deon and Sami on the arrangements, and send us all out in our separate directions.

I barely made it to muster on time. This whole business of rushing to work with that beating stress of being late had to stop or I'd stroke out.

There wasn't much banter or gossip on the way to our assigned vehicles. I looked forward to getting behind the wheel and having the time to breathe while I drove to my AOR. We didn't have dedicated vehicles, but the senior agents always had the newer ones. That left the rookies with the more beat-up units. We normally drove the same one, so agents generally kept the vehicles in the shape they were comfortable living in for ten-hour shifts.

Today, my regular pickup was scheduled for service and I was assigned one from the pool. Not only did it smell like something curled up, died, and haunted the cab, it was strewn with dirt, cactus, and trash. I rolled down my windows and headed to east Tres Bellotas. My blood pressure started to ebb as I drove the roads and let the wind rush through the windows, masking the cab's debris smell with the fresh bite of the damp desert.

Last night's vigil and altercation at Jacome Plaza made the local news. No one was injured and no arrests were made but a couple of people were interviewed. A college professor who supported No Desert Deaths said how disrespectful the anti-immigrant protesters were. A man identifying himself as a patriot commented about the need to protect the nation's borders. Pretty typical stuff.

The thought of Josie on that podium, exposed to the whims of violent people, made me want to throw up. How would I navigate this whole situation without sending Josie into the arms of the likes of Serena? Could I possibly get us through this without losing Ann?

My phone rang and I welcomed the distraction from my circular thoughts. Chris's ID gave me a dose of relief. "I'm glad you called."

"Just wondered how everyone got along last night. Since I didn't get a call from the morgue, I assume no one was murdered."

Very funny. "Josie's at school and I'm back at work. I'm worried about Ann, though."

"Does she have a doctor's appointment?"

I turned off Ajo Highway southbound to Tres Bellotas. "Not worried about her physically so much. I think she's pretty deeply involved with No Desert Deaths. We have to make her stop."

He chuckled. "I can't say I didn't suspect that. But how are you going to make Queen Ann do something she doesn't want to?"

He was right. "After Lacy Hollander's death and that stuff last night, it seems like everything is getting really dangerous."

Chris sounded serious. "I'm not buying the murder was cartel-related. I think there's someone mad about helping immigrants. I spent a lot of years out there and I gotta tell you, the last few have been scary. Some of those militias are getting fired up. Something like this was bound to happen."

I felt a chill. "Do you think Ann's in danger?"

"If we could get her to stay at your place, I'd feel better. Even if they'd find Hollander's killer, it would help."

"You're going to have to convince her," I said. "As long as I'm Border Patrol, I'm the enemy."

He paused and repeated a line that seemed on everyone's lips these days. "You don't have to do this, you know."

I scowled out the windshield, irritated to say it again, knowing I needed to hear it from myself. "My views haven't changed. I doubt yours have. We know there's corruption. You and Manuel were closing in and now you've burned all those bridges. So it's me."

"There are others we could recruit."

"Why are you making me argue about this? Of course there are others who could sniff out the bad guys in the agency. There are plenty of others who could be compassionate and fair agents in the field. But I'm one of them. The good guys. And it feels like what I'm supposed to do."

He sighed. "I don't know whether to be annoyed with your stubbornness or proud."

I sped along rolling hills, the Joshua trees filling the desert. "Do you know Ford Dewlinski?"

He laughed again. "Wow. That's a name I haven't heard for a while. Yeah. Good guy."

Good guy? "I think he's creepy."

"Well, yeah, maybe. But he's fair." Chris paused. "At least, I don't think he's violent or crazy."

"That's not my take. I think he instigated the anti-immigration protest last night."

Chris sounded skeptical. "Naw. That's not his way. He doesn't like crowds. Probably doesn't like people much at all."

"He threatened Josie."

Chris didn't answer immediately. "Are you sure?"

"Do you think he might have killed Lacy Hollander?"

He let out a surprised guffaw. "Damn, Mike. That's a leap. No. He's not—wait a minute. You're not getting mixed up in this Hollander thing, are you?"

"You said you'd feel better if Lacy Hollander's killer was found."

His voice took on an intense note. "Not your job. Do you hear me?"

"Sure, I hear you."

"No, really, Mike. Stay out of this. The sheriff's department will handle it."

I switched gears. "We need to have a family meeting with Ann and figure out what to do about her situation."

Chris went all patriarch. "We'll do that soon. But right now, I need you to promise me to stay out of Lacy Hollander's murder investigation."

I'd promise him, no matter how I decided to proceed. But in this case, he was probably right. A creepy guy with scary eyes, a Tilley hat on a table, and a penchant for showing up at the murder scene didn't make Ford a killer.

The morning passed uneventfully, thank goodness. After lunch I came across one of the newer Border Patrol Tahoes parked in the shade of a tall sycamore on the side of a crumbling one-lane paved road.

I pulled up beside it, not excited to see Brody pull his cap from where it covered his eyes. "How's it going?" I tried to sound as friendly as I could. Which didn't come off as very warm.

His nose turned up in a sneer. "Nice wheels."

"I'll get mine back tomorrow. What are you up to?"

Brody didn't bother to sit up. "Siesta time."

Really? This was how he spent his time. "I thought I'd hike over to that ridge and take a look."

Without craning his neck at all, his eyes drifted to me. "Whatever floats your boat. You'll learn soon enough that it doesn't matter whether you hunt or save your strength. It's all strategy."

Strategy. How he came away jumping so many groups baffled me. It didn't seem possible he was as canny as he claimed. I wondered again about Chris's insistence that Brody wasn't involved in the corruption.

"Well, don't let me disturb you," I said.

He dropped his cap back over his face. It jumped from the movement of his mouth. "I won't. Have a good hike, Grandma."

I gunned my engine but I'm sure it didn't bother Brody at all.

In a few miles I followed a dirt road and parked when the narrow passage threatened to give my beat-up pickup a few more Arizona pinstripes from the mesquite. The sun warmed the cool autumn air and the hike up the ridge was exerting enough for me to warm up nicely. The quail and cactus woodpeckers kept a nice chorus as I climbed, my breath keeping time. The red berries of the Christmas cactus and a few burnt orange grasses added highlights to the khaki and olive tones of the mesquite, creosote, and sage. Always, the cactus flourished with bursts of dangerous needles lying in wait for me to lose focus.

After about a half hour I reached the top and took out binoculars. Nothing seemed to move except the flick of birds performing their daily dance. The soft scent of damp sand from yesterday's rain and the still air made the desert seem placid and generous. Things I knew weren't true.

In the distance a plume of dust rose from a passing vehicle. Maybe Brody couldn't sleep. Poor guy.

It had been too long since I'd been hiking with Sami and Josie. We used to traipse around the Catalinas and the Tucsons. Sometimes we'd venture down to the Santa Ritas or the Rincons—all the ranges hemming in Tucson. I'd never thought to come down this way. Now that I knew what kind of activity took place down here close to the border, I was grateful I'd never brought them here.

I checked my blood sugar level. Definitely time to eat. The last thing I needed was to have an insulin seizure while out on patrol. The crinkle of the protein bar's wrapper coincided with a call from my radio.

Brody's voice hit my nerves. "Tango 572. Backup requested. 10-46 by 4. East of Marieta Wells."

I keyed the mic. "Tango 721, responding."

Brody's voice came on again. "How far away are you, Sanchez?"

I did a quick calculation. Marieta Wells was on the east side of this ridge. I'd have to get my pickup and drive around. "Forty-five minutes at least."

Liz responded. "Tango 321, same ETA."

I pulled out my binoculars again and pointed them to where I thought Marieta Wells should be. With a little searching I located a reflection and spot of white that was probably Brody's pickup. It only took me a few minutes to decide to jog there. With four smugglers, the sooner Brody got backup, the better. I oriented myself and started out at a decent clip. I wouldn't win any medals for speed but I'd be there sooner than if I went back for my vehicle.

I picked up a trail after a half mile and the running eased since I didn't have to dodge cactus and brush. Once I found Brody's pickup, the rumble of men's voices directed me the rest of the way.

I stopped and crept forward, not knowing if Brody was interrogating the smugglers or having a conversation, which seemed unlikely given his general disdain for non-Americans. After several more feet, I picked out a few words and it was clear they were speaking English. I continued toward the patch of sand where Brody and another man outfitted in camo stood in front of four seated men with their hands restrained behind their backs.

Brody saw me and his eyes registered shock. "Grandma. What...?" He glanced around quickly. "Where's Hinkin?"

The man standing next to him spun around. He held an M4 as if it were part of his arm. Without a word he slipped through a small space between a Palo Verde tree and a tangle of scrubby mesquite.

"Who's that?" I nodded toward the guy.

Brody swung his head to where I'd indicated. "Who's what? I don't see anyone."

Oh. Now I understood how Brody managed to jump so many groups. He and the vigilantes were tight. Recon to Reclaim the Desert did all the legwork, and when it was all over but the shouting, they called Brody in to raise his own voice.

"It isn't legal for that citizen to detain people and really not legal for him to do it at gunpoint. That's called kidnapping."

Brody gave me a confused look. "I don't know what you're talking about. There was no armed civilian here. I tracked these men and here they are."

Footsteps in the desert warned us before Liz stepped between some scrub. She studied the four men on the ground ranging from their teens to maybe early thirties. They all wore baggy, dusty jeans and dark ball caps over their black hair, and the ever-present carpet shoes. Only one of the younger men looked upset. The rest wore resigned expressions. They'd been through this before and knew they were in for some time in jail before their case was heard and they'd be sent south. After that, they'd be back at it. Whether it was for the money or because the cartels threatened their families, they probably didn't feel they had much choice. They might be right.

"You collected all four on your own?" Liz didn't hide her skepticism.

Brody pointed to the north. "Bundles are there."

Liz spoke in her usual deadpan way. "Convenient they dropped them all in the same spot right next to where you jumped them. All four. All by yourself."

Brody nodded. "Some days you get lucky."

20

The sun hit its final countdown before slipping behind the western range as I climbed into the Pilot and headed home. Deon and I had passed a few texts back and forth and decided he'd swing by Mi Casa to grab Josie and I'd pop over to Nikki's house to pick up Sami. We'd meet up at El Guero Canelo for Sonoran hotdogs.

With two baskets of chips, a few dishes of various salsas, and a giant bowl of guacamole, we crowded into a booth with plastic benches and chowed down while waiting for our Sonoran dogs. Josie and Deon sat across from Sami and me.

"How is Ann?" I opened the conversation by addressing Josie.

She swallowed and sipped her soda. "Better. According to Donia, she slept most of the day."

Deon wiped his mouth. "Who's Donia?"

Sami ate with gusto, seeming not to pay attention to our conversation.

"One of the residents." Her eyes flicked to me and away quickly. I took that to mean Donia wasn't there legally. "She kept an eye on Ann today. Made her some awesome chicken soup and got Ann to eat a whole bowl and a half." She popped a guac-laden chip into her mouth.

The dogs came and we dug in. Chicago had its deep-dish, Texas had its barbecue, but Tucson had this bacon-wrapped, beans, cheese, chili, chipotle, and desert-magic-doused two-fisted feast. It was enough to keep me living here the rest of my life.

I wanted to grab onto this moment. The four of us in this tight circle, sharing a happy interlude together. No fighting, simply enjoying the food and company. When I teared up, I felt sappy and trite, like every parent and grandparent in the world. The clichés tripped through my head: it goes by so fast—just yesterday they were...

While Sami talked about the plans for Nikki's sleepover, Deon caught my eye and gave me a questioning look. I smiled at him to let him know I was okay.

Josie wadded up her hotdog wrapper and dropped it on the plastic tray. "I need to stop at home and pack some stuff before I go back to Ann's."

Deon whipped his head to her. "You're spending the night with her again? I thought you said she's better."

Josie sucked the last of her soda. "She is better. But she shouldn't be alone tonight."

I swallowed the last bite of my dog, wishing I had another but knowing I couldn't possibly finish it. "You're right. I'll go."

Josie frowned. "I need to."

That made me pause. "Need?"

Deon swiped at the tail end of the guacamole with a chip. Sami poked her finger into the dish and wiped the sides. "Hey!" The two of them laughed and scuffled with the bowl.

Josie said, "I told Serena I'd help her fill the packs for tomorrow's resupply."

Before thinking of diplomacy, I blurted, "Oh, no. I don't want you anywhere near Serena."

Her eyes spit fire. "Why not?"

"Why not? She had you up on a stage as a prime target for any lunatic. And believe me, crazy people are out there."

"I told you. I asked to do that. Serena didn't push me."

Deon and Sami stopped their teasing to watch us.

I'd gone from being in love with my family to hopping mad in a matter of seconds. "I know you think you're mature and can make your own decisions, but you're only fourteen."

Josie leaned into the table. "You're the one who brought up Greta Thunberg. You're such a hypocrite. Age didn't stop you from being a Border Patrol agent even though you're old, so why are you trying to make it an issue for me?"

Deon tried to inject humor. "Who are you calling old? Your mother is younger than I am."

Neither of us was having that, and we kept our focus on each other. "I'm proud of you for taking a stand. But I want you to stay away from Serena."

"Mom." The way she said the word infused it with all the arguments of the ages about the clueless, unfair way of parents.

Bless Deon's heart, he stepped in to help me. "Your mom's right, Bird. Helping your aunt at Mi Casa is a good thing. But getting involved with No Desert Deaths is too much for right now."

She spit out a "huh" and folded her arms, clearly not liking the verdict but accepting it from Deon.

So much for the warm emotional ride I'd been on. We cleared our table, pack backed into our vehicles, and headed home. Within seconds of hitting the kitchen door, the girls high-tailed it to their rooms, doors closing, music pounding through the floor of Josie's room.

Deon followed me upstairs where I threw overnight things and tomorrow's clean uniform into a bag. He pulled me into his arms. "You've got a day off coming soon, right?"

"Day after tomorrow." It couldn't come soon enough.

He kissed me slow and sweet. "Don't worry about Josie. She appreciated you letting her stay with Ann last night and allowing her to go back today. I promise, whatever skirmish you have going, it's not forever."

I kissed him back. "That's what we hope, but we don't know."

The drive to Ann's felt lonely. She wasn't going to take me staying with her well and I didn't feel up for the fight. All my life I'd put up with Ann's bristly ways because she was family. Part of me was staying with Ann now because I loved Josie enough to take care of someone she loved. Circles of family and love. Complicated and necessary.

I drove around to Ann's house but didn't see any lights on. Why would I? Ann wouldn't do the smart thing and stay home. Without Josie to monitor her, she'd go right back to work. Stubborn, as always.

I parked in her driveway and used my key to get in her house to make sure she wasn't sleeping instead of working at Mi Casa. I hadn't had much doubt and I proved myself right. Josie had made the bed and I gave her and myself a gold star. Maybe I wasn't the world's worst mother if I could teach her that much. I dropped my bag in the guest room and let myself out the back sliding door, then walked across Ann's yard and opened the gate.

The courtyard lights shone on a group of twenty people milling around. They looked like the same group I'd seen yesterday. Backpacks and bags sat in the gravel as if they were tourists waiting for the bus.

A couple in their thirties spotted me first. They looked alarmed to see me coming through the back gate. The man put his arm around the woman and they quickly moved to the side of the building in the shadow of a grapefruit tree. More people seemed to dissolve.

Serena was leaning over, her rear to me, stuffing clothing into a backpack. She must have sensed something because she stood upright and spun around to face me. "Where the hell...? What are you doing here?"

I stopped a couple of inches from her and thrust my face toward hers, giving me a psychological advantage since I had a couple of inches on her. "Stay away from Josie."

Serena stepped back and stuck out her chin in a belligerent move. "She's awesome. I don't know how she got so much compassion being raised by a Nazi like you. Guess it's Ann's influence."

"Yeah. Guess so." I poked my finger into her chest and it felt like a soft mattress. "You get anywhere near her and I'll turn you in for arson and vandalism and any other thing I can think of."

She smirked. "And I'll turn Ann in—"

I poked again. "You contact my kid and I don't care if you throw Ann into a bonfire."

She didn't seem at all rattled. "Josie's got her own mind. Forbidding her to do her work will only drive her to it."

I pulled back my hand and glowered at her. "Don't try me."

Before she answered, I strode to Mi Casa's back door and yanked it open.

Ann sat in her office, eyes closed, face pale. I made it to the doorway before she blinked and focused on me. "What are you doing here?" Always glad to see me.

"You look awful. You belong in bed." Back at her with the same lack of gentleness.

She inhaled as if to argue, then slumped. "I feel awful and was trying to get the energy to get there."

"I'm here to help. Gave Josie the night off and I'll stay." I bit my tongue before adding that tomorrow we'd have a discussion on a more permanent solution to Ann living alone.

I tipped my head toward the courtyard. "What's going on out there?"

"You don't want to know," she said, not making a move to rise.

I dropped into a chair facing her desk. "Serena is directing a circus on the patio. I want Josie and Sami to be able to come here and help you out, but I can't let them around that woman. She's dangerous."

Ann nodded. "You're right. When Lacy was alive, she kept Serena focused on moving immigrants from Tucson to safe places around the country. But Lacy's death..." Her voice caught and she paused to get control. "Serena is so angry. Derrick has been trying to calm her down, but he says she's escalating, drawing out the vigilantes and trying to get them to react."

Ann seemed so tired. She'd be surprised if I followed through on my urge to hug her and tell her she was a good person. We weren't that kind of sisters. "You've got to break with her before she destroys everything you've worked so hard for."

Ann rubbed her eyes. "I know. I told her. This is the last group. Most of them are leaving tonight and then I'm done."

"How did she take it?"

Ann smiled without humor. "How do you think?"

"You don't think she'll hurt you?"

Ann waved that away. "No. Derrick will keep an eye on her."

"I didn't see him out there."

Ann sighed with weariness. "He has class tonight so he'll be in later."

"Okay, tonight is the last night, then you're back to legal stuff. You promise?"

A hard gleam lit Ann's eyes. "For the most part."

"Ann." The word sounded similar to the way Josie had said Mom earlier.

She started to smile but a loud crash sounded outside the office door. Electricity slammed through me and without thinking I jumped up, spun around, and burst into the lobby.

Pellets of safety glass were scattered across the floor from the shattered front door. An object lay in the midst of the glass. Looked like a khaki bundle of some kind.

I sprinted across the lobby, my shoes slipping on the glass pellets. The glow of the street light shone through the ragged edges of the doorway. Cars roared past on the four lanes in front of Mi Casa.

Serena barreled through the back door, shouting at the people in the courtyard. "Go, go, go!"

"Get back. Take cover," I shouted at her.

A small Hyundai and Mi Casa's pickup were the only vehicles in the lot. Traffic kept its steady pace. The drivers didn't so much as glance our way. Whoever and whatever had exploded the front door hadn't been a big enough disturbance to gain attention. I raced out to the sidewalk, not expecting to see any fleeing suspects. No one, not even at the bus stop a half block away.

I ran back to the center. Ann stood in the doorway to her office leaning on her crutches, staring at the broken glass. I pointed at her. "Stay there," and ran across the lobby to the courtyard.

Serena came through the gate to Ann's house. After shutting it she advanced on me. "What was that?"

"Is anyone hurt? Where are they?"

She walked past me toward the lobby door. "I don't know who you're talking about."

I grabbed her arm and swung her around. "Don't play games with me. Someone attacked Mi Casa and we need to make sure everyone is safe."

She smirked. "They're safe."

I wanted to punch her.

"Mike," Ann called to me from the doorway. Of course she hadn't stayed where I told her to. Why would today be the first time she ever did what I said? "Leave her alone. Everyone is okay."

I left Serena and stomped toward Ann. "A bunch of people were here. Where did they go?"

Ann exhaled an exhausted breath. "I'm not going to tell you the details. Good people are helping them get to family and friends. This was their first stop but some of them will have a lot more. They aren't here, that's all you need to know."

"An underground railroad?"

Serena snorted. "Brilliant." She pushed past me into the lobby.

Three women and a handful of small children stood at the mouth of the hallway leading to dorm rooms in back. They stared at the shattered glass and turned frightened eyes on Ann when she came back in.

In slow Spanish, Ann told them the others were safe and on their way, and the broken door was nothing to worry about. We'd patch it up for tonight. She told them I was a cop and would be there all night.

Serena obviously didn't speak Spanish or she'd have been all over that exaggeration. Ann glanced at her. "Can you get them settled in their rooms?"

Serena drew in a breath to speak, whether to complain, ask questions, or rage, who knew, because Ann shut her down with, "They need reassurance. Come back when they're calm."

I stood by the front door searching the balls of safety glass across the floor. There. I shuffled to a small bit of something white and leaned over, but didn't touch it. "That's the culprit."

"What?" Ann asked.

I pointed. "A piece of ceramic, like the insulation of a spark plug. You throw that at safety glass and it can shatter. Then they tossed whatever that is inside." I pointed to the khaki bundle. "Then they took off."

Ann's crutches clanked behind me as she made her way toward the object in the center of the glass.

"Be careful," I said, as if she cared about my warning. "That might be a bomb." At the least, she could slip on the glass and fall.

When she kept shambling, I hurried to join her so if the crutches slipped on the glass I'd be there to catch her. She made slow progress, shuffling her crutches and feet to clear the path. I got close enough to take hold of one arm. She didn't shake me off.

One more step and she let out a peep of distress. "No. Oh, no."

I leaned over and tried to see what had upset Ann with the khaki bundle.

She let her crutches fall and clutched me. The object came into focus.

"It's Lacy's hat."

21

Ann sat on a chair at the long table in the lobby, propping her head on her arm. Her eyes were red and puffy, though she hadn't shed many tears. "Please, get that out of here before Serena sees it."

"We can't touch anything until the crime scene investigators process it."

She dropped her arm and glared at me. "You can't call the cops."

"We have to. Someone threw this through your door. It's a clue to Lacy's murder."

Ann rallied to argue. "Oh, please. Do you know how many Lacy hats are in Tucson? That's probably not even real blood on it."

"But they targeted Mi Casa. Someone is after you."

She waved her hand. "We get threats every day. Facebook, our website, mail. With Lacy's murder and everyone so upset, I'm not surprised that someone took it a step further. It's not as big a deal as you're making it out to be."

God, she was so damned exasperating. "You don't know that. Maybe whoever did this is on his way back. I'm calling the cops."

She leaned forward. "If the cops come they'll see Reyna, Donia, and Jimena. They've gone through so much to get here."

"Ann." I stared at her. "Those women with Serena? They aren't legal?"

"They're leaving in two days. Don't call the cops. They've got nowhere to go."

"We have to report this." I felt the anchor of my argument slipping.

"If they deport the women the government will keep their children here."

"No, they won't. You can't hide this."

"Donia's little boy, Juan, he's only five years old. They crossed when he was two and were detained. Donia was sent back to Nogales and Juan went into foster care. After two years she finally got him back but he didn't remember her. He was bonded to his new family who had toys and computers and a swimming pool. He didn't want to be with Donia. She's risked everything to come back here to try to give him the kind of life he'd never have back home in San Salvador."

"Ann..." I didn't have an argument.

"And Jimena. She crossed with her husband and the coyotes kept them for ransom. They couldn't pay any more and the cartel forced her into prostitution. She was caught and deported and her husband is still being held by coyotes in a house in Phoenix somewhere. She needs to get a job and earn enough money to get him out. If she gets sent back, the cartel will kill her husband."

She stared at me. I knew if I said anything she'd tell me Reyna's story and it would be as hopeless as the others. I couldn't turn them in. And I couldn't expose Ann to government charges and maybe jail.

"Okay. Do you have latex gloves in the kitchen?"

She exhaled. "Yes. In the drawer by the sink."

I returned with the gloves and crossed to the hat. How many laws was I breaking to protect Ann and help keep undocumented people from being found? Add this to not turning in Serena and Derrick for arson. Who was I?

I pulled on the gloves and lifted Lacy's iconic hat from the glass. In every poster of Lacy, she wore the Tilley hat. Now, it was smeared with what looked like dried blood. The splotches of deep brown on khaki looked much like the ground under her murdered body. I stuffed it into a paper bag I'd found in the kitchen. Chain of command screwed. But hopefully I hadn't contaminated it and we'd still find fingerprints.

Could I match this to the hat in Ford's house? Or was this, as Ann said, any one of a million Tilley hats floating around Tucson.

Ann had moved back to her office and sat with her chair pushed back from the desk, her head against the wall.

I handed her the bag with Lacy's hat and she slowly leaned forward, opened a lower drawer of her desk, and dropped the bag inside.

"Let me take you back to your house." I stopped before I told her she looked more dead than Lacy.

Ann closed her eyes and leaned her head back. Her voice sounded weak. "If it's the same person who killed Lacy, and it might be the case, they're giving us warning. They have to know we aren't going to stop."

That troubled me, too. "It seems almost arrogant. Like they're taunting you."

She opened her eyes. "Who do you think it is?"

"Ann?" Derrick's voice rang out in the front lobby.

"Here," Ann said.

Footsteps crunched on the glass and Derrick rushed into the office. "What happened? Are you okay? Did something go wrong with the transport?"

Serena appeared behind Derrick. "Thank god you're here." She threw her arms around him.

Saying I was surprised at the show of affection was like saying dogs like bones. I glanced at Ann to see her reaction. She seemed to take it in stride.

When she stepped back, Serena's assertive voice took hold. "We got the group off as planned. But some asshole shattered the front door. It's got to be Recon to Reclaim the Desert. They're probably mad after we visited their camp. The big babies."

"I think it might be a little more than that." Ann opened the bottom drawer of her desk, drew out the paper bag, and set it on the table. Serena lunged forward and grabbed the bag.

"Stop!" I shouted loudly enough to make Serena freeze. I picked up two food service gloves from the pile I'd dropped on Ann's desk. "Put these on."

Serena snatched them, settled the bag on the desk, and snapped them on. She opened the bag and reached in, letting out a cry when she pulled out the hat. "Oh my god. Lacy."

Derrick stared at the hat, his Adam's apple bobbing. His eyes teared up. "Damn it." He spun and stormed from the room.

Serena looked surprised. "Derrick?"

He shot back into Ann's office. "He did this. He killed Lacy and now he's bragging about it."

"He?" Ann said.

"That fucking blue-eyed asshole," Serena growled.

"You think Ford Dewlinski did this?" Did I?

Serena bristled. "Of course he did."

Ann's forehead creased and her lips tightened. She wasn't buying into that and I wondered why.

I addressed Serena. "What makes you think it's Ford?"

She spit words at me. "It's so obviously Ford. Only the damned cops won't listen. I've been in their office every day and no one will even talk to me."

I could understand that. If Serena pushed her way into the cop shop and treated them with the same lack of respect she tossed at me, it's no wonder she didn't get any traction with them. "Tell me why you think Ford killed Lacy and why he'd throw her hat into Mi Casa."

Serena planted her palms on her wide hips and aimed her words like weapons. "Why do you want to know? You don't give a shit about what's happening on the desert. You don't care who lives or dies or what kind of suffering goes on out there. You'd just as soon throw poor migrants into the jaws of hell than see the real need out there. You—"

Derrick laid a hand on her shoulder and she took a breath. To me, he said, "Lacy and Ford knew each other."

I looked at Ann for confirmation and she nodded.

Derrick went on. "She'd been trying to get him to understand what the migrants were going through. She kept going out there to his camps and his house. We told her that she was wasting her time but she kept going."

"Why didn't you tell the cops this?" I asked.

Serena thrust her chin forward. "Are you not listening? They don't care. At first, we didn't want the cops anywhere near No Desert Deaths or Mi Casa. Fine if they want to call this a cartel thing."

Derrick cut in. "We figured we'd find another way to deal with Ford."

Ann's face showed the alarm I felt. "What do you mean?" I asked.

Serena's harsh voice slashed at me. "Not shoot him down like he did to Lacy, if that's what you mean."

"Then what?" I prompted.

She shrugged. "He's bound to mess up out there. Maybe tangle with the wrong people, like they say Lacy did. But we've been following him. He rounds up undocumented people and holds them at gunpoint. I mean, the asshole actually killed a guy a couple of years ago." She pointed at me. "You guys say you will arrest civilians detaining anyone, but the truth is, you let Ford do your work and you take credit. You don't care how many people Ford might kill before he turns the prisoners over to you."

I wanted to argue with her, but people like Brody existed. I couldn't defend that.

Ann didn't say anything, but I could tell she didn't like what Serena said.

"Ford thinks he's all-powerful," Derrick said. "Like he sets the rules and it's his desert. But we're going to show him he's no better than the rest of us. He's not as smart as he thinks he is."

It was the first time I'd seen true passion from Derrick. Until now he seemed to only want to do Serena's bidding. I can't say I liked this side of him. Milquetoast fit him better.

"He killed Lacy, no question," Serena said.

"Then let's go to the cops," I said.

"No!" All three of them spoke at once.

I was outnumbered for sure. "You're willing to let Lacy's killer go free?"

Derrick got more worked up. "That Ford. Thinks laws don't apply to him. So self-righteous."

Yeah, nothing like your girlfriend, Serena.

Ann stared at Lacy's hat. "I don't know."

Derrick's expression hardened. "Don't know about what?"

She made eye contact with Serena. "This doesn't seem like Ford's M.O."

Serena's mouth dropped open.

Ann looked thoughtful. "He tends to go at things headfirst, not send a threat attached to a brick."

Derrick fired up. "I can't believe you. This is exactly what he would do."

Serena faced Derrick. "How would you know? You've only been working with us for a couple of months. We've been dealing with Ford for years. He's dumped our water and shot up our beans, but he's never tried to deny it."

Ann added, "In the last several months he hasn't been destroying our caches."

"Someone has," Derrick said. "Seems like a day or so after we leave them, they're ruined."

"Yeah," Serena said. "It's like someone's been stalking us or listening at our planning meetings."

"It's got to be Ford doing all this." Derrick sounded certain.

Ann clucked. "Lacy told me she thought Ford was backing off of the immigrants and concentrating on smugglers."

Marcy, Dell, and Tim thought Ford had gone soft. "Or maybe it's this John person some of the vigilantes talked about."

Serena gave me an irritated look. "I've never heard about a John."

Different tack. "How do you know Lacy was in contact with Ford lately?" I asked Serena.

"Look, I spent a lot of time with her. We worked together and we roomed together. I heard her talking to him on the phone."

Something about the way her eyes shifted told me she wasn't telling the truth. Serena might be brazen and crass, ready to fight before negotiating, but she didn't seem like a seasoned liar. "She spoke to Ford when you could hear? What was her tone like? Did she seem angry or pleading? Did it sound like they were friends? Or did she sound like she wanted to hurt him?"

Serena considered me for a long moment. "Okay, I didn't really hear her. I saw her texts to him."

"So, you read her texts when she wasn't there?" I wanted to make sure I had it right.

Clearly Serena didn't want to own up to that but I admired her for doing so. "She was acting weird and I was worried. She'd been going out on her own and I didn't like that. I'd asked her to stop but she wouldn't."

Derrick shuffled slightly to put himself closer to me. "I can vouch for how worried Serena was. And rightly so. I mean, we all know you shouldn't be out on the desert alone. Especially at night. Serena showed me Lacy's texts and she definitely had contact with Ford."

Ann asked, "Did the cops recover Lacy's phone?"

I shook my head. "It ended up swimming in a water jug." I turned to Serena. "Did you tell the cops about the texts?"

Serena gazed at the ground. "No. I was afraid if I told them I'd seen the texts they'd want to know why I didn't go with Lacy that night and then I'd have to tell them where I really was."

"And where was that?"

She and Derrick shared a look that held an entire conversation.

I waited, and when she didn't answer I finished for her. "Trashing a vigilante camp?"

Her silence was confirmation enough.

"Okay," I said. "It's late. Can you guys help me get the front door boarded up and clean up the glass?"

Ann said, "There's plywood in the shed."

"I'm taking you to your house." I handed Ann her crutches.

She shook her head. "I told the women we'd be here all night. We can take the room closest to the front, there's two single beds in there."

Of course, that's what we did. Though, for all the rest I got, I could have sat up in the lobby all night.

22

Seeming well rested, Ann sat at the long table in Mi Casa's kitchen while we finished a breakfast of coffee, toast, and scrambled eggs that I'd cooked. "How is everyone at home?" she asked.

I picked up our empty plates and stacked them in the sink. "Deon said Josie is mad I won't let her come back here after school."

"It's perfectly safe—"

I held up my hand to stop her. "Not going to argue with you again. When Reyna, Jimena, and Donia are gone and I can verify everyone else here is legal, we'll talk about the girls maybe being allowed back in the daytime."

She frowned. "They're being transported out today. Leave the dishes. I'm sure the women are waiting for you to go to work so they can fix their breakfast. They can clean up."

Since I was running out of time again, I left the dishes in the sink. I couldn't resist the urge to put my hands on her shoulders, as close to a hug as we usually came. "Sure you're okay to be here today?"

She shrugged from under my hands. "Derrick is coming in around nine. The women keep pretty close tabs on me. We're fine."

I'd have liked to gather everyone up and keep them all safe, but who and what was I protecting them from? "Okay. I'll check in on you after my shift."

She waved me away. "Go."

Muster didn't hold any revelations and we all dispersed to our assignments in short order. I headed to Tres Bellotas, my head a mass of worry. Being on my own without having to listen to Brody's country music or anyone's rambling confessions would normally be nice. Patrolling in the beauty of the Sonoran Desert, with the sun bright in a sky so blue it could make you weep and a soft breeze feeling perfect on my skin, should be heaven. But my stomach churned.

Saturday morning at our house meant cinnamon toast and hot chocolate, maybe a video game with Sami. We'd run errands, do some chores, I'd drive Josie to a friend's house. Everything would feel free without the schedules of school and activities. But here I was, wandering the desert and worrying about things at Mi Casa. Wondering if Nikki would be Sami's friend today or would she go for the jugular. Hoping Josie and I could reach an understanding soon.

The voice on my radio popped me out of my dread. "Agents respond. 10-15 by 65 soft count, south of Margarita Wells. Looks like quitters."

This was the last thing I, or any agent, wanted to hear. These calls always meant a group of people trying to escape poverty or violence in their country and hoping they'd be welcomed here. They'd heard rumors that if they traveled with children they'd be allowed to stay. Their expectations were so much higher than the reality they would face. Criminals often hid in the midst of families, women and children.

I keyed my mic. "Tango 721. I'll 13 that way."

Maybe some large groups of crossers made arrangements themselves, but more likely someone was helping them. That someone knew a crowd of hundreds of immigrants would draw all the agents in the area to process and care for them. That left the rest of the border open.

It took me twenty-five minutes to get to the site. By then, several agents stood guard over about sixty-five immigrants seated in a clearing by the side of a quiet highway. The group of people seemed resigned and peaceful, waiting for transport to take them to the station.

I joined Luke, who stood in line behind another agent at the back of a

BP van. He lifted a case of water in plastic bottles. "Looks like we'll be here for a while. As soon as we get them water we need to start with the field forms."

I hefted a flat of water and we walked several feet down the group of immigrants. Brody came up behind us with his own case of water. "Isn't this grand? We're here babysitting these losers and somewhere down the border the cartels are walking through shipments of heroin and Fentanyl."

He was probably right.

Luke handed out water bottles to people who appeared grateful. Even if it wasn't the horrible heat of summer, the sun and dirt made for a big thirst.

Liz came by with a stack of field forms. "Transport is sending some dog catchers but a few of you will still need to take some to the station."

Luke sighed. "I can."

Brody spoke up. "They aren't gonna stink up my rig."

I followed Liz to the group and handed out water.

One young woman rocked a fussy baby while a toddler hung on her back and whimpered. She spoke to the little boy but whatever she said didn't make him feel better. He sat down next to her, opened his mouth, and howled. Fat tears squeezed out his eyes and made dusty streaks down his round cheeks. The baby she held let loose in solidarity and started to sob.

I set a bottle of water next to the woman, not knowing what else to do. When one of my babies or toddlers was this upset, I'd been able to walk with them in my clean, air-conditioned home. On a hot day, I could ease us into the pool and that usually quieted them down. Maybe they needed something to drink or eat, or just a safe, soft place to lay down and sleep. This mother, and so many others in this group alone, had none of those luxuries. I had nothing to offer.

The sound of a squeak behind me made me turn. I could have dropped dead with surprise to see Brody holding a teddy bear in his palm. The tiny pink toy was fist-size, and when Brody clenched his hand it let out a cute squeak. He squeezed it again and the little boy stopped howling and stared. The baby kept up her cries, though. Brody squatted in front of the toddler and pinched the little teddy with two fingers. He held it to the little boy's cheek and made it squeak while pursing his lips in a kiss.

The toddler's trembling mouth turned into a smile. To the sound of the baby crying, Brody made the teddy kiss the little boy's other cheek, producing a giggle. He took the boy's hand and placed the toy into his pudgy fingers. Then, to my even greater astonishment, he held out his arms to the woman and offered to take the crying baby.

She drew back but Brody gave her a gentle smile. She cast questioning eyes to me, but I couldn't give her much help. I wouldn't trust Brody with a ten-year-old strip of jerky. But this wasn't the Brody I knew.

Exhaustion settled onto her face, the sun-burnished skin gray with dust and smeared with dried sweat. I didn't see anyone with her, a sister or friend, to help with the children, a husband to support her. She seemed completely alone, in a country with strange customs, herded into a group and seated on the ground, not knowing the language. I'd never experienced her level of misery. Not many of us had.

There wasn't much fight left in her. With her little boy now happily squeaking and kissing his teddy, she allowed Brody to slip his hands under her squalling infant and lift the baby from her arms.

It took effort to keep my jaw from dropping, and one glance at Luke told me he was fighting the same battle.

Brody seemed oblivious to us. He stepped back from the immigrants seated at his feet and gently jiggled the baby. He lifted the baby swaddled in a dirty blanket to his face and cooed at her, maybe even singing. Gradually, the baby quieted.

Brody settled the baby into the crook of his arm and took in Luke and me watching. "What? I can't stand to hear kids cry. Gives me a headache. Don't you have forms to fill out?"

Still keeping the baby in his arm, he bent over and pulled out a bottle of water with his free hand before dropping it into the lap of a middle-aged woman. She didn't make eye contact but took the bottle and twisted the lid.

Luke turned his attention to a young man. In Spanish he asked the man's name and date of birth, writing the answers on the field form. He paused to give Brody another once-over, as if confirming the unbelievable event he'd witnessed.

Liz came along beside me and pulled out another form. "He's not all bad." She squatted to ask a woman her name and birthdate.

Nope. Not all bad. But pretty near.

We spent the next three hours getting all the immigrants numbered and field forms filled out. The transport vehicles arrived to take them to the Tucson station for processing. Most of those seeking asylum would be turned out over the border in Mexico to await their trials. That would be a shock since they'd been told by coyotes or others who'd crossed before them that they would be released in the United States. Those were the good old days. Others would sign a form admitting they'd broken the law by crossing and agreeing to leave. They'd also be dumped out in the Mexican side of Nogales.

Brody held the baby the whole time. When the infant started to fuss in his arms, Brody shifted her to his shoulder. The next time I looked, the baby was sound asleep, her little pink lips puckered and a fine film of sweat curling her soft dark hair.

The woman kept her eyes on Brody while she spoke softly to the little boy, who had moved to her lap. Only when she was ready to climb into the cab of one of the agent's pickups did Brody relinquish the child. He laid her gently in a car seat and strapped her in, placing his palm over her head before turning and striding away.

"Who knew you were such a softy?" Luke said as we stood back and watched the pickup pull away.

Brody scowled at him. "It's not the kids' fault their parents are idiots to bring them here. That alone should prove to anyone how unfit they are as parents and should have their kids taken away for endangerment."

He yelled at a group of young men climbing into the back of a dog catcher. "No. Can't you count? Eight seatbelts. You can't put nine of you in there." He grabbed the last guy in line and jerked him back, shoving him toward another dog catcher. "Over there. Get in, buckle up. We've got better things to do than rustle your sorry asses."

Luke and I hurried to the back of the truck and got everyone settled without any more temper tantrums.

Brody stood by his pickup, arms crossed and prune face puckered.

I walked to him. "Can I ask you something?"

He gave me a nasty side-eye. "No."

"Okay. I heard that Lacy Hollander turned in Recon to Reclaim the Desert for having IEDs."

He snickered. "Where'd you hear that?"

"Were you there when they raided Ford's house?"

He stopped and faced me. "Lacy Hollander was a troublemaker. Is that what you wanted to hear me say? She poked her nose where it shouldn't have been and it got her killed."

"Maybe she knew Ford had weapons he shouldn't have. Maybe she knew he got them illegally. What if she wasn't killed by smugglers but by someone who didn't like her messing in his business?"

Brody laughed. "Gonna have to change your name from Grandma to Nancy Drew. Really, Sanchez, you've got no idea what you're talking about."

"But you know Ford pretty well. Do you think he's dangerous?"

He rolled his eyes. "Only if you're a drug smuggler, trafficker, or terrorist. And I'm not sure Lacy Hollander didn't fit some of those categories."

Now I scoffed. "Right."

He pointed at me. "No. Really. Who do you think slashed tires of vigilantes or tried to burn Ford's house? She was after him. Yeah, she turned him in. But if Ford has any contraband, he's sure as hell not going to keep it at his house."

"Wait, someone tried to burn his house?" I thought of Serena and her disposable lighter.

Brody gave me a "duh" look. "Ford was sure it was those No Desert Deaths righteous pricks."

The last of the transports took off. Luke drove by and waved at me. I turned back to Brody. "So, Ford's got contraband? Where would he keep it?"

"You know what, Grandma? I tried to teach you the wise ways with Recon and you didn't want anything to do with it. I'm cool with that. But I'm not giving away Ford's secrets so you can use them against him. Go bleed that heart on someone else."

He threw himself into his pickup and let his tires give me a dirt shower. I jumped back and watched him drive away. I didn't care what Liz said, he was an asshole.

I had about five hours left of my shift so I climbed back into my own pickup. More and more I thought Ford might be Lacy's murderer. Maybe I'd go back to the site where we'd found Lacy. There might be something I missed.

My phone vibrated in my breast pocket, surprising me that we had a signal. I pulled it out and wondered at the ID, both happy and worried to see Josie's number. She wanted to talk to me, a very good thing. Or she needed to talk to me, maybe not so good.

I punched it on. "What's up, Bird?" I hadn't intended to use her old nickname, it slipped out.

"Mom." Her voice sounded watery, sending all the hairs on my body at attention. "We're at Ford Dewlinski's house. Hurry."

23

I gunned my truck, speeding through the afternoon and leaving a trail of dust behind me. With my free hand, I dialed Josie's cell. No connection. Had Ford caught her calling me? Had he punished her?

Those cold blue eyes held such rage and violence. My stomach cramped to think of them focused on my daughter. What would he do to her?

My brain spun and swirled. What was Josie doing anywhere near Ford? How had he gotten hold of her? Did she go to Mi Casa after I'd told her not to and he'd found her there? Was she out in the desert? None of it made sense. My little girl should be at home today or hanging out with her friends. Not in the hands of a violent man.

My back tires slid on the loose dirt as I rounded a corner and stepped harder on the gas pedal. At best it would take me another ten minutes to get to Sasabe. It seemed like an eternity where so many things could go wrong for Josie.

I keyed my radio. "Tango 721 calling for backup. Possible hostage situation in Sasabe at Ford Dewlinski's house."

Liz answered immediately. "Tango 321 responding. On my way. What's the situation?"

Situation? Josie was in danger, but I had no more details. "Don't know. I got a call from someone saying they were at Dewlinski's house."

A couple more officers responded. But with several agents transporting the group of quitters to the station, there weren't a lot of hands to spare.

Liz sounded skeptical. "Someone called? Who?"

Would it make agents more or less willing to respond if I told her? I guessed Ford had working relationships with more than Brody. "My daughter. She didn't say much and then her phone went dead."

Liz came back with, "Your daughter is at Ford's house? Why?"

I could almost hear other agents snickering. The situation was losing its urgency. "I don't know."

Liz's response came after a second. "Okay. I'll be there in ten minutes."

Sasabe slept as it always did. I sped through the center of town and slammed on my brakes down the road from Edna's cabin. Her dogs didn't set up any racket I could hear.

With my M4 in hand, I stepped out of my pickup and clicked the door closed. In a town this quiet, the door slam might carry. Not that the sound of me barreling into battle hadn't already registered.

It took only a few minutes to run along the road to Ford's driveway. I kept to the cover of dilapidated sheds and abandoned houses. The gravel crunched beneath my boots and the sun cast short shadows from the dusty structures. An old sycamore rustled in the slight breeze.

Nothing moved in Ford's yard except a lizard the size of my hand doing pushups on the top of a bench by the fire pit. Ford's ATV sat outside by the road so they must still be inside. Would he have them tied up?

Another vehicle roared from down the road. It sounded like it parked next to mine. I assumed it was Liz and she didn't hesitate to slam her door. Her boots were like explosions as she ran toward the house. I guess she didn't see the need for stealth.

I signaled to her from the cover of an outbuilding next to Ford's house. She veered off her direct route and ran toward me. Out of breath, she asked, "Are they inside?"

I watched the sparkling windows on Ford's front porch. "I assume so."

She assessed the house. "Is anyone else here besides your daughter?"

God, I wish I knew. "I don't know. She's not answering her phone."

"But you're sure she's here?"

Josie wouldn't lie to me about this. "I'm sure."

"Is Ford the only one holding them?"

"Probably."

"But you don't know."

No. I didn't know. His partner, John, might be with him. I could barely keep myself from storming up the porch, guns blazing.

Liz stared at the house, her eyes scanning from left to right. "It'll be a while before anyone else gets here. Our best bet is to keep watch and wait for backup. When they get here, we can surround the house and contact Ford."

That wasn't going to work. My daughter was inside that house with a crazy man. No way was I going to wait for backup. I gripped my M4 closer to my chest and sprang from behind the building. "Cover the back," I said over my shoulder as I ran full speed toward Ford's house.

I expected fire so I zigged and zagged. I heard nothing behind me so I assumed Liz stayed where she hid, with a view of the front and back. That seemed the best. My total focus zeroed in on the door. Maybe I was super-woman and could beat it down with a single kick, storm in and grab Josie. I'd shoot anyone standing in my way.

My feet hit the concrete step and someone shouted from my left. I hadn't heard Liz move from her hiding place.

"Stop now." The voice came at me, not loud, not strong, a warbling voice of an old woman.

As soon as my foot landed on my leap I swiveled around to see Edna standing at the edge of Ford's yard, her ceramic chihuahua cradled in her arms. She wore the same purple sweatpants and black hoodie, her wrinkled face drawn in a fierce frown.

I waved my arms at her. "Get away."

She advanced on me. "No. You get away."

I jumped down the steps and grabbed her scrawny arm, tugging her toward where Liz had come from behind the shed. "He's got hostages. Leave now."

Edna jerked her arm away from me with more force than I'd expected. "I thought you were a good one. But you can't be here. This is not right."

I heard the fear, anger, and desperation in my voice. "My daughter is in there."

Liz made it to us and took hold of Edna as I'd done. "Come with me." She pulled.

Edna dug in her feet and leaned back, clutching the ceramic dog to her chest, her face set.

The front door opened and Ford stepped out on the porch. "What is going on?"

Edna succeeded in yanking her arm free from Liz. "They're up to shenanigans."

I held up my gun, pointing it at Ford's center mass. "Where is my daughter?"

His eyebrows dropped over those icy eyes. "Put that gun away."

"Mom!" Josie dashed out the open doorway, running for me. Her dark hair flew behind her and her hiking boots pounded on the dirt of Ford's yard as she raced to me.

I didn't drop my gun but took one hand off to grab Josie and shove her behind me, then I aimed the gun at Ford.

Liz tried to contain Edna again and the old woman slapped at her, keeping Liz from getting a grip. Edna never let loose of her chihuahua.

With my gun focused on Ford and all my fury directed his way, I yelled, "You're under arrest."

He raised his arms and let them fall. "What for this time?"

Edna backed away from Liz like a boxer on the balls of her feet. Spry didn't seem to cover the spirit of that little old woman.

"Mom," Josie started. "He…"

Ford stepped out farther into the yard. He advanced on me. "I didn't kidnap anyone."

Serena stomped out the front door.

What? Serena had brought Josie to the desert. I didn't know if I'd rather shoot Ford or Serena first.

"You asshole," Serena said to Ford, pointing her finger. "You had no right to take us. Kidnapping is what it is. Arrest this piece of shit."

That was enough for me. Leaving Liz to deal with Edna, who ducked and dodged as if playing tag, I advanced on Ford. When I got close, I used one hand to pull the zip tie cuffs from my belt. "Turn around and put your hands behind your back."

"Mom," Josie said again.

Serena kept up her ranting at Ford, calling him vile names. "You're inhuman. You're a monster. I hope you have kids someday and someone rips them from your arms and throws them in a cold jail cell." Apparently, she didn't see the irony in her humanitarian heart.

Ford only registered annoyance as he might a persistent fly in his face. "This is the second time I've had to protect your daughter. What are you thinking letting her wander around out here? Don't you know Lacy was killed? Shot like a dog for doing exactly what your daughter was doing."

I burned with fear for Josie. "By you. Now turn around."

The anger in those eyes was almost physical. "You think I shot Lacy? You're the stupidest woman on the planet. Why would I kill her?"

"Because you hate the work they do."

Serena's tirade continued. "Life means nothing to you. Shoot him like he shot Lacy. See how he likes it."

He glared at me. "You don't know anything."

At that moment Edna let out a banshee howl and rushed at me. With all her five foot two, one hundred pounds she plowed into me, throwing me off balance.

That was all Ford needed. Without hesitating he sprinted away. I shoved Edna back and gained my balance, then glanced behind me to see Liz jumping up from the ground and fumbling with her gun.

I took off after Ford. He raced behind his house and I kept with him. He wore lightweight hikers and I had my heavy-duty boots, but they had good traction and I dug in. Sasabe was a town of shadows and abandoned buildings. Crumbling fences and piles of junk where people had moved out and never returned. This was Ford's town and he knew where to hide.

He ran through an alley and behind an old shed. Clutching my gun, I kept up; the only object in my vision was Ford and staying with him. That son of a bitch killed Lacy and put my daughter in danger. I wasn't going to let him go.

He rounded another corner into an enclosure probably used for a milk cow or hogs. Three sides were built of corrugated metal and the other a three-strand barbed wire fence that opened into an alleyway of dried grass and tumbleweeds with a thicket of brush and cactus on the other side of a wood planked fence.

Ford ran straight for the barbed wire fence. With the grace of a gazelle, he cleared that sucker. I had done some hurdles in high school and didn't hesitate. Using all my strength, I thrust myself like a rocket to carry me over the barbed wire. I nearly made it.

The toe of my boot caught and drew my back leg down. The barbs stuck into the fabric of my pants and tugged enough for me to lose balance. I crashed to the alley floor and rolled. Sand and grit collected in my teeth and scraped my chin, the burning sting making me wince. My gun slapped against my chest, the strap cut into my shoulder. I landed on my knees with a painful thud, then fell to my wrist, bending it back in a painful twist. Gravel and dirt grated my skin. With my good hand, I shoved myself up from the ground in time to see Ford's hands disappearing from the wooden fence where he'd propelled himself over.

The crashing and thrashing on the other side told me he was working his way through the brush, but the noise subsided before I limped to the fence. With my injured wrist, I couldn't scale the seven-foot barrier. I slammed my good palm into the fence and it held firm. Probably the only structure in the whole town, aside from Ford's house, that had any strength.

By the time I trudged back to Ford's house, Edna, Josie, and Serena were sitting on the bench by the fire pit.

Liz paced the yard. "You didn't get him?"

Obviously. "He's out there. Maybe call air backup. But he knows this country better than anyone. My guess is he's gone."

I stopped in front of Josie and assessed her. "Are you okay?"

She nodded, her face set, maybe in defense of whatever I was about to say.

I slapped the bench next to her. "Where is your head? The desert is no place for you."

She bit back, "But it's fine for you. You can run around here doing what you believe in but I'm supposed to go to school and play my sports and forget people are dying out here."

"That's right. People are dying. Like Lacy Hollander. When you're old enough to understand the consequences, you can make your own decisions on what it's worth to you."

Liz glanced from Josie to me, then changed the subject. "Just as well Ford took off," she said. "I don't know that we've got anything on him."

That got my attention. "What do you mean? He kidnapped my daughter."

Josie looked up at me. "He didn't, really."

Liz affirmed with a slight nod. "According to them, they were setting out water and someone slashed their tires."

"Ford?" I asked.

Serena, her face stern, said, "Of course."

Josie shook her head. "I don't think so."

"Why is that?" I asked.

"Because he showed up and got all mad. He was yelling that we shouldn't be out there because someone was killing people like us and he ordered us to leave."

"Asshole," Serena said.

Josie ignored her. "He was scary but not like he wanted to hurt us. Like mad he had to protect us. He kind of, like, made us climb on his ATV, but he didn't, like, drag us there."

"Forced march," Serena said.

"Did he pull a weapon?" Liz asked.

Serena folded her arms over her chest. "He might as well have."

Liz turned to Josie, who shook her head. "But he was like this big ball of energy. Scary energy like a bomb that could go off."

"He needs to be locked up," Serena said.

I wanted to tell her to shut up and thought maybe Liz was close to doing that.

"But he acted like he was really surprised at the flat tires. Like maybe even upset or whatever." Josie looked at Serena for confirmation.

Serena rolled her eyes. "That's when he made us get on his ATV."

As if someone couldn't bail on an ATV if they weren't tied on.

Josie took up the story. "He said we weren't safe and he was going to take us to his house. When we got here he made me call you."

"Why didn't you answer when I called you back?"

Her cheeks reddened. "I had to pee and forgot the phone was in my back pocket. I dropped it in the water."

Such a teenage thing to do. Something so innocent and thoughtless. She shouldn't be out here dealing with death and loss. She should be home hanging out with her friends worrying about what to wear to school.

Liz gave me an unamused smile. "See. Nothing here."

I sighed. "Okay, I'll drive them back to Tucson. I'll leave it up to Serena how she wants to get back to repair the tire."

"Mom," Josie started.

I held up my hand. "Not now. I need to talk to your dad before you and I get into this. But you can be sure your time volunteering for No Desert Deaths is over."

"Mom. Nothing happened. Everything is okay."

She didn't seem to get it. If I started talking to her now, I knew I'd lose it and the ranting and hollering could possibly end up in me chaining her to her bed. More or less. My blood pressure needed to come back down before I could do anything more than haul her home.

"Come on." I lifted my arm to Josie and Serena. "Let's go."

Serena let out an irritated exhale. "So you're just going to let him go? He's a criminal." She stood up and put her hands on her hips, as if protesting.

Liz shook her head and turned to her pickup.

Serena wasn't done. "And you"—she pointed at me—"need to respect this young woman. She's got a good mind and can make her own choices."

I stared her down. "Shut up."

Of course, she didn't. "It's so stupid to take me all the way back to Tucson to get repairs. Don't you and the other death patrol agent have spare tires? Aren't you here to protect citizens? You should—"

I took a step toward her, ready to escort her to the pickup. "Look," I started. But that was all I said before a shot cracked the air.

24

The first thing I noticed was Josie squirming underneath me, followed closely by Serena screaming, "I'm hit!"

As the initial recognition of gunfire hit me, I'd tackled Josie and scooted her closer to the front porch. Now I jumped up and shoved her at the front door. "Get inside."

Liz was already at Serena's side, looping Serena's arm around her neck and half dragging her toward me. Blood soaked Serena's hiking pants below her knee. I ran to get the other arm.

Dust puffed from the yard as the schwing of air sounded a split second before the crack of a rifle. The shot ricocheted from the ground and pinged off a metal chair.

It didn't seem possible but Serena's screaming ratcheted up more. Josie stood in the doorway waving her arm. "Hurry!"

Liz and I leaned into the job and in no time lurched up the steps and burst into the house with Serena dangling from our arms. We settled her on the floor.

She cried and grabbed at her calf, swearing and screaming in a whirlwind of noise. "He shot me. The motherfucker shot me. This is exactly what happened to Lacy. I don't want to die."

Edna stood in the middle of the living room with her ceramic dog. How had she made it inside so quickly? She looked annoyed.

Liz crouched to the side of the doorway with her M4 pointed out. She spoke into her shoulder mic about shots fired and our location.

I leaned over Serena's leg and stuck my thumb into the hole in her pants. I yanked on the thin fabric to tear it and studied the wound. Blood flowed out, but the bullet had entered the fleshy part of her calf and exited.

I spoke with the same tone I used when Sami fell off her bike and scraped her knee. "You're not going to die." Though I'd never been shot, I could only imagine how bad it must hurt. But I really wanted her to take it down a notch.

Edna stepped closer and looked over my shoulder. "That's gotta sting."

"Josie, go to the kitchen and get a towel. Try to get a clean one."

Serena's face was blotchy red and white, covered in tears and snot. She rocked back and forth, her hands clutching below her knee.

"I'm sure it hurts like hell but I don't think there's a lot of damage." I tried to sound nicer than I felt.

"Damage?" she screamed. "He shot my leg. My leg!"

"I know."

Edna clucked. "If he was trying to kill you, he failed."

Josie returned with a couple of towels and bowl of hot water. "Perfect." I dipped a rag into the water and wiped away the bulk of the blood. Josie took the other towel and pressed it to Serena's wound as she wailed.

Edna addressed Josie. "She always so loud?"

Josie kept pressing the wound but I swear she fought a smile.

A Tahoe rounded the corner, roaring to a stop out front. The green and white Border Patrol logo on its side made me relax. Liz spoke into the mic. "The shooter was on the hill behind the house. I think he's probably gone now. Be careful."

Through the front door I saw Brody slide out and point his gun to the north. He inched around the front of the pickup and waited. When nothing happened, he stood up and sauntered toward the front door.

Liz muttered under her breath, "Idiot."

Brody must have heard her. "Hey, I've known Ford for a long time. He's not going to shoot me." He kept heading toward the house.

"Ford is not out there," Edna said with conviction.

Serena yelled at Edna, "He shot me! He's a whacko."

Edna drew her head in as if offended. "I'm old, not hard of hearing."

Serena didn't lower her volume. "But you must be senile because you saw him shoot me."

Edna stroked her ceramic chihuahua. "Wasn't Ford."

"Shut up," Serena spat at Edna. "Just shut up."

Liz stepped onto the porch and surveyed the hill behind the house.

"Okay," I said to Serena in a calm, authoritative voice. "We're going to load you up and take you to the hospital."

Brody stomped up the porch steps and into the room. "What happened?"

Liz gave him a rundown, ending with Ford escaping and shooting at us.

Edna moved past Brody on her way out of the house. "Ford didn't shoot anyone."

Brody put an arm out to stop her. "What are you doing here? I told you if I saw you again I'd deport you."

Edna glared at him, muttered something threatening in an indigenous language, and said, "I'm Ford's friend. I belong here."

Liz gave Brody an irritated look and asked Edna, "How do you know Ford didn't do this?"

Edna's look was one of supreme irritation. "He didn't. That's how I know." She stared down the road and cocked her head. "I've got to calm the dogs down. All her yelling is stirring them up."

Serena whimpered and swiped at her wet face. Josie and I helped her to her feet.

"Damn, it hurts," she yelled. "That asshole is going to pay. I swear it." She leaned heavily on us, her weight more than me and Josie combined.

"It wasn't Ford," Brody said.

Serena glared at him. "You and that bat-shit old lady. You weren't here. You didn't see his crazy eyes. He kidnapped us and he was going to kill us."

Josie and I shared an exasperated glance. Serena put some weight on her leg and shrieked.

Ignoring that, I said to Brody, "You know where Ford might go to hide. We should send some agents to bring him in."

Liz stepped closer, focusing on Brody. "Ford's got a hideout? Would he store weapons there?"

Brody pulled back and laughed. "He doesn't have a hideout like Butch Cassidy's Hole-in-the-Wall Gang."

"You said he did," I countered.

He laughed again. "It's a joke, Grandma. I never thought you'd take it seriously."

Liz turned away and Brody smirked at me.

Brody watched us struggle with Serena as we made our way toward the porch. "Ford has a mission. He's a professional. He's here to protect the border, so he doesn't have time to kidnap interfering do-gooders like you. Whatever you think, it wasn't Ford."

Serena managed to shout at him between sobs. "He killed Lacy. And he planned to kill us."

Josie sounded as if she'd had enough. "He wasn't going to hurt us. He was trying to help us."

Serena twisted her head to shout directly at Josie. "You're so naïve. How can you say you don't think he meant us harm? He herded us to his four-wheeler with intimidation and brought us somewhere we didn't want to go. That's kidnapping. And then he shot me. You get shot and see how it suddenly makes everything clear. I might have wondered about Ford killing Lacy before, but now I know he did. He tried to murder me, too."

Liz was keeping watch out the front door. "I think he's gone."

We struggled to get Serena out the door. Brody grunted behind us and a loud thumping made me turn around.

Edna stood in front of him, legs apart, slightly crouched. "You don't belong here. Get out of Ford's house."

Apparently, she'd shoved him and he'd stumbled into a wall. He pulled himself up. "You *are* nuts." He lowered his face to her level and sneered at her. "I'm the law around here. You don't tell me where I do and don't belong."

"You aren't my law." She lunged at him.

She hit with such force Brody took several steps back and nearly fell. She backed up and started another rush, but Brody held out his hand and placed it on her forehead, stopping her before she could attack again.

"Take her," I said to Josie, and slipped out from under Serena's arm.

Brody raised his fist and pulled back his arm, looking for all the world as if he was ready to punch an old woman in the face.

Before he could let loose, I lunged toward him and grabbed his arm. Though his punch didn't connect, holding onto his arm launched me a few feet, surprising me with its force. He spun toward me, ready to go at it.

I backed up and gave him a shaming look. "You weren't going to hit an unarmed citizen, were you? A woman old enough to be your grandmother?"

"Fucking Death Patrol," Serena screamed.

His face red with rage or embarrassment, he barked at me, "She attacked me. You saw her."

Edna narrowed her eyes at Brody and muttered her dark curses while stroking the ceramic chihuahua.

I looked around for corroboration, but Liz was somewhere in the yard with her back turned and Josie had taken Serena to the bench out front. "What I saw"—the sound of reproach was deep in my tone—"was an agent harassing an elderly citizen."

Edna stopped her rumbling and eyed me.

"You're taking the side of a crazy woman," he said.

I started back toward Josie and Serena. "We need to take care of this injured citizen."

"You old crone," Brody said.

The threat in his voice sucked me back and I reeled around to see him advancing on Edna in Ford's living room.

She held her ground and growled at him like a fierce little dog.

"Brody!" I yelled.

His hand shot out and he grabbed Edna's arm, the one clutching the chihuahua. He yanked, sending the ceramic pup tumbling to the ground.

Edna screamed and lunged for the dog, but Brody dropped quicker, grabbed it by its head, and flung it to the front porch. It hit a metal support and exploded into a dozen pieces.

All color faded from Edna's face, leaving her ashen. She approached the broken bits and knelt on the ground.

I gave Brody a murderous look on my way to help Edna gather the pieces and place them in the hoodie she'd pulled up to form a basket.

Liz walked back to us and I swear I heard her say, "Asshole," as she passed Brody and helped Edna stand up.

Brody stood on the porch and glowered at us while Josie lowered Serena into a chair and came to help. Even Serena seemed to understand the weight of Edna's loss and lowered her noise to whimpers.

Edna trod with her head down toward her house.

I returned to Josie, and we helped Serena up and started toward the parked vehicles.

Brody gave us a skeptical look. "Where are you going with her?"

We made our way down the porch with Serena howling at each step. "We're going to load her into your Tahoe and take her to Tucson."

He hurried to block me. "Oh, no. She's not going to bleed all over my ride. Call an ambulance."

Serena's predictable temper rose. "I'm injured. I could bleed out and die waiting for an ambulance. I'm getting in that truck right there."

Liz came over and made moves to transfer Serena's arm from my shoulder to her own. She probably didn't want to mess up her ride, either. "Go get your pickup. You take these two to Tucson and Brody and I will try to find Ford."

Brody shook his head. "I'm telling you, Ford isn't the shooter."

Liz nodded. "Okay. Maybe not. But someone is out there shooting at civilians and we need to find him and stop him."

I left them to argue about it and jogged to get my vehicle. The radio came to life as I drove the few blocks back to Ford's. Liz put out a call for agents to help in the hunt for Ford. She requested air backup. Whether the Black Hawk would arrive to assist was up for grabs. It depended on if it was already working some other section and how likely it would be to catch our guy. The expense of flying had to be weighed with the seriousness of the situation.

Liz and Josie had Serena waiting at the road when I pulled up. Brody was in his Tahoe, the engine firing up.

I opened the passenger door of my truck, and amid Serena's squalling and crying, Josie and Liz managed to get her inside. Josie took off around the front of the truck to crawl in and sit in the middle.

"Where's he going?" I asked Liz.

She slammed the door and eyed Brody driving away, then spoke quietly so no one else could hear. "Someone named John called. Brody's on his way to intercept a bunch of crossers and claim he tracked them single-handedly."

"Are we going to let him get away with it?"

She shrugged and started toward her own pickup. "The job gets done. Doesn't matter who gets credit."

"So everyone is going to chase after those quitters while Ford gets away?"

She nodded. "Bird in the hand."

I got in my pickup. Josie had already arranged Serena so her leg was elevated. It took an hour to get to the hospital and Serena didn't let up the whole way. She cursed and sputtered, cried about the pain, and generally made everything worse than it already was.

Since Serena had lost her phone somewhere along the line and Josie's had taken a dive, I had the only lifeline. I called Deon to meet us at the hospital and take Josie home.

Trying to keep my temper under control, I dialed Ann and started with, "Everyone is okay."

She answered predictably, "What's wrong."

Serena shouted, "Okay? I'm shot. How is that okay?"

Ann sounded alarmed. "Shot? Serena is shot? What happened?"

I couldn't hold back. "Are you crazy letting Josie go out on the desert?"

Josie piped up. "Mom, I can make my own decisions. You—"

I gave her my most demanding Mom Stare and she stopped talking. I still had some authority.

Ann came back equally strong. "Josie was there? Oh my god. What's going on? Is Josie okay?"

"You didn't send her with Serena into the desert to drop off water and supplies?"

Ann sputtered, "Of course not. She's too young to do that. Tell me what you mean?"

I explained in shorthand, promising to fill her in later. When I hung up I turned on Serena. "You irresponsible stupid asshole. You brought my daughter into a war zone."

Josie and Serena both erupted with angry retorts and pleading. I gripped the wheel, tuning them out. Eventually, they stopped and we rode the rest of the way to the music of Serena's moans.

Deon met us at the emergency entrance. Since Serena's injury wasn't life-threatening, they made her wait. Deon wanted to take Josie home and I had to get back to work. Recon to Reclaim the Desert was striking too close to home and I wanted to put a stop to it. Even if Ford didn't shoot Lacy Hollander or take shots at us today, he was a boiling pot of rage that needed to be quieted. And if he and his partner, John, were working together, I figured it was high time I meet this guy face to face.

Brody had a call from John. If I hurried, I might be able to intercept Brody and John where they held the migrants. I could see what John was like and maybe get them to tell me where Ford's hideout was. If Brody and Edna were right and Ford didn't shoot at us, who did?

Josie tugged at my arm. "We can't leave Serena here alone. I need to stay with her."

"Have her call Derrick. He's supposed to be her boyfriend," I said.

Josie lowered her voice. "She tried to call him on your phone but he's not answering."

Deon watched this exchange. I read his expression and knew what was coming next. "We can stay, Bird."

Damn him. I wanted Josie far, far away from Serena, Ann, and No Desert Deaths. But I couldn't explain it all to Deon now and I didn't want to break our steadfast rule to present a united front...again. If Josie was with Deon, she'd be okay. With a kiss to both of them, one accepted and returned and the other brushed on a cheek and barely tolerated, I headed back to the desert.

25

Clouds dropped low and thick, making it seem much later than it was. I pulled up to where Brody had called in the group of quitters and counted six vehicles parked by the roadside, including two dog catchers that could transport eight each in the back. It must be a big group.

I followed the beaten brush and murmur of voices. Twenty people stood together, their shoelaces and belts removed. They were linked together and in line, ready to walk to the transports.

Luke stood with a couple of other agents while the migrants filed past me. Young women, some fighting tears or crying, a few children, more men from teenagers to graying, every one of them looking defeated, exhausted, and dirty. I'd only been an agent for a short time but I didn't think seeing people in such misery would ever get easier.

It hit me with force again. What was I doing out here? Was I protecting or torturing?

Luke nudged me. I hadn't noticed him approaching me. "Busy day, huh?"

I located Brody. "Yeah."

"I mean, I'm glad we're working. You know, those days hanging at the checkpoints really kill me. But, man, I've gone from one thing to another all day. A few of us are going for a beer after shift today. I feel like I need to debrief, you know? So, want to come along?"

I smiled up at him. He wasn't young enough to be my son but I hoped wherever his mother was, she was proud of him. Not for wanting to go for a beer, but for being so open, hard-working, willing, and a really good guy. "It sounds great, but..."

He nodded. "You've got a family to get home to. I knew it but I wanted to ask." He followed my line of sight. "You should have seen Brody earlier."

I snapped my attention back to Luke. "Why?"

He leaned closer to me. "You know I've never liked that guy. He's such a racist."

I didn't add my two bits about him being a misogynist, too.

He glanced at Brody then lowered his voice even more. "But there's some good in that guy somewhere."

Okay, I'd seen him calm a toddler and make a baby feel safe. Still, I'd seen him almost clock Edna and then smash her ceramic dog.

Brody must have felt us talking about him because he turned toward us and glared. I wanted to keep my eye on him so I could talk to him.

Luke looked around to make sure no one else was listening. "I was the first one on site when he called for backup. There was this guy here, one of the Recon to Reclaim the Desert guys."

"Did Brody call him John?"

Luke nodded. "Do you know him?"

"Heard he's Ford's second in command."

"Probably not anymore. At least after Brody talks to Ford."

"Why is that?"

"So I show up and John takes off, like they do. Brody is acting all important and treating the people like he's their warden."

"Even the kids?"

That stopped Luke and he considered it for a second. "I didn't notice him talking to the kids, but when I got here they all had little stuffed toys. Like the kind you buy in bulk to give away at carnivals."

It would take more than this to make me like Brody.

"Anyway, this John guy takes off and Brody is acting all smug and stuff. He has me count the group and I told him twenty-two."

Brody watched the line of migrants as they slowly made their way to the waiting vehicles. His face still looked like a bowl of prunes.

"He gets all annoyed at me and makes me count again. He says there should be twenty-three."

I needed Luke to wrap this up because Brody started walking after the group. In a moment he'd be in his Tahoe racing back to the station for the end of the shift.

"I tell him twenty-two again and he's getting all puffed up like he's going to explode when we hear this sound. Kind of a muffled cry just behind a bunch of rocks and brush."

Brody waited at the end of the line of migrants, his M4 dangling casually in his hand.

"Brody takes off. I swear I didn't think he could move that fast."

I shifted my gaze to Luke, wondering what was coming next.

"Rodriguez and his trainee got here just then so I ran after Brody."

Agents closed the doors on the first dog catcher and Brody instructed the next in line to load into the second one.

"When I got to the rocks, Brody was beating the shit out of this guy, John. There was a girl, maybe fourteen. I don't know. It's hard to tell ages. But it was pretty clear what John had in mind. Her T-shirt was ripped and there were scratches on her arms."

Damn it. The cruelty and horror of what the immigrants faced every day felt like a sucker punch.

Waves of anger flowed off Luke. "I can't even. I mean, these people have been through enough. And to do that. It makes me sick."

How could I not think of Josie? Fourteen years old. On a journey through heat and thirst, hunger and pain. At the end of her endurance. Only hoping for a chance at a decent life. Dreaming of sleeping in a bed with clean sheets, somewhere safe. I wanted to beat John myself.

"What happened to John?"

"He managed to get away. I think Brody might know where he hides out."

Bingo. I grabbed Luke's arm. "Let's go with Brody to find John."

A few cold drops of rain dropped on my cheeks.

Luke looked uncertain but followed me anyway. With the clouds blocking the sun, twilight had turned to nearly full dark while Luke told me about Brody and John. Our shift ended soon but we were a long way from calling it a night. I pulled out my flashlight and Luke did the same.

The last migrant climbed into the transport and Brody slammed the door behind her. He stood back out of the way of the dust as the van drove away.

Other agents wandered past and one by one their vehicles fired up and they drove away, leaving me, Luke, and Brody alone. This was what I'd been waiting for. If I had any chance of convincing Brody to go after his partners, it would have to be in private.

Keeping my flashlight pointed down, I approached Brody. "We need to find Ford and John."

Brody looked away in disdain. "Look, Grandma, you don't tell me what I need to do."

"You know they're out of control."

He took off his green BP cap and wiped his head, even if the night chill probably made sweating unlikely. "I don't know anything like that. John and his crew caught twenty-three migrants and turned them over to the good guys."

How could he keep defending these men? "Ford had my daughter and who knows what he intended to do with her. He shot at us. And John tried to rape a girl."

Brody swiveled to Luke, and even though his features were hard to see at night, I knew he was giving Luke that puckered-up glare. I had news for Brody: his most threatening expression couldn't come close to my severe Mom Stare.

Luke stood up taller. "It's true. At least the part about John."

Brody gazed off into the dark desert. "They're decent guys. They've caught more smugglers and traffickers than anyone else out here."

"I guess it depends on how you weigh decency. Is it worth catching a hundred bad guys if you hurt or kill ten people? One innocent young girl?"

Brody turned back to me. "Do you really think Ford killed Lacy Hollander?"

I told the honest truth. "I don't know."

Brody laughed. "The great and wise Grandma admits to uncertainty. Someone mark this on the calendar."

"Knock it off," Luke said.

Brody looked as if Luke's outburst surprised him as much as it did me.

The rain picked up, cold and unpleasant. Too bad I'd left my poncho at home. Too much going on with Ann and Josie to think about packing for my own day.

Luke sounded less sure. "It doesn't do any good to be a dick. If you know where Ford and John might be hiding you should take us there."

Brody gave us his back and walked a few feet into the desert beyond the circle of our flashlights.

Luke sent me a questioning look and I shrugged. Nothing to do but wait for Brody to make a decision. I felt the clock ticking. Maybe Ford and John had something planned. They were a menace that needed to be stopped before someone else got hurt.

Finally Brody strode past us on his way to his Tahoe. "If you're coming, let's go."

Luke and I hurried after him. Taking all three vehicles seemed ridiculous, but leaving one so far out here in the desert wasn't an option.

Ford and John had morphed their role as protectors of the border into conquerors with impunity. They were no better than the ruthless and cruel cartels, taking what they wanted without consideration of the people they hurt.

My hand closed on the handle to my pickup door when Luke's voice rang out. "What are we going to do if we find them?"

Brody hoisted himself into his Tahoe. "There are lots of ways to get justice on the desert."

26

We caravanned north from the border to catch a dirt road heading west. Dust swirled in the headlights as I kept close to the red taillights of Brody's vehicle. As it can in the desert, the night closed in black and dense. The rain clouds from earlier had scuttled away, leaving a sky rich with the gems of stars. I doubted the night sky could be prettier anywhere else on earth. Though tonight wasn't a time for star gazing. The chill air was lush with the damp smells of sage and creosote. If you weren't a migrant concerned about your life or an agent tracking bad guys, it might be a beautiful night. Right now, I'd prefer bright sunlight.

I called Deon. "How's it going?"

He sounded tired. "Good. It took them forever to get around to seeing Serena. We're picking up dinner at In-N-Out and then I'll take Serena to Mi Casa."

Hot and juicy, with tomatoes and sauce, French fries fresh from the fryer, salty and warm. Dear god I was hungry. That reminded me to check my blood sugar and grab something from my cooler. It wouldn't be as satisfying as animal style and maybe a chocolate shake.

A car door slammed on Deon's end and I supposed he was going inside instead of the drive-through. "Serena's really a piece of work. Dedicated and vocal about it."

"I'll be glad to get Josie away from her."

Deon laughed. "Good luck with that. Josie seems nearly as devoted to the work as Serena. Although she acts more like Serena's big sister than the little one."

I didn't want to discuss this on the phone. It would take more than an offhand conversation to make my case that, though it was admirable Josie had passion and energy and talent, we, as parents, needed to step in and force moderation. The work she did on the desert couldn't continue. I wouldn't allow her to be in that kind of danger. Even if we captured Ford and put him away, there was too much out here, from bad people to weather, plants, animals, insects, and reptiles, that would delight in damaging my little girl.

"I'm just glad Josie wasn't hurt and Serena isn't any more injured than she is." I closed my eyes against the image of Josie being the one with a bullet hole in her calf. I couldn't let myself see that or even think about it. That's why I wouldn't allow her to keep going out here.

Lightning flashed like bombs exploding on a distant battlefield. I glanced up to see a gray billow of clouds curtaining the stars. Another storm. I instinctively counted. One-one-thousand, two-one-thousand and made it to five before thunder rumbled.

Deon chuckled. "Honestly, she's doing pretty well. When I was shot I pretty much fell apart."

The thought of Deon bleeding and in pain two years ago curled around my gut and twisted tight. I couldn't take one of them being hurt again. "You've never fallen apart. But I'll be happy if you or our girls are never shot at again."

"Are you on your way home?" Sounds of people talking filtered behind his words. He must be in line at the counter.

"I'm going to be late tonight."

He sounded distracted, probably reading the menu and planning his order. "Too bad. I won't get you a burger then."

I was glad he didn't ask what kept me at work. I'd been prepared to lie and tell him I was processing a big group of quitters. He didn't need to know I was tracking a killer.

We took a few more turns that I'd be hard-pressed to repeat in the daylight. Brody stopped his Tahoe and shut it off. Guess this was the place. Brody stood outside his truck, and when I stepped out of mine, he said, "Tack up."

I hadn't expected to be working after dark so hadn't checked out night vision equipment. I'd have to make do with my flashlight. Luke parked behind my truck and caught up to me as we approached Brody.

Brody eyed my flashlight attached to the strap. This time his mouth cocked in derision, but he didn't say anything about it. "We're going to make our way up this wash for about a mile, mile and a half."

Three strobes exploded in rapid-fire. One-one-thousand, two-one-thousand, three-one-thousand.

The wash he indicated was filled with sand still damp from the earlier rains. Any footprints would have been swept away by a small flash flood roaring through the wash. Puddles still pocked the deeper parts of the channel but would be absorbed in a matter of an hour or so. Brush clogged either side of the shallow banks and grasses grew in pockets along the edges. With the recent rains, everything sprang up, ready to grab at loose clothing or gear.

Brody studied me and Luke. "You've got night vision." He pointed at Luke, then gave me an irritated look. "Keep your flashlight off and walk between me and Luke."

We formed a short line and Brody led the way. It was slow-going with the deep sand and darkness. The bushes on either side made the trail narrow and wet. We didn't speak. When we'd walked for about ten minutes, Brody held up his hand to signal halt. We gathered close.

"We're still a ways from the cave. Keep your eyes open. It's hard to spot. The opening is about ten feet above the bottom of the wash, kind of hidden by a couple of good-sized mesquite trees. Ford usually throws some brush across the entrance for good measure. It's hard to spot in the daytime, so I don't know how much luck we'll have at night."

Luke turned his head up to survey the sides of the wash. That's when I realized we'd wound our way close to a cliff that rose above us. We were somewhere in the Altar Valley but I had lost track of where.

Brody turned to continue. Luke reached out to tap him on the shoulder but Brody had already stepped out of range. Luke spoke aloud, his voice a bomb blast in the silence. "How far do you think—"

The whizz of the bullet hit my ears before I heard the report of the rifle. Luke called out a single cry and crumpled.

Brody jumped into the brush at the side of the wash. I threw myself at Luke. Another shot pinged the sand a hair's width from my face and I couldn't help throwing my arms over my head and planting my face in the wet sand. Immediately, I grabbed Luke under his arms and lunged my weight backward.

He was a tall guy, and even if he was mostly bones, there were a lot of them. I yanked backward again at the same time another bullet hit the side of the cliff behind me, followed almost immediately by the crack of the rifle.

There was a lot of distance between us and the shooter if I heard the bullet strike before the shot. He had pretty sophisticated sniper equipment to shoot that well in the dark.

After I had Luke hidden behind a thicket of creosote and Christmas cactus, Brody ventured from behind a rock and grabbed under one of Luke's armpits. Together we lugged Luke to cover behind the rock. He let out a weak moan. Thank god he was alive.

I leaned close to Luke and flinched as lightning broke open, revealing low-hanging clouds roiling overhead. One-one-thousand, two-one-thousand.

I pulled out my flashlight and held it close to Luke before turning it on. It didn't take long to find the wound. Blood pulsed from a hole somewhere around the top of his right ribcage. Did it puncture a lung? Hit some other vital organ? No way to tell.

Luke squeezed his eyes closed and grimaced so I knew he was conscious. I whispered to him, "You're fine. I know it hurts. Hang on."

A shot pinged off the rock and ricocheted into the darkness.

I pressed on the wound. "Call for an ambulance. We've got to get him to the road so they can help him."

Brody didn't hesitate. He spoke into his shoulder mic and gave our coordinates.

I leaned over Luke. "It's okay. We're going to get you some help."

Luke nodded slightly, his breathing shallow and rough.

"Hold pressure here," I said to Brody. "I'll use my shirt for a bandage."

Brody switched places with me and I stripped off my uniform shirt and whipped off the green T-shirt underneath. The brisk wind cascaded instant goosebumps over my skin but I didn't care. Together we bunched the shirt on the wound. I secured it with my belt.

Brody sat up. "He hasn't fired for a while."

The night weighed deep and heavy. I slipped my shirt on and pulled my damp coat over it.

Brody shook his head at me. "I didn't think Ford would shoot at me. That woman was right. He's crazy."

The world exploded in brightness, and before I finished the first one-thousand, the thunder boomed like a kettle drum in my back pocket.

I moved away from Luke and crouched behind the rock, poking my head out. Nothing but dark and darker. I might as well take a chance. I stood up and moved beyond the rock cover. The shooter didn't react. He might be waiting for us or he might have taken off.

"Come on," I said to Brody.

He didn't move for a couple of seconds.

"We can't wait for an ambulance. It could take them an hour to get here."

"If we move him, we could cause more damage," Brody said, his natural sense of self-preservation making sense this time.

"If we can get in a truck and head out, we could meet the ambulance that much sooner. I think we have to try."

"What about the shooter?" Brody said.

"If he's still there, he'll shoot at us. Or he'll shoot at the rescue squad. I need to do everything I can. Are you with me?"

I reached down, put my hands under Luke's armpits, and clenched my fists together. I'd damn-well drag him to the road myself if I had to. But god, I hoped I didn't have to because that much jostling would be bad for Luke.

Brody stood up and wrapped his arms around Luke's knees. He made eye contact and said, "Ready?"

We lifted Luke and he moaned again.

Flash-boom. My eyes closed and I ducked. My heart climbed my throat.

I'd never been to war but this instant panic didn't make me anxious for battle.

"Easy," I said, as if that would make it all okay. I prayed to every spirit and god I could think of. Luke would be okay. He had to be.

We eased our way into the center of the wash just as the skies opened up and rain pelted down on us.

Maybe the storm chased the shooter away and that was something to be grateful for. But the cold drops ran down my neck and I worried it would make things worse for Luke. My back strained and ached. My arms throbbed with trying to keep Luke close enough that his head rested on me. I didn't know how far we'd hiked from the vehicles.

Brody's face was set in stone and he kept moving. He had the lighter side but I was sure he felt the pain, too. Water started to rise in the wash. If this kept up we'd have to climb out and find another way to the vehicles.

In no time Luke's hair was drenched. In the lightning flashes I caught sight of the water dripping down his face. His clothes collected rain, adding to the weight. Even through the downpour, blood seeped through the T-shirt covering his wound. Carrying him might have been a mistake.

But keeping him here would have been worse. Brody's radio burst into sound. "Dispatch Tango 572."

We couldn't set Luke down in the wash because the water covered the sand about six inches deep. We struggled to the side of the wash and gently set Luke down under the branches of a tall Palo Verde tree. I wiped his face and checked to make sure the T-shirt was snug against the wound. He'd passed out, probably a good thing.

Brody answered. "Tango 572 go ahead."

"The ambulance can't cross a washout and had to reroute."

Brody keyed the mic. "Tango 572 10-4. We'll 13 to St. Mary's."

We were on our own to get Luke to the hospital. It seems we'd made the right decision to leave when we did.

With the slight break we took off at a quicker pace and in another ten minutes made it out of the wash that now ran with about a foot of water. Icy rain filled my boots and soaked my clothes. The cold November night made me shiver and my teeth clattered. Since Luke's pickup was last in line and the easiest to back out, we loaded him inside.

I wasn't surprised when Brody said, "You stay here and wait for backup. I'll take Luke." I'd have been surprised if he offered to hang out and wait instead of driving to a warm, dry hospital and then ending his shift.

"Be careful," I said, wiping Luke's face once more. In the pickup's dome light he looked so young and pale. I wanted to kill Ford.

As I watched them drive off, water running off the tip of my nose, I thought that might be exactly what I'd do.

27

Damn Ford. He couldn't keep getting away with this. First he killed Lacy, then he took shots at Josie and Serena. Now Luke. I had to stop that son of a bitch and I couldn't wait around for backup that might or might not arrive through the flooding desert.

Equipped with Luke's night vision gear I headed back to the wash. By now, water ran freely, and I splashed through. The cold flow rose to my calves where the wash ran next to the cliff. The rain kept a steady rhythm and my anger burned away the chill trying to seep into my skin.

I passed the rock where we'd taken cover. Lightning flashes kept my progress in strobes, but the thunder sounded farther away. I counted three-one-thousand between the flash and boom.

The level of the water made it too hard to keep sloshing through the running flood, so I climbed the east side of the wash and crashed through the bushes and grass, my progress slowed. The temperatures had surely dipped lower though the constant battle through the brush kept me warm. The rock cliff rose to the west and I needed to stop and study the side, looking for two big mesquite trees that might hide a cave. The journey seemed to take years. Ford was probably dry and comfortable inside his cliff hideout. Water ran down my neck and soaked my clothes.

No telling how long I battled the wind and rain and the stupid ocotillo, barrel cactus, Palo Verde, and mesquite. The desert was my home and even though it could be harsh and cruel, I'd always loved it. But not tonight.

The night vision glasses gave everything a green glow as I scanned the cliff wall and spotted two mesquite trees. Brody said Ford usually placed brush covering the entrance, but from where I stood looking over the running water, the gaping black hole looked open.

I unholstered my pistol and splashed into the water. With the thunder, the racket of the rain hitting hard ground and rock, and the roar of the flooding wash, sneaking up to the cave didn't cause much concern. Ford wouldn't expect anyone to return after we'd taken Luke to the pickup.

The trail to the opening started out as a narrow path, slick with greasy mud. Tall grasses grew thick and hid the path from casual hikers. Using the grass for a handhold, I grabbed and pulled until my boots hit more rock than mud. From there, I bushwhacked the next several feet from one rocky point to another, always keeping watch to make sure Ford didn't come to the cave's mouth and open fire.

No ledge led to the cave. I would have to leap from the highest rock and land in the opening, leaving myself vulnerable to Ford if he lounged inside. But if he didn't expect anyone, I'd have the advantage and could shoot before he even drew. I pictured it. Lunging from the rock, gun ready, landing with the grace of a mountain lion, ready to open fire.

I studied the black opening. If Ford was hiding inside wouldn't there be some light? He'd probably shot Luke and taken off. I was wasting my time. I gripped my gun and crouched, ready to jet into the cave's mouth.

A flash of lightning illuminated the opening, momentarily blinding me because of the night vision goggles. When I could see again, I made out a figure on the cave floor. He was sleeping, confident he couldn't be touched. My advantage.

Without any more planning, I coiled and sprang. With my gun in front of me, finger on the trigger, I shouted, "Freeze!"

I'd been right. The long, lanky body with a grizzled buzz cut was definitely Ford. But instead of grabbing his gun and challenging me, or zeroing in with those blue laser eyes, he barely moved. A noise came from him, more groan than roar.

My flashlight still dangled from the strap. I snatched it and flipped it on while ripping off the night vision gear.

The cave created a room more than twenty feet wide, the stone ceiling curving back into darkness. Ammo boxes lined one wall, along with a few cases of bottled water. I assumed food and other provisions filled some of the ammo cans. I didn't see a stash of weapons. Ford lay on the well-packed dirt floor.

I knelt next to him and he opened his eyes.

Still blue, still icy. "What are you doing here?"

"I came to kill you." Maybe. That certainly held a possibility for me.

A faint smile tilted his lips before he said, "Where's John? Did you get him?"

I thought I'd better see how badly he was hurt before I launched into interrogating him. "What happened? Are you shot? Bleeding?"

Ford swallowed and moved his arms and legs a few inches as if testing them. "Don't think so. That bastard conked me on the head."

"John?"

He twisted his neck, turning his face to one side, then the other. "Of course John. Who else?"

With some effort Ford pushed himself to sit and immediately bent to the side and threw up. "Got me pretty good, I guess." He gingerly touched the back of his head.

I let him sit for a second and scooted around to shine my flashlight on his injury. Yep, a stream of blood was nearly dried on the back of his neck. Goose egg looked to be about the size of a golf ball.

He stirred around and rolled to his knees.

"Hang on there, cowboy. I don't think you should get up right now."

Ford growled, the sound telling me what he thought of my advice.

I didn't think I stood much chance of convincing him to take it easy, so I clasped his upper arm and let him use me for support. "How far away is your vehicle?"

He succeeded in pulling himself to stand but bent over and rested his hands on his knees. His head hung between his shoulders and his breath chuffed in ragged sequence. He fought the nausea and slowly straightened. "I have an ATV in a clearing a few yards from here."

I checked outside the opening. "The rain's let up some. Let's get to your ATV and I'll drive us to my truck and take you to the hospital."

Ford staggered toward the cave opening. "Screw that. I've got to find John before he kills someone else."

I thought about pushing Ford out of the cave and letting him tumble on the rocks before crashing into the wash. With any luck, he'd land face first and not have the strength to lift his face from the water. "How 'bout I find John, you go to the hospital, and after that, we can discuss who killed someone."

Ford seemed to gain more strength. He stumbled toward the ammo cans and slammed the metal clasp first on one end, then the other. He flipped the heavy top and it landed with a plop on the dirt floor. After rummaging inside he pulled out a pair of night vision goggles.

I watched him replace the lid and secure the clasps, then I laid it out for him. "You're under arrest for the attempted murder of Luke Manifold and Serena Lewis and the murder of Lacy Hollander."

He waved me off and started toward the cave opening.

I grabbed his arm and spun him around, dangling wrist restraints in front of him. "I'd rather not cuff you but I will."

Those blue eyes stabbed me. "I don't have time for this. John is out there and he's crazy. I don't know what he's going to do but I know he's got something planned."

"How do you know this?"

He inhaled as if a sharp pain hit, closed his eyes briefly, then looked at the ceiling for a moment. "He told me, okay? Right before he knocked me in the head with his flashlight. His exact words were, 'I don't take orders from you anymore. I'm working to save America.'"

"I'm supposed to take your word for it?"

He took a few steps back from me. "If you want to stop John from doing something bad, you're gonna need to."

"From what I hear, John is your second in command. Why wouldn't I think you're working with him?"

Ford scowled. "Where did you hear that?"

"Dell, Marcy, and Tim. They hadn't seen you for days, but they'd been talking to John."

Ford rubbed the side of his head. "Those aren't the brightest bulbs in the chandelier."

That was my assessment, but I wasn't ready to buy his goods. "What about Lacy? We know you contacted her the day she died. How mad were you that she turned you in for IEDs?"

His face lost all emotion as if a door slammed shut, hiding whatever he felt. "Yeah. I knew Lacy. And she didn't turn me in for IEDs. That was our friend John."

It wouldn't do any good to talk to him about this. "I'm sure we can clear all this up later. Right now, you need medical attention for that concussion."

"I'm not going with you."

I held up the restraints. "Then we'll do it the hard way."

He gave his head an arrogant tilt. "Or not at all."

Without fanfare, he slipped into the night. Guess he'd recovered quicker than I'd thought.

I ran after him. My flashlight beam caught him as he edged through some brush. He knew where he was going so he moved faster than I did. I hadn't chased him far when the roar of his ATV sounded above the water rushing in the wash. By the time I rounded a rock, his taillights disappeared over a hill heading south.

I didn't hesitate but turned around and ran the mile-plus back to my truck, splashing and slipping in the receding water. No backup had arrived yet. They were probably working their way around flooded areas. I called on the radio and told them Ford had taken off. No need to bring anyone to this location. We might as well spread out and search on our own.

I bounced and splashed down the road, hitting deep ponds and sliding in the greasy mud. Not sure where to go, I decided to try Edna. Maybe she'd know where Ford might be.

After too much time I slid into Sasabe. The rain had stopped here some time ago but the eaves of Edna's house still dripped. I let myself through her rickety front gate and rushed to her porch, banging on her door and calling her name. No ceramic dogs lined the porch. A light shone through the curtains shielding the small windows in the front of her cabin.

The floor creaked inside, the porch light flicked on, and Edna's voice rose. "Who's out there?"

"It's Michaela Sanchez. Border Patrol."

The lock clinked and Edna opened the door inward. She pushed the screen open to let me in. "Something's wrong with Ford," she said by way of greeting.

"How do you know?"

She blew air from her nose and gave me a stern look. "The dogs. They know things."

Behind her all the dogs circled around a five-gallon plastic bucket. "You bring them in at night?"

She looked at me like I was bonkers. "Of course. It's cold out there and I don't want the coyotes messing with them."

She turned an admiring gaze on her pack. "You caught us at supper time." She frowned and scurried over to the dogs, repositioning the big dalmatian and snugging a black scottie in its place. She tsked as she came back to me. "He don't always stand up for himself." She folded her arms. "Why are you here?"

"I need to know more about Ford, where he might go if he was in trouble."

She snapped her fingers. "I knew it. He's hurt. Isn't he?"

I nodded, not wanting to tell her he might be heading to cause more damage. "Yes. But he took off before I could get him medical care."

She eyed me with some skepticism. "He probably went to his house."

This wasn't getting me anywhere. "Is there someplace else?"

She put her arms out and started to shove me backward toward the door. "You don't want to help him. You want to hurt him."

"No, I—"

"You think he shot at that loud-mouthed girl. But he didn't. He is a good man. You need to leave him alone."

"I'm trying to help people. Trust your dogs. They like me."

She had me backed to the door. "They're only glass and pottery. You'd have to be crazy to think they're real."

She opened the door and had me outside in a heartbeat. The lock clinked back in place and the porch light went out.

The air stung the tip of my nose. This night was too cold for anyone to be out. But I knew the desert hid people, even in this weather. Some bad people, for sure, but also families with nothing but hope. Was I helping any of them?

I climbed into the truck and cranked on the heater. My shift had long since ended. Weariness crept into my bones along with the cold. My monitor showed my blood sugar was diving so I grabbed a peanut butter and jelly sandwich from my cooler. A real meal would be better, but this would do for now.

With no plan, I radioed duty commander and told her everything I knew. She told me to come back in and she'd send out other agents to patrol and search for Ford. They'd do as good a job as I could, probably better because they wouldn't be so worn out.

Since I had service, I dialed Deon. "How's everything going?"

He sounded warm and well fed, or maybe that was just me projecting. "Sami and I are watching *Elf*. Again."

Deon hated that movie so I knew he was working hard at making up to Sami. "How's Josie doing?"

He paused. A sound I hated. When he started again, I knew I was right to dread. "She's doing great. She wanted to spend the night with Ann."

"Deon..."

He quickly added, "I know. You want her home and safe. But listen a minute. Serena is her friend, even if we hate it."

"Serena is twice her age and a mess. She took Josie into the line of fire."

"Sure, sure. But Josie is concerned. Ann is still weak and Josie's worried about her, too. She wouldn't have rested at home. It seemed like the best thing was to let her go."

I shouldn't have said it but it boiled over. "And you want to be the good guy. You're the father, Deon. This is what being a parent is all about. You aren't supposed to be her friend."

I heard footsteps that sounded like he was going upstairs. He wouldn't want Sami to hear us disagree. His voice came through hard. "You're out on the desert following your passion. I support you, you know that. But that leaves me here to be the parent. I'll do it my way."

"But your way is them running all over you."

"And your way is to hold them under your thumb."

We both stopped for a moment. The line went silent as I waited for both of us to calm down. Then I said, "I'm sorry. You're right about me trusting you to parent. But I don't think Josie should be at Mi Casa tonight."

He sounded much calmer, too. "Is there a reason for your worry?"

Ford was on the loose. And if he was right in his accusation, John was the dangerous one and he was also on the loose. Ann had assured me the last of the undocumented immigrants had left earlier today. No one had a reason to go to Mi Casa. Even if they did, Ann and Josie were safe in her house. "No. I'm being paranoid and controlling."

He laughed. "You love your family. That's good."

"I'm worried about Josie. She's only fourteen. That's too young to take the world this seriously."

Deon sighed. "You have yourself to blame for that, *mi corazon*." Ah. After all these years Deon could still get me with as little as one word of Spanish. "You raised her to care. And to be a rebel."

I was proud of her. But I'd be just as proud if she stuck to soccer and quiz bowl. After telling Deon I'd be home as soon as possible and that I loved him, I hung up and dialed Ann's number.

She answered as if already in conversation. "Josie is fine. We're at my house. She's hovering over Serena like a regular Florence Nightingale."

I sighed. "How are you?"

"Me?" She sounded surprised I asked. "I'm feeling better. Derrick was around most of the day and kept a good eye on me. Wouldn't let me get out of bed."

"Is Derrick there now?"

"He left this afternoon. I don't know where he went but it must be important or he'd be here to take care of Serena."

I wanted him there. With Ann sick and Serena injured, that left Josie as the only able-bodied person. "Maybe give him a call and see if he can hang around there tonight."

Ann shot back, "We're fine. We've got the doors locked and everything, just like you taught us."

I didn't need her patronizing tone. "I'm not happy Deon let Josie stay with you tonight. I can't do anything about it now. But we're not done with this. So go ahead and be all superior and confident. We're going to talk tomorrow."

"Fine. We'll see you then."

Maybe big sisters will always find a way to poke under your skin. Ann loved Josie. No doubt. But did she love her the way I did? Josie and Sami were as close as Ann would get to having a child of her own. She couldn't love them any less than I did, could she?

I put the pickup in drive and eased away from Edna's house. It would be another hour or so before I got to the station and another hour after that before I curled up next to Deon in our soft, warm bed. I checked the dash clock. That would leave me maybe three or four hours before I got up and started all over.

Tell me again why I wanted to be a Border Patrol agent.

I drove a few yards to the intersection, prepared to make a U-turn and head out of town toward Tucson. When I glanced to the right, I slammed on my brakes.

A light shone from the front windows of Ford's house.

28

I pulled the pickup to the side of the road and shut it down. Gun in hand, I jogged to Ford's house, dodging puddles. My feet crunched on the damp sand.

Through the front windows I watched Ford moving from one room to another. He walked slowly and leaned his head to the right. Trying to keep as quiet as possible, I snuck up the porch steps and advanced to the door where I lost sight into the house. I listened with my ear close to the door.

Suddenly it swung inward and I pulled my gun up to point at Ford's chest.

He glanced at it then me. "No need to lurk out in the cold. Come in. Did you have a good chat with Edna? She's a little off but she's good folk."

I kept my gun focused on him. "Are you ready for me to take you to town?"

He picked up a sheet of paper from the desk. "Why do you think I was waiting for you?"

That surprised me. "Okay then. I don't need the restraints?"

He didn't answer the question but handed me the paper. "This is the address. I'm sure it's near the university."

Keeping the gun pointed at him I took the paper and glanced at it. It seemed to be an application of some kind. "What's this?"

"It's John's information. I make them fill out the form when they apply to Recon to Reclaim the Desert. I should have known from the beginning John wasn't right for us. At the time I was building my forces. We needed the manpower. This was when the cartels were running over the border like it was a garden fence."

"You and John aren't partners?"

He glared at me, those eyes like weapons. "Are you crazy? John is a loose cannon. Always was. I gave him the benefit of the doubt because we were short-handed but the guy couldn't follow orders. I had to kick him out."

"And he didn't take it kindly?"

Ford propped himself on the desk then the wall as he moved to a locked closet. "I don't give a shit what John thinks. Recon to Reclaim the Desert is my company. I run it how I see fit. Our mission is to protect the border and I don't give a shit if John has a different idea. He's not one of us."

"What was his idea?"

Ford pulled a key chain from his pocket and sorted through several keys, settling on one. "John wants to kill things. He came out here with a whole arsenal. Guess he thought we were free to shoot at anything that moved."

"You have standards, though."

He sniffed at that. "Oh sure, you go ahead and judge. I'm on your side. You wear a uniform and so do I. I was in the Army for three tours in the Middle East. I swore an oath and just because I'm no longer active Army doesn't mean I'm off the hook. I patrol and track and hunt the bad guys. When I find them, I alert Border Patrol. That's my job."

"What did John think was his job?"

Ford unlocked the padlock and slipped it off the door. "We've been over this."

I scanned the tabletop. "What happened to her hat?"

Ford squinted at me in confusion. "What?"

I pointed to the table. "Lacy's hat. It was here two days ago and now it's gone."

He stood perfectly still. "What do you know about that?"

His focus unnerved me. "When I stopped by to talk to you no one was home and I looked through the window and saw it here."

He rubbed his forehead as if it hurt. "Yeah. It wasn't hers. Just some copy like everyone has. I brought it here and then it was gone. Thought maybe I was losing my mind, like PTSD or grief what-have-you."

"It might have ended up sailing through a broken window at Mi Casa."

"Mi Casa? Doesn't make sense to me."

I tried a different trail. "So why did you contact Lacy on the day she died?"

He stopped his frantic action and rested his arm against the door, dropping his head. "She should have listened to me."

"About what?"

"I told her we had to stop. Someone found out about what we were doing."

It took a second to register what he said. "The two of you? You were working together?"

He flopped to the side to put his back against the door, then slid down to sit, as if his bones dissolved. After a second he said, "Yes. We were working together."

I hadn't considered this. "You and Lacy weren't enemies?"

His eyes traveled from the floor to me. The sadness in their depths matched the tone of his voice. "No. We weren't enemies."

I sat down a few feet from him. "Tell me about it."

He seemed to consider whether I was worth his confession. I must have met some measure because he started. "The first time I saw her, she was putting water out on the desert. It was one of those summer days when the temperature climbed well over a hundred and the air had been still. There were three of them, that Serena and another guy, and I'd been following their progress up the valley. Serena and the guy gave out. But Lacy didn't have the word quit in her. She took their water and hiked on.

"I followed but kept my distance. There was a monsoon rain heading our way, but if it didn't get there soon, as hot as it was, I thought she might pass out. I didn't know the strength of her determination then.

"She hiked at a pace that impressed me. Leaving jugs at several stops. Usually they set more out, but she did what she could going solo. It might be the difference between someone living and dying."

"You left the water there?" I asked.

He frowned at me. "I'm not a killer. Those migrants out there, they're people. They suffer to get to this country. I don't approve of them sneaking in and not abiding by the laws. But I don't want them to die trying to find a decent life for themselves or their families."

He seemed sincere but I wasn't sure I could trust it. "Didn't you shoot an immigrant a couple of years ago?"

He pointed a finger at me. "A cartel scout. And it was self-defense. That son of a bitch shot at me first. That's a whole different thing."

"But some of them are forced to work for the cartels to protect their families."

He nodded. "That's true. But I don't tolerate the cartels. No compromise."

I guess everyone had their line in the sand. "Go on."

"That monsoon rain hit hard. It came sooner than I expected and I think it caught her off-guard too." He stopped and his eyes glazed over as if he was remembering the day. His voice grew gruffer. "At the first drops Lacy shed her pack. She pulled her shirt over her head and unsnapped her bra."

Wow. The way he said it made it seem like an erotic movie.

He closed his eyes and I had no trouble believing he saw Lacy in the rain. "She unlaced her boots and pulled off her socks. By then, the rain fell hard. Steam rose from the sand as she pushed her pants down her calves and stepped onto the sand. Water soaked her hair and ran down her body and she held her arms out, head tilted to the sky."

He swallowed and waited a moment. "It was the most beautiful thing I've ever seen." I knew he meant it. He opened his eyes, a little watery but no real tears. "I can't believe she'll never dance in the rain again."

This was good drama, but I needed to know more. "How did she get you to start working with her?"

He acted as if I weren't there and kept going. "I couldn't resist her. Before I knew what I was doing, I'd gone to her, dropped my pack, and pulled off my own shirt. Because of the roar of the rain, she hadn't heard me approach. When she opened her eyes, there I was, a half-naked man staring at her."

Jesus. That would have freaked me out.

"Any other woman would have been terrified. But not Lacy. She had a moment of being startled, then she smiled at me and said, 'It's no good unless you take it all off.' So I did."

I didn't know if this was a porn movie or some romantic fantasy.

"The rain pelted us in this almost painful way. But we both let it beat on us and we stood there with our arms out to get every inch of our bodies saturated. And we looked at each other."

Okay, this was weird.

"When the storm moved on we draped our clothes over a mesquite and sat on our packs." He seemed to remember I was in the room with him. He smiled, a true smile not tainted with sarcasm or bitterness. "That must sound crazy to you."

"A little."

He nodded, the smile sad again. "It was. But so right. Lacy said we were bound together in past lives. I don't know about that bullshit. I do know I felt filled up. Satisfied for the first time in my life."

I must have looked skeptical.

He thought a second. "It's like if your whole life all you've ever had to eat is oatmeal. It keeps you from being hungry and you've never eaten anything else so you don't know what you're missing. Then, someone puts a steak in front of you and you suddenly find out the world is so much better than you ever thought possible."

"Lacy was the steak."

He looked away, as if embarrassed. "Lacy was everything."

I waited to let him get back to the story.

"We talked until our clothes dried and then we walked back to where Serena and the other guy waited in the pickup. I held back so they wouldn't see me. By that time Lacy had me convinced to help her save migrants."

"By putting out water and supplies?"

He straightened his back. "I never did that."

"What did you do?"

"Lacy and I worked out an underground railroad of sorts. She had all the contacts and I was only one piece. But I was the bit that had been missing. There is a humanitarian group over the border that helps people from

Mexico and Central America. Family groups terrorized by cartels, who don't have the power or money to save themselves but refuse to work with the cartels. She had someone on this side willing to hide the migrants until arrangements were made to move them farther north."

Mi Casa. That's why Ann kept defending Ford. She knew he'd been helping Lacy. And she hadn't told me.

"She needed someone out here who knew the trails. Someone familiar with cartel routes and the workings of Border Patrol. Tough and smart as she was, Lacy couldn't do it alone. For one thing, she hated guns and wouldn't touch them. You can't protect anything in this remote country without a gun."

"So you joined her."

A warmth seeped into his cold eyes. "I might not have been totally convinced it was the right thing to do, but I'd have done anything to protect Lacy. She'd already started doing this without me. It was only a matter of time before she got hurt."

He seemed to realize what he'd said. He swallowed again and his Adam's apple bounced down his grizzled throat. "I didn't protect her. Instead, I brought the danger to her."

I wanted to reach out and pat his hand or touch him in sympathy but Ford wasn't the kind of person who would accept that.

"John must have discovered we were going to meet and found her before I could get there. When I arrived, Border Patrol was all over the place and Brody wouldn't let me near her."

"So you're saying John beat you to where you were going to meet Lacy, killed her, and then, what?"

He slammed a fist into the wall. "I don't know what. He's slippery and smart. Lacy and I knew someone had infiltrated No Desert Deaths because as soon as they'd leave supplies on the desert someone destroyed them. John must have been working with someone at No Desert Deaths and that person found out Lacy and I were working together. Either the No Desert Deaths spy or John killed Lacy and John came after me. He's who shot at your daughter and her friend."

He dropped his head back against the wall, spent.

"Let me take you to the hospital. A doctor should look at that lump."

He pushed himself to standing. "We need to go."

"Where?"

He pointed to the application. "To stop John."

"From what?"

He stared at me. "I wish I knew."

29

With Ford resting beside me, I drove the white Border Patrol pickup back to Tucson, the wet roads shiny in my headlights. I called Brody and was relieved to hear they'd made it to the hospital and Luke was going to be okay. I was shocked to find out Brody was staying until Luke was brought to his room. Still didn't make me like Brody but I noted the good deed.

With the heat turned up, I started to dry out but the chill seeped deep into my bones. We made our way past downtown to the crowded areas surrounding the U of A campus. Houses ranged from tiny, rundown bungalows inhabited by students to stylish adobes refurbished and landscaped behind tall stucco walls. A handful of blocks north of campus we pulled into an apartment complex with two floors surrounding a hard-packed center with a few blades of grass that would thrive with the recent rains.

We parked and Ford clutched the handle to jump out of the pickup. I grabbed his arm before he could leave. He snapped back to me as if ready to do battle.

"Easy, cowboy," I said.

He glared at me. "Let's go get him."

"Sure. We're going up to talk to him. No guns."

Ford's nostrils flared but he didn't say anything.

"I mean it. We don't know if he has anything to do with Lacy's murder. And we're not cops."

"Right. We're not cops so we don't have to play by those rules."

I held up my phone. "No guns or I'll call the real cops and we'll risk the chance of losing him."

Ford stared at me for a couple more seconds, then pulled his pistol from his jacket and pushed it under the seat.

"Is that all?"

He exhaled. "What? You think I'm a 007 and carry a spare everywhere? I have a knife, but you aren't going to get that away from me."

Working with Ford was exhausting. "Okay, but you can't use it. Are you sure you're up to this? I still think I should take you to the hospital."

He growled in what I already considered typical Ford fashion. He might have lost his heart to Lacy and turned all soft and gooey about her, but that didn't translate to the rest of the world. Without more conversation he threw himself out of the pickup and headed for the stairs.

The apartment doors opened into the courtyard and John's address said he was on the second story. I followed Ford as he climbed the stairs. His head must have been like granite because he didn't seem to have any fallout from getting clocked.

John's apartment was at the end of the top floor. Ford didn't lean on the cheap wrought iron balcony as he continued with a determined gait. I was a few steps behind him, expecting him to stop in front of the door and wait for me.

That wasn't the way Ford wanted to play this. A few steps before reaching John's apartment he sprang forward and propelled himself at the door, turning so he hit it with his shoulder, putting all his weight and momentum into it. It takes a lot to break a door down, and even taking into account cheesy student housing, I didn't expect it to give.

I was wrong. The jamb cracked and broke and the door burst inward. So much for abiding by the law. If John had been home, he couldn't have missed our entrance. Ford was already up and moving into the room when I got there and found a light switch.

Ford stood in the middle of the room and drew in a breath. "Holy shit."

That didn't begin to cover it. The room looked like an ammunitions dump. John had no couch, chairs, or TV, even threadbare, secondhand stuff. Three six-foot fold-up tables, like the kind I'd bought for Ann at Costco, took up the center of the small living room. Guns, hand grenades, bullets, and all manner of weapons filled the tabletops.

"This guy is certifiable." Ford made his way into the room. Tactical gear was stashed in every corner. The guy had thousands of dollars wrapped up in his army of one. The arsenal sent a chill through me. John meant to kill. And I didn't think he'd settle for one person.

I mentally tallied the rounds of ammunition when a *ting* sounded from the other room that must be a bedroom. Ford had gone in and flicked on a light while I'd been staring at the terrifying sight of all that firepower.

He shot out of the room holding up his phone. "He sent me a text."

"John?" I lunged for the phone.

See who's commander now.

I handed it back to Ford. "What's that mean?"

The phone's screen lit up as it *tinged* again. Ford held it out for me to read. **Traitors die.**

Ford picked out a message. **Where are you?**

John's message returned before he could have read Ford's. **Either you protect the US or you betray it. You chose your course.**

Ford finished typing. **Why did you kill Lacy?**

We stared at the screen until it *tinged* again. **She had to die. She was aiding and abetting the enemy. And so are you.**

Ford's fingers tapped slowly, nothing like Josie or even Sami would do. **What do you want?**

For traitors to die.

Ford didn't look up as he answered, **Come and get me.**

The dots indicated John was typing. It all moved so slowly I was holding my breath. **It's not that easy, SIR. You will see what happens to the others.**

I couldn't wait for Ford to peck and grabbed his phone. I fired off: **What others?**

The others betraying the US.

I quickly shot a reply. **But I'm the one in charge. Come get me.**

You'd like that. Mr. Hero.

Ford stared at the screen. "We need to figure out where he is."

I already had my phone out calling Ann. She picked up, sounding groggy. "Michaela? What's wrong?"

Damn it. I hadn't considered the time. "I'm checking on you. Is everything okay there?"

As if too tired to talk, she mumbled, "It's fine. We *were* asleep."

"And Josie's okay?"

She exhaled. "We're all okay. Derrick came over after his class. Josie's in the guest room. Serena's on the sofa, and Derrick is watching TV in the living room with her. Okay? Can we get back to sleep now?"

"Yeah. Sorry. I'll swing by sometime tomorrow."

She hung up without another word.

We had an apartment filled with enough weapons to stage a coup in a small country and a lunatic on the loose. This was bigger than the two of us could handle. "It's time we call the cops."

Ford stared at his phone. "Yeah. Who knows where John is and what kind of firepower he's got with him."

Not that it made any difference, but it was good to have him agree with me for a change.

While I gave 9-1-1 the address and basic information, Ford kept going back and forth with John.

I hung up the phone, paced to the front door, and looked out. Where was John and what was he planning? Whatever it was, we needed to find him in a hurry.

Ford's phone signaled another incoming text. Ford cursed under his breath. "Come on," he said, passing me in the entrance. "I know where he's heading."

I ran after Ford onto the balcony. "Where?"

Ford stopped and gripped the railing. "He's...he's..." Ford's eyes locked onto mine in shock. His mouth contorted and he gasped before toppling over at my feet.

30

I called 9-1-1 for the second time in a matter of minutes. I gave them as much information about Ford as I could, which wasn't much since I didn't know his age or medical history. All I knew is that he had been cracked on the head several hours ago and he'd passed out. While I waited to hear the sirens of police or ambulance, I knelt by Ford and spoke to him in a reassuring way. I didn't know if he could hear me—probably not—but if he could, I didn't want him to think he was alone.

Meanwhile, I rifled in his jacket pocket for his phone. He knew where John was heading so he must have figured it out from the texts.

I pushed the on button and Ford's phone lit up. The password screen mocked me. Damn it. There was no way I could get into it and find the texts. "Come on, Ford. Open your eyes and tell me what you know." Of course he didn't.

A few students wandered out of their apartments, curious about what happened or wondering if we needed help. I asked them to please stay inside because the ambulance would be arriving soon.

It seemed like an eternity while I spoke to Ford and tried to work out what to do next. But eventually the sound of sirens warned of the ambulance. The responders raced up the stairs. Again I answered what questions I could, frustrating them and me because I didn't know more. It didn't take long for them to strap him onto a gurney and whisk him away. All I could do now was hope he'd be okay.

The first two cops on the scene from my first 9-1-1 call pushed past Ford on the stairs. I'd hoped I might know the officers from my time on the force, but they were new to me. I showed them John's apartment and explained our fears and why Ford had broken in. John's creepy apartment spoke for itself and detectives were called.

The officers wrote notes and seemed to take me seriously when I insisted John was out there planning harm.

As a Border Patrol agent, I had no role to play in finding John. My job ended when the cops showed up.

Despite it being after three in the morning, I needed to know my family was okay. The world felt out of order, tilting toward chaos. I couldn't shake the feeling that people were going to die at John's hands before the sun rose, and I needed to make sure none of them were mine.

I dialed Deon. It rang three times before he picked up, panic in his voice. "Michaela? Are you okay? Where are you?" I must have pulled him from REM sleep and he'd only had a chance to glance at the clock.

Guilt at my selfishness flashed. "I'm sorry I woke you. I'm fine. I just wanted to know you and Sami were okay."

"Yeah. Fine. Why wouldn't we be?"

"No reason. Go back to sleep. I'll be home in a little while."

He sounded more awake and I feared I'd ruined the night for him and he'd be up for good. "Is everything okay? Why are you out so late?"

I tried to sound soothing, maybe relax him a little. "It's been a long night. I'll tell you about it when I get home."

All trace of drowsiness was gone from his voice. "Okay. I suppose you'll still have to work your shift tomorrow so we'll talk after you get home tomorrow night."

"I love you. Go back to sleep."

"Love you, too." He hung up but I doubted he'd go back to sleep.

Another day before I could be with my family.

I thought of Lacy and what she'd given up to help others. Had Ford made sacrifices to do what he thought needed to be done? I had no intention of losing my life defending the border, but was I giving up too much?

I craved the warmth of my bed and comfort of Deon next to me. Chances were he wouldn't be snuggled in anymore. I'd probably destroyed any chance he had for sleep and he was reading a brief or something. Maybe I could share an hour or so with him before he got ready for work. I didn't think it'd be too hard to convince him to come back to bed. That idea brightened my mood.

But knowing John was out there somewhere pushed away any good feelings about my plans. There must be something I could do. Maybe hang out in the hospital and wait for Ford to come to and tell me what he'd figured out. That didn't seem like a great plan.

With no new ideas, it was probably time I called it quits and ended my shift. It didn't take long to sign in my pickup and weapons. I felt light without the weight of my duty belt with my gun, flashlight, and other necessities. I craved sleep but considered staying up. By the time I drove home I'd only have a couple of hours before I had to get up and start again. Waking from that short of a nap might be worse than pounding down some caffeine and fighting on.

How was Josie doing? I wished my family were all under one roof tonight. Tomorrow I'd call Chris and we'd force a meeting with Ann after work. We needed to come up with a plan for Ann's care that didn't include my fourteen-year-old as caretaker. Maybe we could hire Derrick on a more formal basis.

Sudden, unreasoning anxiety dropped into my gut at the thought of Josie caring for Serena and Ann all alone. Probably born of fatigue and guilt at being a bad mother. Still, it wouldn't hurt to swing by Ann's to get eyeballs on Josie. I didn't want to repeat my mistake with Deon by calling and waking Ann and risk wrecking her sleep again. With the streets nearly empty I cruised through Tucson, making it to Mi Casa in less than fifteen minutes. I turned at the alley next to the building and drove to the street behind the main thoroughfare, parking my Pilot in Ann's driveway.

Heavy night air pushed down on me, dampening the noise of the occasional car on the normally busy street just a block away. The neighborhood smelled of wet sand, not the usual scents of car exhaust and cooking I associated with Ann's neighbors. No dogs barked, no birds sang, no shouts of kids at play. Just a deep silence as complete as the darkness of night. My boots thudded on her walkway as I made my way to the door.

The screen squeaked when I pulled it open and keys jingled when I pulled them from my pocket. They clanked against the knob when I inserted one and turned it. I'd never noticed how much noise going into a house could make. Instead of sneaking in and sparing Ann a startling phone call, I'd probably make her think she was being burglarized and earn another call to 9-1-1.

The door opened into her small square foyer, with one side leading to the kitchen, the other to the tiny living room. A short hall veered just past the living room and led to two small bedrooms and a bathroom. Moving as quietly as possible, I slipped down the hall to Ann's room. Now that I'd probably terrorized her, I ought to let her know she had nothing to fear.

I pushed her door open and whispered, "Ann? Are you awake?"

No answer. Damn it. I'd done it again. First Deon, then Ann. She wasn't awake now but I was committed, and decided to gently wake her so she wouldn't hear me in Josie's room and panic. Darkness covered the room as I made my way gingerly to her bedside. I reached out to place a hand on her shoulder, hoping I'd find her in the lumps of the down comforter she preferred in the winter. My palm touched the pile and I pressed into it, searching for her. But I kept pressing until my fingers hit the mattress. "Ann?" My voice rang out harsh with fear.

She didn't answer and I lunged back to the door, slapping on the light switch. The bedside lamp lit up to reveal an empty bed, the comforter heaped in the center as if Ann had risen in a hurry.

I ran into the hallway and took the couple of steps to the guest room. Not bothering to save Josie a jarring waking, I shouted, "Josie!" and hit the light switch. Her bed was empty and equally messed.

It took a second to grab my phone from my pocket and hit Ann's number as I ran down the hall to the front door. I didn't know where I was going but I had to find my daughter.

The phone rang twice before it connected. "Ann? Where are you? Where's Josie?"

The voice on the other end wasn't Ann. I didn't recognize it. "Michaela. It's Derrick."

Why was Derrick on Ann's phone? Forty disasters ranging from Ann having a stroke to Josie's appendix bursting made me nearly shriek, "What's going on? Is everything okay?"

Derrick sounded calm, which helped. "It's fine. All good. I didn't mean to scare you."

"Why isn't Ann answering?"

"She's in her office and her phone is in the kitchen. She asked me to answer so she didn't have to get up."

"Is she okay?"

He responded quickly, as if wanting to reassure me. "Oh, sure. She's fine. Just a little tired. Where are you?"

"I'm at her house. Josie isn't here either and it scared me."

He chuckled. "I'll bet. Don't worry. We had a little problem here but it's all okay."

"Where is 'here?'"

"Sorry. At Mi Casa. Reyna got up for a midnight snack, I guess, and smelled gas. She called Ann and we came over to check it out."

I spun from the front door and headed to the sliding door in the dining room. "You need to get out of there now and call the gas company. I'm on my way over."

He spoke quickly. "No, no. You don't need to come over. We opened the windows and it's all aired out. Serena, Ann, and Josie are having some hot chocolate. They got all worked up coming over here and are trying to relax before going back to bed. You should go home. We're all fine."

It was late and if I went over there I'd probably get Josie mad and she'd never get back to sleep. Probably just best to head home. "Yeah. Okay. Tell Josie I'll stop by in the morning and take her to school."

He sounded cheerful for three o'clock in the morning, but maybe that was youth. I'd need at least twenty-four hours of sleep to feel that good again. "I sure will. Take care." He hung up and I slipped my phone back into my pocket before taking a few steps toward the front door.

I hesitated. With my nerves jangling and a fatigue headache threatening, a cup of hot chocolate didn't sound half bad. I checked my blood sugar monitor and decided a treat wouldn't do any harm. Maybe it didn't make sense, but I'd sleep much easier if I at least set eyes on Josie first.

I let myself out the back door and crossed the wet grass to the rickety wooden fence that bordered Mi Casa. The gate stood open, reminding me that Josie and Ann had hurried through here earlier. I left it open in anticipation of helping Ann return to her house soon, hopefully before the sun rose.

Lights shone onto the courtyard from the kitchen and Ann's office. I slipped under the grapefruit tree and passed the sandbox on my way to the glass back door, so much like the front door that was shattered by a protester. I'd have to get Ann to replace this with something more secure.

Predawn chill sank deep into my bones and the hot cocoa sounded better and better. I pushed the door and it whispered open. A security light set the lobby in long shadows.

Voices came from the kitchen and I looked forward to sitting down and relaxing. I called out, "Heat some up for me, I'm coming in."

Derrick's voice stopped. A clatter sounded from the left. I hadn't realized the kitchen door was closed until I heard it open and slam shut again. Before I took three steps, Derrick popped out from the corridor leading to the kitchen.

Air left my lungs as if someone kicked my gut.

Derrick flashed me a friendly smile. Of course, only the left side of his face responded. The other half was a bloody, mangled mess.

31

My brain felt as though it slammed into a brick wall as I struggled to make sense of what I was seeing. Luke said Brody had ruined half of John's face.

John and Derrick. The same person. A reel of the last week spun through my mind, all the times Derrick had been at Mi Casa, with Ann, with Josie. Derrick knew when and where all the supply drops were made. He knew Lacy planned to meet Ford that day. This monster who had killed Lacy Hollander and somehow weaseled his way into Ann's life now stood in front of me.

At least now I knew where he was. "John."

The half of his face that had animation looked delighted. "John Derrick Fowler, not that we need introductions. I'm practically one of the family."

I didn't see a weapon so I started toward him, intent on getting to the kitchen.

He stepped in front of me. "You don't want to go in there."

The kitchen used to be a conference room. Mostly through donations and deeply discounted appliances and supplies, Ann had made the transformation. The last company to occupy the offices had donated the long, polished conference table and chairs. Ann covered the surface with butcher paper and provided Crayons. She encouraged the residents to decorate the covering. The padded, rolling chairs had been sold second-hand and used to purchase plastic chairs as you'd find in a hospital cafeteria. Windows ran from about four feet from the floor to nearly the ceiling along the whole room's border with the hall. Over Derrick's shoulder I looked into the kitchen.

Reyna and Jimena sat in chairs facing the windows. Donia was across from them, turned away from the windows. Her hands were clasped behind her back and secured with zip tie restraints like those I carried. Donia's ankles were also secured to the chair's legs. Reyna and Jimena must be tied to their chairs as well. Ann said they'd be gone by now. More lies.

The five children huddled on adult chairs shoved together. Zip ties had been formed into bands around each of their necks and a nylon rope threaded from one child to the next, connecting them all like beads on a necklace.

No Josie, Ann, or Serena. I tried to shove Derrick aside. "What are you doing?"

Derrick placed his palm on my chest and pushed, knocking me a few steps backward. He whipped his other hand from his pocket and held a disposable lighter over his head. Derrick was the firebug, not Serena.

That's when I noticed the smell of natural gas. Oh my god; the locked kitchen door. "You can't."

He swayed slightly before laughing. "They're in the country illegally. They're sucking off America's tit. Not paying taxes. They'll take our jobs, use our medical system, sponge off social security, and I'm tired of paying for that."

He planned on torching them. Children. Mothers who had risked all and suffered to cross the desert with the hope of a decent life for their families. "Where are Ann and Josie and Serena?"

The one good eyebrow popped up. "Oh, them? I saved the best for them."

Icy fingers closed around my heart. "Don't hurt them."

He shook his head. "They're traitors. They're ruining this country, allowing vermin to invade and take over. You've been to Mexico, right? You see the way they live? Trash, buildings with broken windows or no roofs. People begging on the streets. They don't take care of anything. If you let these scum into our country, they'll bring it down, just like they've done to their own."

Wouldn't it be great to have my utility belt with my gun. I had to try anything to calm him down. "Right. I'm with you. Why do you think I joined Border Patrol?"

"For the same reason I'm with No Desert Deaths. You get to be on the inside, keeping your enemies closer, as they say. You're like Ford. Pretending to stand up for America but sneaking in the damned Mexicans."

"No, that's not true. I'm protecting the borders, like you." Where was Josie? From where we stood in the lobby the offices stretched back on two separate wings. They'd been converted to dorm rooms. Beyond the kitchen were five units, and the other wing contained five and a storage space. Ann's office opened behind me. The door had been closed when I came in. The door she always kept open.

When I'd talked to him on the phone Derrick had said Ann was in her office. He must have locked them in there. Getting into the office would mean I'd have to get the key from Derrick. He didn't know the power of a protective mother.

Derrick swayed again and blinked his good eye as if trying to focus. His momentary weakness gave me a chance.

I sprang forward, swung my arm in a wide arc, and connected with his injured face. Blood and other body fluids smacked from the impact. Warm splotches hit my cheek and lips.

Derrick screamed. He threw a punch that landed full force under my chin and snapped my head back. I reeled backward, sputtering as the pain wrapped around my head, and tried to get my throat to work. The attack had cost me, but his retaliation had taken a toll on him, too. He advanced on me. I took another couple of steps back. In a few feet I'd be able to touch the office door. The keys must be in Derrick's pocket. Whatever it took, I'd have to get them.

His mouth split open in a ghoulish grin. "You don't amount to much without your uniform and weapons."

Like a magician pulling a pigeon from his coat, Derrick flourished a knife from a sheath on his calf.

Derrick had all the toys of a soldier but did he know about hand-to-hand combat? I'd been through the police academy as well as the Border Patrol. Not to mention all the self-defense classes I'd taught. But he had a huge weight advantage. And the knife tipped the scales too far in his favor.

I braced for his attack.

Blood trickled from his wrecked face down his neck, soaking the collar of his shirt. "Want to know what I have planned for your daughter and Ann and Serena?"

"It doesn't matter. I'm not going to let you kill them."

He leered at me. "You can't stop me."

"Oh, I'm going to stop you."

"You're a woman. I'm a man."

His taunting smile looked like a grimace. Using his free hand, he pulled the lighter from his pocket and held it up like a groupie at a rock concert, flicking the flame on. "See those sleeping angels?"

Through the kitchen window I saw the children had tumbled together like a pile of napping kittens. The carbon monoxide in the gas must have put them to sleep. Even if Derrick didn't ignite the room, the fumes in their little bodies would make them sick. Maybe kill them.

Reyna had succeeded in freeing herself from the restraints. She banged on the door, screaming and crying.

Derrick watched with an amused grin. "She's the ringleader. Spending so much time with your bossy sister, I had a chance to get to know all these wetbacks. I just wish that last bunch hadn't cleared out before today. Can you say barbeque?"

Reyna picked up a chair and bashed it into the window. It bounced back and landed on the table, crashing into it before falling on the floor, not so much as nicking the glass.

I lunged at Derrick. He swiped the knife through the air, managing to penetrate through my shirt and the skin of my stomach. Blistering pain leaped out in a widening circle, but within seconds my mind shifted away from the wound to Derrick. He seemed surprised he'd stabbed me, giving me the opening I needed to grab hold of his arm. I brought my knee up and rammed his wrist into it. His bone snapped. The crack sounded like a branch breaking in an autumn forest.

Derrick wailed and fell back. The knife clattered to the floor. Cradling his arm he howled and dropped to his knees.

Glad to have my heavy uniform boots, I kicked out with all my rage, catching him in the chest and toppling him flat. My fingers closed on the knife. I planted a knee on his chest and he writhed and shrieked below me. His earlier injury combined with the pain from his wrist drained him of strength. Thrusting my hand into his pocket while he wriggled in agony wasn't easy, but I succeeded in pulling out Ann's ring of keys.

Keeping the knife leveled at him, I quickly pushed myself to stand and backed toward the office door. For the first time the broiling from the slash in my side grew more intense than a simple sting. My knees started to buckle and I gasped for breath. Blood I hadn't noticed earlier saturated my midsection. The waistline of my jeans felt sticky. I'd thought the knife had only slid through skin and muscles. Had the blade hit something vital? Breathing took effort.

Derrick kept rolling and crying, not paying attention to anything but his own misery. Like every bully.

My blood made the keys sticky but I quickly found the one to Ann's office and slipped it into the lock.

Josie and Ann were tied and gagged, sitting together on the floor, secured to the desk. Serena lay next to them. Blood matted her hair, her face bloated with bruises, scraped skin, gore smeared across her cheeks. Derrick must have decided to shut her up.

I glanced at Derrick, still on the floor, wrapped in his private hell. "Is Serena dead?"

They frantically shook their heads.

Josie's muffled shouts mingled with Ann's. They couldn't move. If I slid the knife to them, they couldn't use it. I watched Derrick writhe on the floor, frustrated because I had no rope or restraints. My best solution would be to walk back to him and bury the knife in his heart. I took the second-best choice.

I dashed to Josie and used Derrick's knife to slice her restraints, then quickly did the same for Ann. "Get outside now. Call 9-1-1."

They had to help each other because I needed to keep an eye on Derrick and get the people from the kitchen.

My mind said I jumped to my feet but my body didn't take the direction. Bones and muscles seemed like cold mud. Behind me, Josie and Ann shouted but I couldn't understand.

Everything felt heavy. My slashed side screamed with pulsing fire. Clouds drifted behind my eyes and I wanted to drop back, rest for only a second.

No. I couldn't quit. Derrick's screaming changed. Instead of his cries coming from where he lay on the ground, they sounded less direct. He was on the move.

I had a knife.

But he had a lighter.

The keys dangled from the office door. I'd need them to free the women and children locked in the kitchen. As I pulled them free, my feet slipped and I crashed to my knees. My guts felt as if they were spilling from my wound as I pushed myself to stand and struggled to draw air. Derrick had murdered Lacy, harmed my family, and there was no way I'd let him kill more innocent people.

Where Derrick had been lying was only a smear of blood. Cradling his arm, he stumbled across the lobby, making his way to the kitchen. Why hadn't I grabbed the lighter at the same time as the keys?

I strained to run after him, gripping my side and hoping I had enough life in me to stop him. He glanced over his shoulder to see me and pitched to the side, banging into the wall and slipping to his knee.

In slow motion I made it to him as he pulled himself up along the wall and took another step toward the kitchen, the lighter still in his hand.

The knife was too heavy. My fingers couldn't stay clasped around the handle. I watched it slip from my hand and crash to the tiled floor. Somehow, I managed to clutch the keys. I couldn't let Derrick hurt those children.

My brain told me to keep going, to lift my foot off the ground for another step. But the black boot stayed on the floor while splotches of thick red splashed on the tile and the toes of my boots.

"Stop," I think I shouted, but couldn't be sure.

Derrick leaned against the wall. Maybe his ruined face grinned at me. I couldn't tell because he seemed to warp and shift in front of my eyes. His laughter was unmistakable.

"You never had a chance at stopping me. Everyone tries but I'm better than them all. Better than you."

I slipped to my knees and then onto all fours.

He was going to set Mi Casa on fire. Reyna, Donia, Jimena and her children would fry. I prayed Josie, Ann, and Serena got out in time. I was going up in flames with the rest. I'd never see Deon or Sami again.

I ordered myself to forget about the knife wound. *Get up. Fight. Don't let this happen.*

Derrick's face receded as he started toward the kitchen.

A scream came from behind me. The battle cry of a righteous woman. A streak of shining black hair flashed by me.

I wanted to cry out, "No!" I needed to stop Josie. Derrick would kill her, too. My cheek lay against the cold floor tile and I fought to keep my eyes open. Legs and arms were nothing but useless bags of sand. I fought to pull air down my throat and into my lungs. *Run, Josie. Get away.*

Josie hit Derrick like a train, slamming into his back. He flew into the kitchen window, leaving a smear of gore on the glass.

He spun around to face her. His bad arm dangled at his side and he gripped the lighter in his other. He couldn't have much strength left. *Take the lighter, Josie.*

She went in again, kicking his knee. Derrick cried out. He gripped the lighter and held it in front of his good eye as if wanting to see how it worked. If he lit it now, he'd blow himself up with the rest of us.

Josie let loose another kick, this time to his groin. Bravo, self-defense class.

Get the lighter.

Derrick dropped to his hands and knees but rocked back and raised his good hand. His thumb worked and he focused on the lighter.

Josie stood over him and slapped the lighter away. It skittered across the floor and stopped a few feet in front of my eyes.

Derrick crumpled to his side. He lay halfway across the lobby from me, his mangled face like a volcanic ruin in the shadow of the security light.

Josie ran to me and snatched the keys from my motionless fingertips.

32

Sticking to the paved roads, the trip to Sasabe in my Pilot seemed like sailing on smooth waters compared to bumping through the desert in a Border Patrol pickup. The sunshine through the windshield kept us warm enough we didn't need the heater, though the desert temperatures in December weren't exactly tropical.

Josie had kept the conversation going, something that warmed me, but I didn't tell her that. She switched gears from school drama. "So, I think it's a really good thing we took off alone together today."

I did, too. The more time we spent doing fun things together, the better we'd do wading through the controversial stuff. "Why's that?"

Josie sounded serious. "Dad and Sami haven't been getting along that well lately. They really need to spend time together doing something fun. So, Dad taking her to practice and then lunch while we're out here will be a good start."

Ah, so wise. "As long as we've got some time, maybe we should talk about No Desert Deaths."

Josie tilted her head with impatience. "You win. You got Aunt Ann and Serena on your side. They won't let me take water and stuff out anymore. All they're going to let me do is help out at Mi Casa." She sounded annoyed but not rebellious.

"Perfect. I'm sure there's plenty to do at the center." I paused. Would I get a straight answer? "Ann swears she's not hiding undocumented people anymore. That's right, isn't it?"

Even Josie's stink-eye wasn't as nasty as it used to be. "Yes, Mom. I hope the Border Patrol is proud of themselves for sending Donia and Jimena and her kids back."

It still felt like a punch to my stomach. "I know I'm not. But Reyna and her kids are working toward citizenship."

"It's not enough." Josie folded her arms across her chest.

It never was. "We're lucky Mi Casa didn't get caught for harboring felons. So maybe be glad the center can stay in business and still help people."

She was quiet, not liking my answer.

How could I explain it to Josie when I didn't understand it myself. "The border is a tough place. It's not fair. I don't like everything I do, but I've got to believe I'm helping."

"By sending innocent people back to desperate situations?"

I shook my head. "By trying to keep criminals out. And by saving people who are suffering or dying in the desert."

"Because the walls and checkpoints force them to cross in dangerous—"

I held up my hand to stop her. "I know."

We didn't say anything for a moment and then I started again. "How is it going with Serena?"

Josie sighed. "She and Aunt Ann fight all the time. Aunt Ann can't stand it that Serena has a different way of doing things and Serena hates to take orders. But Serena is helping out a lot and I think maybe Aunt Ann feels better, even if she won't admit she needs Serena's help."

She thought a moment. "Plus, Serena feels super bad about bringing Derrick into No Desert Deaths."

"She should."

Josie gave me a grunt that told me she disagreed. "How was she supposed to know he was a psycho?" She hesitated. "He's not going to get out of prison, is he?"

What an awful thought. "There's so much evidence against him I'm sure he'll be locked up for life." If the justice system worked as it should, which wasn't always the case.

I steered the Pilot into Sasabe, around the curve and past the sycamore. I stopped in front of Edna's cabin. The dogs sat in their usual places, staring at the bare yard. I picked up the box wrapped in red Christmas paper with a cheerful bow.

Josie opened her door and slid out. We both swung our doors closed, the sound echoing through the deserted town. My scar stung, reminding me that healing completely would take time. Edna popped out the front door as we made it to the dilapidated metal gate. She wore her purple sweatpants and a heavy red cardigan that looked as if it'd been made by Edna's great-grandmother about the time the first Catholic missionaries invaded her tribal lands. Edna pointed to the dalmatian and gave him a disciplinary frown. "Shush up, you." She squinted in our direction.

"Morning, Edna." I tried to sound cheerful though I felt a little nervous.

Edna stepped down from the porch and met us. "It's you." She didn't offer a smile or any other sign of warmth. Josie caught her attention and Edna nodded her way. "And you."

Josie stepped forward and pulled a small wrapped box from her hoodie pocket. "Serena sent you this. She wanted to come see you, but a group from Nicaragua is coming in this morning and she needed to stay at Mi Casa and help them get settled."

Edna took the box. "She's the loudmouth one. Did her leg heal up?"

Josie grinned at Edna's description of Serena. "She doesn't even limp."

Edna pocketed the box in her sweater and held her skinny arms out to me. "Is that mine, too?"

Suddenly, I double-guessed my decision. I wanted to deny the box and hide it in the car. But for better or worse, I was committed now. Without a word I handed it to Edna.

She scurried up to the porch. Josie and I shared a look and followed. Edna set the box on a rickety wood table and snatched the ribbon from the top, smacking it on the head of a German shepherd. She tore at the bright wrapping.

My stomach twisted. It's never a good idea to give someone a pet unless they've asked for one and chosen it themselves. I knew better.

Edna ripped the lid off the box and stepped back, her mouth hanging open. She stared at the contents for a few seconds, then shuffled forward, dipped both hands into the box, and brought out the ceramic chihuahua. About the size of a loaf of bread, it was curled up just right to sit on a lap or in someone's arms. This little guy was light brown with dark facial features and soulful eyes.

Edna cradled the little ceramic creature. "You poor thing. They put you in that dark box. I won't ever do that to you." She scowled at me.

Josie seemed to enjoy Edna's reaction. "What are you going to name it?"

Edna held up the little dog and stared into its eyes. I admit to curiosity over whether Edna saw a boy or girl. She pulled the dog back into her chest. "Peanut, of course."

Luckily, I hadn't expected a thank you.

"How is everything else?" I asked. "Do you need any help? Can we bring you something from town next time we come?"

Edna petted the back of the dog while she looked at me. "Good thing I don't rely on you. You haven't been to see me since that day."

Josie jumped in to defend me. "She just now got cleared to drive."

Edna eyed me with a measure of skepticism. "Ford said you got stabbed by that man. You look fine to me."

Compared to the surgery, a few days in the hospital, and four weeks of rehab, including dealing with a weepy wound, I did feel fine. "Much better, thanks." Luke, with his youth, had healed quickly and was already back at work.

"Hmph," was all Edna had to say. "Ford's been bringing me firewood and groceries. But next time you come, bring me Funky Monkey ice cream."

The crunch of boots on the gravel made me turn to see Ford walking through Edna's gate. His icy blue eyes took in Josie and stopped on me. "Thought I heard someone drive up. You look whole again."

"I'm cleared to go back to work next week. Although they're making me stay with processing at the station." The conversation felt awkward and stiff.

After a moment he said, "Well. That's good."

I smiled and waited. Then said, "How 'bout you? No lingering problems from the concussion?"

Ford shifted his vision down the road. "Nope. Good as new."

"I hear Brody single-handedly stopped six heavily armed smugglers last week carrying over a ton of heroin."

Ford's face took on a look of boredom. "You don't say?"

Josie glared at Ford but he didn't look her way. Edna cooed to the newest addition to her pack, and Ford and I focused on everything but each other.

Finally Ford cleared his throat. "Okay. Just wanted to see if you're okay. So, I've got stuff to do."

"Glad you're fully recovered."

"Yep." He strode back the way he'd come and Edna retreated through her front door without a good-bye.

Josie gave me an incredulous look. "That's it? He's just going to keep doing what he's been doing? Rounding up people and calling you guys to haul them in? After Lacy and Derrick, nothing's changed. You all get up the next day and do the same thing."

The wound in my side throbbed and I was ready to head home. "Yeah, but that dope Brody confiscated last week won't hit the streets. Reyna and her kids are alive and on their way to getting citizenship." I hoisted myself behind the wheel and started the Pilot.

Josie whipped the seat belt across her chest. "It's still so unfair."

I turned the Pilot around to head back to Tucson. "We can't change the whole world, Bird, but we try to leave our corner a little better."

She rolled her eyes and I laughed at the cliché.

THE DESERT BEHIND ME

The mind never truly forgets. Even when it wants to.

When a teenaged girl goes missing in Arizona, retired New York cop Jamie Butler is frantic to find her. Haunted by the brutal murder of her own daughter, Jamie is convinced that this girl has been abducted in the same way.

But while others are slow to take alarm—the girl's mother believes she is merely off on a lark—Jamie sees inexplicable similarities to her own daughter's abduction. Connections that seem impossible. Because her daughter's killer is long-dead...

Already doubting her own grief-fractured mind, Jamie struggles to convince those around her of what she fears to be true. And as her search for the missing teen intensifies, new evidence comes to light.

Evidence that implicates Jamie herself.

In a race to save the missing girl Jamie must finally confront her dark memories and unearth the long-suppressed secrets of her forgotten past.

Get your copy today at
severnriverbooks.com/authors/shannon-baker

ACKNOWLEDGMENTS

Some books are harder to write than others (in my experience, none of them are easy). Writing this book felt like when I learned to water ski as a kid, and I was too determined or too stupid to let go of the rope when I lost my skis. I got drug under and ended up with so much water in my nose and mouth I thought I'd drown. So, I'm grateful to the good folks at Severn River Publishing who, when the rope was finally ripped from my hands, circled around and pulled me from the waves. A more supportive bunch you'll never find, especially Amber Hudock, Andrew Watts, and Randall Klein.

A huge shout-out goes to three Border Patrol Agents who took several afternoons to discuss issues and protocol over beers and lunch. I'm in awe of what they do for a living. The border is unforgiving and complicated, at times beautiful, other times brutal. Anyone compelled to judge their actions should spend a week on patrol with them.

The best thing about being a writer of fiction is that you don't need to solve the world's problems, only the universe you create. I so admire all the volunteers spending countless hours and resources to help immigrants. Their love and caring saves lives and reduces suffering. I am also grateful for the Border Patrol defending and protecting our country. Often those two missions run parallel. Sometimes, they collide. My story isn't meant to pick who's right and who's wrong. I only wanted to see how it played out for the people who live within these pages.

Thanks to Piper Bayard, Wendy Terrien, and Janet Fogg for help with the title. That's always so hard for me. Janet Fogg and Alan Larsen are the best critique partners around and I owe them a debt for their unfailing advice.

Despite it making me giggle to think of her in the outfit, Terri Bischoff is the best cheerleader a writer could ask for.

Rocky Mountain Fiction Writers, Sisters in Crime, Desert Sleuths, Writers Unwritten, and The Sun Voodoo Coven are writing lifelines for me. I'm not sure it's called enabling or support, but you all keep me from slamming down the computer lid permanently and heading out to the trails or lakes.

As always, a big thanks to my daughters for their constant faith, even if I can hear you rolling your eyes during our phone calls when I tell you once again how I'll never be able to write another book. The biggest thank you of all is to Dave, constant and unwavering.

ABOUT THE AUTHOR

Shannon Baker is the award-winning author of *The Desert Behind Me* and the Kate Fox series, along with the Nora Abbott mysteries and the Michaela Sanchez Southwest Crime Thrillers. She is the proud recipient of the Rocky Mountain Fiction Writers 2014 and 2017-18 Writer of the Year Award.

Baker spent 20 years in the Nebraska Sandhills, where cattle outnumber people by more than 50:1. She now lives on the edge of the desert in Tucson with her crazy Weimaraner and her favorite human. A lover of the great outdoors, she can be found backpacking, traipsing to the bottom of the Grand Canyon, skiing mountains and plains, kayaking lakes, river running, hiking, cycling, and scuba diving whenever she gets a chance. Arizona sunsets notwithstanding, Baker is, and always will be a Nebraska Husker. Go Big Red.

Sign up for Shannon Baker's reader list at
severnriverbooks.com/authors/shannon-baker

Printed in the United States
by Baker & Taylor Publisher Services